MW00423073

Peter Wacks is a talented w
Watch out, readers!

Kevin J. Anderson – International bestselling author

There are no single chapters in Peter's stories. If you read one, you are compelled to read them all, beginning to end in one sitting.

Steven L. Sears, Writer/Producer; Xena - Warrior Princess, The A-Team, Walker - Texas Ranger, and others

A roller-coaster read the melds mystery, history and the destiny of humanity in one wild ride. A page-turner from start to finish.

Brooks Wachtel – Emmy Award winning writer/producer and novelist

Peter's vision of time travel reveals a hauntingly believable future and he brings it life in a way that will have you holding your breath with each split second.

Mark Ryan, bestselling co-author of Bloodletting

Peter Wacks writing has a way of grabbing your attention and not letting go and though you can try...you will fail. An amazing talent who's Bram Stroker nominated graphic novel Behind These Eyes is reminiscent of a young Harlan Ellison. Sit back and enjoy the ride!

Jeff Sturgeon - award winning illustrator

Second Paradigm is like the amusement park ride that spins, pins you to the wall, and drops the floor out from under you—except it does that to your brain.

Sam Knight (Jim Sams) Author of Whiskey Jack and a Murder of Crows, and others.

SECOND
PARADIGM

TIME IS WHAT YOU MAKE OF IT...

SECOND
PARADIGM

Peter J. Wacks

WordFire Press
Colorado Springs, Colorado

SECOND PARADIGM
Copyright © 2014 Peter J. Wacks

Originally published by Book Surge Publishing, 2008; Dreamzion 2011;
Fantastic Journeys Publishing, 2012

ISBN: 978-1-61475-180-9

Cover artwork images by Shutterstock

Cover design by Kevin J. Anderson

Book Design by RuneWright, LLC
www.RuneWright.com

Published by
WordFire Press, an imprint of
WordFire, Inc.
PO Box 1840
Monument, CO 80132

Kevin J. Anderson & Rebecca Moesta Publishers

WordFire Press Trade Paperback Edition May 2014
Printed in the USA
www.wordfire.com

EPILOGUE

The crowd screamed, panicking. Police drew their guns, pointing them at the ground, ready to take down the shooter if they could spot him. The man stood back up from where he had fallen, looking around in wonder. Silence encapsulated him, a pinpoint beacon of sanity amidst the contagious fear of the crowd. Sensation was still tricky, confusing him. Had something hit him from behind and pushed him to the ground right before the gunshot? The other way, the other reality, was fading, but for half a heartbeat he traversed both.

Hidden like a viper, coiled and ready to strike, the knowledge of what might have been gnawed at him. Fighting to push it to the back of his mind, he took stock. He stood still amongst the whirlwind of motion surrounding him, frozen in place while people ran for cover.

"No man is an island." He spoke it like a mantra, reminding himself that he was a part of all this, not just the eye of the storm. People around him pointed up and behind him, so he looked back. A window leapt out of the background for him the second his eyes lit on it. An empty tripod stood in the window, some type of clamp attached to the top of it, spinning in its joint. His gaze fell to the ground below. How could he see that far with such clarity? The thought lazily drifted across his mind.

He knew the defenestrated woman too well, from his trial if not his memories. The fall had broken her neck. On the ground next to her lay a Glock, with a shattered scope affixed to it. The gun pushed at his memories and a glimmer of understanding dawned on him. He squeezed his empty hand. The understanding did not come to him as an epiphany; it was not a cataclysmic opening of his mind to the truth. Rather, it was a thief in the dark of night sneaking into his mind and settled in: as though it had always been there.

And once it arrived, it *had* always been there. He smiled and calmly walked away from the crowd. What had been done was now undone. And the Origin … was once again safe. And now he understood what that was, and that it existed. With a simple motion, just pushing another man down, he had determined exactly what the future was to be. Hard though the choice had been, there truly was no other choice. He left and went back to living his life, walking through the reflections of the Origin into his future.

RELATIVITY SYNCHRONIZATION:

THE FIRST CAUSE

2620: The Fine Line Bar, Tucson, Arizona.

Particles of hops floated through the beer, catching rays of the evening sun shining through the window, refracting the light through the dark amber liquid. Alexander Zarth watched the play of light with fascination. Subtleties of the environment, little details that so many people missed, never failed to amaze him. He took a sip of the bittersweet ale, enjoying the chill and the thick weight of it on his tongue. Putting the glass down, he stretched back in his seat and looked at the man across the table.

Leaning back in the booth till his shoulders hit the cushion, he got comfortable. Despite the man's apparent youth, an illusion cast by curly blond hair and boyish features, he had piercing eyes and clearly defined muscles visible beneath his shirt. Wiping away the ring of condensation, Alex lowered his beer. Someone watched them both from the kitchen. He extended his senses and felt a time traveler's signature there, one that he recognized all too well. Smiling to himself, he leaned forward again, ignoring the noise from the house music and other drinkers in the bar.

"So let me get this right. Twelve commandos from two C's up the line have all taken failed shots at me, and you," he paused to look into the eyes of the man across from him, "you manage to find me faster than any of them. On top of this, you have an out of time 'mission' you'd like to hire me for. A mission which puts me back in the crossfire, by the paradox standard of those commandos out to get me, and makes me killable. If I accept this I have to leave the safety of my own time, when they cannot kill me, and go somewhen else—which makes me a target. Do you think I'm stupid, friend? Or do you think greed motivates me past the point of caution?"

Alex locked gazes with the man. His eyes gave him away. Holding a surprising depth; their pure emerald caught Alex in an almost hypnotic spell. Alex had trouble reading him, itself a rare thing. But then again, his eyes gave him away. He was a stone cold killer, and lying through his teeth. Not that Zarth had a problem with lying. Everyone did it, and it was a useful tool.

The man nodded. "That is, looking at the smallest possible picture, correct, Mr. Zarth. It does make you 'killable' by their standards. And no, I do not think you are stupid, or greedy, for that matter. If I did then I would not have bothered coming here. Frankly—you are the best there is in the time travel business. I've been up and down the line from C forty-five back to the C twenty Origin and there is no one else who can do this. Not even me. And please believe me when I tell you that I am the second best 'dox spinner ever. Ever. Do not accept that compliment lightly, or think that it is flattery. It is a simple statement of fact, a statement of your résumé, and why I am attempting to hire you for this task."

Alex took another sip of his beer, finishing the glass off, then—with a quick burst of power—switched the empty with the full glass he had been holding fifteen minutes ago. Thinking hard about the term the man had used: 'dox spinner' while drinking the same beer a second time, he tapped his foot against the ground. Alex had never heard the term before, but he immediately liked it. He made his decision, mainly guided by the presence of the traveler observing from the back room.

Alex raised his glass. "Here is to paradox, Mr. Smith. And the free beer it entails you. All right, I believe you. But why should I accept the job? My odds of survival are low, and frankly money is not a problem for me. And, you should know, there is another who is as good as me. Hell, he's probably better. If this situation is as big as you say, then in all likelihood this man will be opposed to me once my presence is known."

Smith smiled at Alex, and something odd lurked in that smile. "To be frank with you, you don't survive the mission. You change the objective and die in the process. But somehow, it all ends up working. Whatever it is you do—it works. And I'm not good enough to figure out what exactly it is that you do. But as to why you accept the mission, I can only suppose that it is because it is the greatest challenge you will ever face."

Alex raised an eyebrow.

"And because Mr. Zarth, as trite as it is, only you can save the world. And your trick just now, circumventing the block I put on your ability to travel, only goes to reinforce the point to me that you are the best. That you can do what I could not."

With a grunt Alex raised his fresh glass of beer to his lips then set it back down without drinking it. Thoughts ran through his head.

"Hmmm. I die? You really know how to upsell, don't you? You might as well drop the block you have on me, all it's doing is annoying me. I've already shown you I can slip it." The other traveler meant something, but the block on his nanotech was messing with his ability to figure out what that was.

The heads up display on his contacts started flashing information as his nanotech fired back to life. Alex grinned. "So you want me to go on a mission that is a secret, bring me against my worst enemies, and get me killed? Yeah, you're right. I'm probably in. Leave the dossier with me."

The look of surprise in the other man's eyes gratified him. "Trace my last jump and you'll find a list of what supplies I need and when I need them dropped. If you can't trace the jump, find someone else for the job, Mr. Smith."

2003: The Pawn Sacrificed

"I ..." Chris flushed, anger pushing through his blood roughly. He could feel every heartbeat in the tips of his fingers. But looking to the jury and seeing sympathetic eyes staring back at him helped calm and stem his rising pulse rate. He answered the question, asked in a different way for the dozenth time, with the same reply. "... I don't remember. I'm sorry."

The prosecuting attorney, James Garrett, flashed a tight, humorless grin at Christopher Nost, and his cold gray eyes bored into Chris's, sparking a fight or flight reaction. Words arced through the connection of their eyes. *I've got you. There's no way out for you this time. This has to finish it.* Chris felt bile rise in his throat. Fearing he would to throw up all over the witness box, he swallowed it down. The acrid taste burned at the back of his throat.

"What exactly do you mean, you don't remember, Dr. Nost? Do you or do you not have an alibi for the night of August thirteenth, nineteen ninety-seven, or was it, in fact, you who murdered Lucille Frost at the office building you both worked at?" Garrett's voice gained volume as he turned towards the Jury. "How can you know you are not guilty? Your mental condition seems awfully convenient—something that you could easily take advantage of in a situation that played out exactly as this one has for you. I urge you to look deep inside yourself. You ca—"

"Objection, Your Honor." Chris' defense attorney, Alan Dunwich, rose, both fists planted on the long oak table in front of him. "Dr. Nost's memory loss condition has already been established to the jury. At this point the prosecution is badgering the defendant and building straw men!" Livid, his face flushed as he glared at the prosecuting attorney.

"My client has a rare form of mental defect that inhibits PKC Zeta, here documented by Dr. Eric Jorgensen, one of the world's foremost neurologists. As was previously explained—" he drew out the words while staring at Garrett, as if speaking to a young child, "—Dr. Nost can remember concepts and ideas, hence his ability to continue his work in the field of Aerospace Mechanics and Astrophysics, but new experiences and faces fade after a little more than a year, rendering his long term memory useless. The court has already heard Dr. Jorgensen's testimony. I request that the prosecution's question be struck from the record." Dunwich waved a manila folder toward Judge Miller, but he still glared at James Garret.

Chris's head swam and Garrett seemed to blur for a second as his vision went fuzzy. *Hold it together,* he fought the fear rising in his gut, a wave of nausea burning his stomach, *here is not the time or place to break down.*

"Objection sustained, defense. Recorder, please strike the last question from the record and the jurors are instructed to ignore it. Mr. Garret, you have been warned once already about bringing up Dr. Nost's disability in an attempt to discredit it without actually bringing a witness to the stand over it. If you continue to ignore the rules of this courtroom I will hold you in contempt. Now, would you like to spend a night in jail, or do you have any other real questions for the defendant?"

Dunwich looked at Garret in triumph, but the lawyer only shrugged, seemingly nonplussed, and said, "I apologize, your honor, it must have slipped my mind. The prosecution rests." Garrett walked back to his seat at the prosecution table and sat, trying to hide the smug smile flitting across his face.

Bastard. Dunwich couldn't conceal the thought so obviously going through his mind. Chris imagined he could see the words scrolling through his lawyer's mind. Inadmissible or not, prosecuting council had planted suspicion in the minds of the jury. It was a dirty tactic, one that ignored actual innocence or guilt in favor of getting a conviction.

Allen glanced covertly at the jury. The defense attorney could see it in their faces; the seed of doubt would grow. Where five minutes ago there was sympathy for Chris etched in their eyes, some now looked doubtful, others loathing—the ones that had already made their decision. The damage had been done, right when Dunwich thought he had this trial clinched.

He clenched his jaw in frustration, gears already spinning on how to turn this around in the closing statement. *Damn him,* Alan glanced at Garrett, *an unknown who relies solely on playing dirty. How did this asshole land this case? Is the District Attorney stupid? I can nail him in an appeal and it will be easy.*

Judge Miller looked around the courtroom, his gaze lingering on Chris as he walked back to the defense table and sat. "Then this court will adjourn for a one hour recess. We will reconvene at—" he glanced at the round, institutional clock hanging above the jury, "—three thirty for closing statements. Bailiff, please take Dr. Nost to his holding cell. Dr. Nost, you will not be summoned to this courtroom again until the jury's announcement of the verdict. Do you understand that?" He met Chris's eyes with the last question.

Chris nodded to the judge. He did understand. It meant that he would have to suffer alone in a cell until the jury finished deciding his fate. As the guards led Chris from the courtroom he saw a man stand up in the audience benches and push his way through the milling crowd, waving to Judge Miller. He wore a plain blue suit and thick black-rimmed, military style, birth control, glasses. The last thing that Chris noticed as the guards pushed him from the courtroom was that the man clutched a small stack of folders stamped with a red "**CLASSIFIED**" across them.

Do I know that man? Chris wondered. A spark of recognition flared and, though he wracked his brain, he couldn't remember.

• • •

Chris waited in the holding cell for over three hours, staring out to the world through a three-inch thick Plexiglas window. The glass, besides obscuring what he could see because of its thickness, also had some sort of thin metal woven through it in a diagonal pattern that formed diamonds, ostensibly to stop prisoners from smashing through the three inches of transparent plastic, squeezing through a tiny window, taking out armed guards, and escaping down the sheer wall. *Just in case I had a hope of escaping they had to reinforce it with metal,* Chris thought bitterly. Every moment of those three hours dragged by like an eternity as he watched the seconds creeping along on the wall-clock behind the guard, who was ignoring him while reading a science fiction novel at a desk.

It looked like the same clock hanging in the courtroom. *How long will it take them?* he thought over and over. *How long?* He fantasized about moving time forward to get it over with, but soon gave up on the idle daydreaming, knowing that it was futile to try and distract himself. *It could be days*, he thought ... *or even weeks*. Anger welled in him over this unfair situation, a throbbing tide in his blood, eaten away by a corrupting fear. Conflicting emotions ate at him until he became so lost within himself that he didn't even notice when tears ran down his cheeks.

Chris's stomach lurched when the external door opened. His hopes and fears were answered as the bailiff walked in and, with a quick glance at him, began speaking to the holding cell guard. Chris took a deep breath, trying to make the nausea settle. *It's not going to be good.* He tried to banish the cancerous thought, but it entrenched even before they opened his cell door. A certainty lay in his stomach like a lead weight. *It's not going to be good.*

As the holding cell door opened, the guard noticed the despair in Chris's eyes and handed him a small stack of napkins. "Here. Wipe your cheeks off."

The guard looked away for a moment to give Chris a chance to compose himself. "I know it's scary for you right now, but don't give up. Me and the other guards have been watching your case on the TV and none of us think you did it. We can't be the only ones thinking that way."

Their eyes locked for a brief moment. Truth gazed back at him from those eyes and with crystal clarity Chris, realized that his life had finished. *Hope ... they know I've lost, too. It's not just me.* As he focused on centering himself, trying to retain some shred of his dignity, he looked once more to the guard.

"Thank you," he said with no emotion in his voice, no fear, no hope. As they walked down the hall the guard once again became all business, but as Chris entered the courtroom and started walking towards his attorney, he felt a slight, reassuring pat on his back from the bailiff. He knew it should be consoling, but it only served to reinforce the hopelessness in his mind.

It seemed like he had been through this scene a dozen times prior—and nothing he could do would change the scripted outcome of this play. As he took his seat, his lawyer leaned towards him. Alan Dunwich, a man who surprised him with his humanity and friendship. The man was older, in his sixties with pure silver hair. He was large, not necessarily fat, but headed in that direction as a lifetime behind a desk caught up to him. In many ways Chris thought him to be truly larger than life. "Something has happened," Dunwich whispered. "I don't know what, but as soon as you left a guy came in to talk to Judge M—"

"All rise. The honorable Judge Miller is presiding." The bailiff interrupted. Chris and Alan stood. Judge Miller emerged from the antechamber wearing a troubled demeanor, sat, and banged his gavel. He looked around the hushed courtroom, then turned towards the jury and sighed.

"Foreman of the jury, have you reached a verdict?"

"We have, Your Honor." A wormy man with a greased comb-over and a Freddy Mercury moustache stood and handed the bailiff a slip of paper. The bailiff, in turn, relayed it to the judge, who unfolded it and read. His eyes gave away nothing.

My life is on that paper, Chris thought. *My continued existence hangs balanced on a thread of twelve people's interpretations of the words of two men.... A man who cares deeply for me, and a man who hates me.*

Judge Miller frowned once as he looked again at the slip of paper, and then handed it back to the bailiff who returned it to the foreman. "Please announce your verdict to the court."

The foreman of the Jury looked at the watching crowd and cleared his throat, "We, the Jury, find the Defendant, Dr. Christopher Nost, guilty as charged of First Degree murder in the case of Lucille Frost."

Chris' mind went blank as a wave of numbness crashed into his soul. He felt like he still waited for something. He could almost see it, hurtling toward him in time, something that he could not quite grasp. Looking deep inside himself, he knew he hadn't done it.

A susurrus swept through the watching crowd as people started to whisper their opinions to each other. Christopher Nost, a condemned man, looked up to the ceiling. It took everything he had to stop himself from bawling like a child in the middle of the courtroom. Even so, a few solitary tears made their way down his cheek.

Judge Miller banged his gavel again, calming the stir of the courtroom. Chris had not been aware of the noise until it once again fell silent. "I am now in a position I have not before found myself in twenty years of serving as Justice of this state. I received a visit from someone who has shown me evidence that the likelihood of Dr. Nost's guilt is very small, indeed."

He clenched his jaw, thinking. "This evidence, however, remains inadmissible. Therefore, this court will waive the lifetime sentence and reduce it to the minimum of ten years. Furthermore, this term will be carried out in a minimum-security prison in which Dr. Nost can continue to work with his employer, GeoTech, Inc., and will be provided with any and all equipment necessary to carry out his duties."

Judge Miller sighed and rubbed the bridge of his nose, then continued. "Dr. Nost is to continue his sessions with Dr. Jorgensen in an effort to find a cure for his condition. And one last point: as a ward of the state, all of Dr. Nost's medical expenses will be paid by Colorado."

Judge Miller looked at Chris. "I personally very much hope that someday you will find your memories returned to you, and I wish you the best of luck, Dr. Nost. This court is now adjourned."

So that's it, then. Chris thought as he nodded to the judge in thanks. His lawyer said something about an appeal but Chris wasn't listening. The feeling of waiting remained. If anything, it had intensified. *The sentencing is over*, he told himself. *The waiting is done. You got off with your life, which is a hell of a lot more than you expected. Relax.*

Got off how? another voice within him asked. *I'm sure I didn't do it. I couldn't do anything like that. I'm going to prison for ten years for a crime I didn't commit.* The feeling of shell shock wouldn't go away.

Guards marched Chris into the high, marble hall that led to the front doors of the courthouse. Despite the judge's lenience, he counted six guards escorting him to the waiting prison van. *Do they really think I'm that dangerous?* he wondered. *Yes,* he answered his own question. *In their eyes I am a convicted killer. I am a dangerous person to them.*

Then he began to hear something over the empty echo of their footsteps on the checkered black and gray marble floor, and saw, in the light at the end of the hall, (*end of the tunnel* he thought) more guards, facing outwards.

He heard someone shout, "Here he comes!" and the footsteps were drowned out by the roar of the media circus outside. Dozens of voices all clamored to be heard over each other. Dunwich stepped in front of Chris to attempt to fill in as crowd control against the impending mob of media.

Funny, he thought, *you'd think that in a city like Denver a simple murder wouldn't draw the attention it has.* But the world didn't work like that.

Because of his memory condition, this case had become a sensation. Chris grimaced as his memory flooded with the headlines he had read about himself over the last few months. With no distant past to connect to, this trial was all he remembered of his life. No family, no memory ... the mystery murderer ...

One of the guards leaned in and tried to reassure him by squeezing his shoulder. The guard handed him his jacket, but Chris was lost like a deer frozen in headlights and didn't hear as the man said, "You might want to put this over your head ... you know ... they can attack like vultures when they smell blood." He waited, watching this unstoppable, unnamable event hurtle towards him through time.

What's happening to me? His head spun as he felt something beginning to awaken in him. *What is this ...*

Chris stepped out, brilliant sunlight blinding him, and questions and cameras immediately assaulted him. *Why didn't they give me something to cover my face?* He wondered, and waived his hand in attempts to still the mob, the feeling of something about to happen churning his stomach as he did so. Dunwich stepped up to the forest of microphones and the cacophony quieted. "I would like to remind those gathered here, and the viewers at home, that Judge Miller offered his condolences to my client after sentencing—so convinced was he of Dr. Nost's innocence. Furthermore, I would like to point out ..."

The waiting was over. Potential had become real. Chris saw a glint from behind one of the crowding news anchors—a woman wearing a red dress and matching lipstick, a permanent, plastic smile molded to her face even as she jostled those around her to catch Dunwich's words. The woman, the moment, the waiting, his body sang in anticipation as his vision swam. *What the hell is going on?*

I can stop this. The realization hit him below his conscious mind and he felt a primal power begin to surge through his veins. His heartbeat gained a crescendo and the rest of the world faded into silence. His blood caught fire and pumped through his body, surging and ebbing like the tide, orchestrated by the rhythm of his heart.

Duck! Chris felt his blood scream to him, and everything began to move in slow motion. His knee buckled, and he fell down the stairs.

At the same moment he heard a loud crack and felt something hit him hard in the face. Whatever had been fueling him fled, chased off by the gunshot. The world sped back up and the cacophony of the city hit him full force, harder than the bullet that had just lodged itself in his brain. "Murderer!" someone shouted. "Murderer, murderer!" in a familiar voice … and all went black.

2873: Discoveries

Garret sipped lukewarm coffee and studied the results of the latest tests. A handsome man in his late forties, his body had a muscular look, but he was not heavily built and tended more towards wiry. Close-cropped brown hair, lightly streaked with silver, framed his cold gray eyes—eyes that flickered back and forth across the papers in his hand. The datapad with the same results on it was discarded to the side. He was hopelessly lost in the past, preferring the anachronistic aesthetic to the modern.

This made no sense at all. Whatever methodology he used to produce the nanomachines, it should yield the same results—a temporal circuit machine that piggybacked the body's mitochondria. The entire effect should produce an internal machine that linked all of the body's cells together and gave them the ability to manipulate temporal energy. In short, time travel. But this last batch, which he had engineered with his new process, didn't pass the performance benchmarks. Specifically, they weren't jumping the way they should. He sighed and put down the papers. They pushed out no energy at all. A complete failure.

He popped in his steel grey control contacts and injected a test batch into his arm to rerun the benchmarks and tests. The hypo hissed and he felt a sting in his forearm as the injection pierced his skin. The contact lenses flickered to life, showing a Heads Up Display, or HUD, and outlined the circuitry for him, creating a floating ghost image, which, only he could see. With a small effort he activated his primary system travelers and hopped back one day into his safe window.

As he appeared in his isolation chamber, the HUD threw up a diagnostic report on how the new nanos handled the jump's energy spike. Nothing seemed out of the ordinary in the programming, except that the new nanos were not contributing to the jump. The system he had injected should have fused perfectly with his old system. Instead it was nonreactive. Rerunning his isolation routines, he separated out the new nanos and pushed an energy spike through them to hop forward to his 'home' time.

Time froze. His HUD showed time running at a ratio of four to one Terra to personal. Garret gaped. If this was right, he was moving very, very fast. He cautiously opened the chamber's door and walked into his lab. Back turned to the chamber, he moved at about a quarter of the speed he should be. Garret grinned and pushed on the new system—hard. He shot up to an incredible speed. Everything around him appeared to be frozen in place. The light coming through the large bay windows shifted from light blue to lavender. Garret decided to stress test the new system and leave the closed environment of the house. His mind raced, leaving him feeling like his thoughts were moving even faster than his newfound speed. The implications of what he had discovered staggered him.

Blue light shimmered around him as he jogged down the highway, passing cars that should be going over a hundred miles an hour like they were standing still. After jogging for a couple of hours of his relative time, he turned off on a country exit, leaving the city behind for a more rustic area where he could perform a few experiments. As he trotted off the road into a field, he stopped for a few moments to think things through.

Stopping revealed another surprise of slow time. He moved faster than the air around him and standing still too long depleted the supply of breathable air, forcing him into motion again. Once he dealt with this discovery by walking in circles, he got back to his main line of thought.

What would happen if he interacted with an inert object and then reintroduced the object to the environment? Nothing for it but to try, he figured as he picked up a rock. With a quick flick of his wrist, he threw the rock and watched in amazement as it slowed to a standstill about two inches from him and turned red.

Intuition screamed at him, and with a few ideas about what might happen when he released accelerated time he stepped back about twenty feet then phased back into normal time flow. The rock exploded in midair, throwing fiery shards in every direction. Garret threw himself to the ground. Shards of the stone shot over his prone form, and puffs of dust erupted around him. Luckily, he escaped with only a few minor scrapes, mainly from throwing himself to the ground.

He stood back up and dusted himself off. A grin tugged at the corners of his mouth. Turning on his datastats app, he reviewed the physics of what had happened on his HUD. The reaction was not what he had expected, but it did make sense. The forces exerted upon the object as it moved between time speeds was spread evenly across the molecules of the stone, not just across the surface. The rock just hadn't been able to withstand the pressures, at least not without the buffer of the nanites which he had in his system.

His own shortsightedness had nearly caused him to be badly injured. He resolved not to repeat that mistake. Stretching his will again, he phased back into 'fast' time. Picking up another rock he glanced over it with the HUD and imprinted its structure on his nano's object orientation subsystems. The HUD contact lenses had been one of his more inspired inventions; created one day when his wife argued with him about how much paper he left lying around the house. It was a little piece of history he had trouble giving up, his love of paper. Something about the visual layout of something being in front of him appealed his senses. But the HUD gave him a similar layout without having to waste hours a week on the 3D printer creating paper.

Time to redo the experiment—but with a few altered conditions. This time around, he transferred a small batch of his nano machines into the rock, then threw it as hard as he could. The nanos in the rock acted as a field extension and the rock moved like a bullet through the frozen landscape. He pushed against the resistance, reaching out to the nanites now in the rock, increasing the rock's ratio of time acceleration. Turf rippled in slow motion as the rock sliced through the earth, burrowing a hole about thirty feet long. Ripples in the ground continued to spread like aftershocks once the rock stopped moving and Garret had phased back into standard time to watch the results.

Dirt and grass exploded upwards as time snapped back to its normal passing, the after effects of the high speed stone leaving not only a trench in the ground, but once the dust had settled, a full a crater. Garret walked up to the point of impact and started digging until he held the rock in his hand. He stared down at it, and then recalled the nanos back into his system. Filled with warring thoughts over his discovery, James Garret jogged back towards his laboratory, moving into the future about a hundred times faster than anyone else on the planet. But his eyes were on the past.

Time: The Past, 4th dimensional Cartesian coordinates classified
Location: Classified
Operation: Classified.

Wanda Garret was a damned good time traveler and she knew it. Besides her husband being the best causality control theorist in the world and her personal trainer in applied causality theory, she was the best hopper ever tested. Only thirty-four, her skill allowed her to transfer her grid points on a three-dimensional plane instead of having to utilize the fourth.

Effectively, this gave her the ability to teleport herself on the world grid without hopping forward or backward through the time stream. That wasn't her only advantage as an agent. Her strong jaw and cheekbones, yet soft face, luscious almost-brown amber hair, and warm eyes helped her fit into any era as a good looking woman, and good looking can get you far.

So it made a certain amount of sense that she had been the one given the mission to assassinate the most important figure in history— at the time he was meant to die. If, for any reason, this mission was messed up, then the paradox she had been sent back to fix could shatter history. Once again she reviewed the mission dossier.

History was on the brink of destroying itself in one nasty moment of time. The brass in the Time Corp had isolated the incident that created the instability in the time stream. This was the alpha and the omega of all paradox.

The target somehow escaped an assassination in the late nineteen hundreds, surviving through an indeterminate time afterwards and destabilizing the time stream. Recorded history, and the initial time monitoring databanks, all said that he died. For nine hundred years, the world had been hanging under the modern equivalent of Damocles' Sword.

But she had doubts nagging at her. Undoing nine hundred years of history in order to undo a class six paradox seemed like it might be more harmful than helpful even though, since the incident of that giant paradox, nothing greater than a class two paradox had occurred. There had to be something missing from her files.

Once again she did the math on the situation and it returned results in the positive. Just like the countless other times she had done the math since accepting the mission. She sighed and rubbed her temples. If only she could disclose this to her husband and have him review the results. Deep in her gut, she had a feeling she, and everyone else, had missed something important about the equation.

But then again, according to the algorithms the computers spat out, this guy was meant to die here and now. The disparity between her gut and the facts was maddening. Ultimately, her job was to be an agent. It created a certain focus, simplifying the choice. And when it came to simplicity of form and action, it had a certain beauty as a form of conflict resolution. She followed orders.

Following orders didn't leave her a lot of choice. She settled down in her seat to watch the trial and to try to piece together the reasons that the missed death of the man who created time travel served as the greatest paradox in all of history.

RELATIVITY SYNCHRONIZATION:

THE SECOND CAUSE

2003: The Sea & The Swimmer

"...bullet appears lodged in temporal bone, possible meningeal and or brain penetration. Blood is flowing freely. Continue open IVs with lactated ringers. Blood here? Good. Nurse, clamps and sutures. He's tachycardic, tachypneic. His eyes are moving, he's shocky ... I think he's waking up!"

Chris didn't understand. He couldn't see and his face itched. He tried to remember the last thing that he had done, but organizing his thoughts was like digging in mud with a butter knife. He tried to reach up to scratch the itch on his face, but for some reason his arm wouldn't respond. Why couldn't he move? Was something holding him down?

"I need suction now. Damn it! Anesthesia? Get him back under now! How's his paralytic? Intact? If he moves we're d..."

"...up again? What are you doing? Get him under and keep him there! Are you a first year resident or what? Do you want a malpractice suit on our hands?"

"Doctor—any more and I'll bottom his pressures out. His body's burning through everything five times faster than anyone I've ever seen. I'll start him on presso ..."

Both infinite and stagnant, time formed not a line or a circle, but a sphere. And along the curve of that sphere were an infinite number of planes, overlapping, intersecting, and warring for space. The surface was measurable, but it was larger on the inside, creating an infinity of possibility inside the construct.

Spinning along the planes of existence were motionless solar systems, people, planets, every conceivable perspective. Each of them projected a sheath, protecting it from the other planes of existence.

An entity moved through the sphere, swimming in the substance of time, at first without awareness. As time passed—a misleading statement, since within the substance of time things that happened instantly also took eons to transpire—it became aware that it was a "he."

At the same, and yet separate, time, he became aware that he served as part of a greater sum. In the bright darkness and silent roar of the substance of time he sought anything that could be identified as himself. He ranged and spread throughout the infinite sphere until he found an anchor—a mass of flesh and matter (the word 'man' entered into its thoughts, then, 'I am a man.'), both within but outside the Time Sphere.

It could sense a boundary between 'he' and 'himself' and he briefly wondered if he had found the edge of time, but quickly discarded the idea. This was something else; a veil that allowed the substance of time to ooze through to the other side, but not enough to create or destroy the dual purpose of time. It was only enough to ... progress.

He studied the veil and became aware that it was indeed porous: that, in fact, tiny holes that allowed the raw substance of time to seep into the universe covered the whole of the Time Sphere. With this understanding came awareness that on this side of time, he had no body, and, therefore, the size of the pores did not in the least bit matter.

With that realization he moved toward himself, and reached through the veil at the sleeping figure on the other side. While what he saw and understood was wrong, it built a picture that allowed him to pretend at understanding, and it was enough for him to find his way back.

2873: James Garret's Laboratory

James sipped his coffee, going through the motions of his day. His mind and spirit fought each other, and somewhere amidst the joined battle his heart had slipped in and stole the victory out from beneath the two combatants.

Since his discovery of the "Down" Nano a week ago, allowing him to alter the speed of his personal time stream, his thoughts had been trapped in the past. With an all too vivid recall, his mind went over and over the death of his wife. Replaying for him the scene when the message had arrived from the Corps that she had died while on a mission. He now had to deal with a pain he thought he had buried years ago. But now ... the picture had changed. He had a new tool at his disposal that went beyond the scope of the Agency.

The Time Corp Agency had refused to share the details of her death with him, insisting that undoing it would create a class five paradox. All of the details of the mission were listed as classified. The suspicion that had gnawed at him back then was that they had classified it to keep the details from him. They were afraid that he would make an unauthorized jump to try to fix the outcome to result in her survival.

Garret knew that he was the best analyst that the world would ever see and it was not a source of pride. It was simply a stated fact within his soul. And because of this, it drove him into a near fury every time he thought about the Corp's refusal to allow him to take a crack at figuring out how to save his wife. If anyone could find a better solution, he could, but they were so damned afraid that emotion would rule him that they wouldn't let him work on the files.

With a sigh he put down his cup of coffee. He made his decision. Stretching time would make it rather difficult for them to stop him from getting the details for himself. Since they would not allow him to work out a solution with them, he must follow a different course of action. The more he thought about it, the more the idea crystallized in his mind.

He knew what he had to do, and he even thought that he knew how to do it. With more than a little nervous excitement he began preparing himself. There were several things that he did not yet have.

He wrote out to-do lists, started preparing to rebuild technology that had not existed in a long while, and started pulling information from his dead wife's computer, which he had hacked long ago. It was an arduous task, preparing to pit himself against the Time Corp, but he would finally be getting answers.

Time: Classified
Operation: Classified

Wanda sucked in a breath between clamped teeth as she watched her husband walk into the trial in place of the prosecuting attorney. What was he doing here? Had he seen her? She had to fight the urge to abort the mission on the spot. What the hell was he doing here? She looked closely at him and was surprised to see that he looked about ten years older. His frame was about the same, no weight lost or gained, but his hair had started to go to a silver-white in streaks here and there. And his eyes ...

His eyes were very different. They were not the warm playful eyes that she remembered. Instead, they now looked like the eyes of a lifelong insomniac, with permanent dark rings below them. His smile wrinkles were gone. She used her Optical HUD contacts to confirm his identity. It was a positive match. Ten years older. Well then. Perhaps field control had given him a secondary mission. But why would they send a scientist into a field situation? Her HUDs weren't showing him as chipped with an active mission, so odds were against him being here on legitimate business.

The only conclusion that she could jump to was that he was acting independently as a time rogue. She shook her head in horror at that thought and clamped her fingers over the bridge of her nose. She had developed the habit to help herself stay silent when she needed to. Just what the hell happened in the future to bring about this series of events? As tempting as it was to contact him and ask, she knew that the results of talking with him alone could create a huge paradox and piggybacking even a class two onto a class six could have devastating results on the stability of the time stream. Contact was not a viable option and she summarily dismissed it. Puzzling out the situation from secondhand and observational facts would to have to do.

Could procedure have changed so much in the ten years separating them that he would be allowed to come back here? That was an easy answer: no. James was on an unauthorized leap, trying to alter the time stream without field command's knowledge. She didn't even really need logic for that one. He would have sent a message via the HUD if he were here on a legitimate mission. So, logic followed that her husband's motivation was either born of desperation or that he was hell-bent on destroying the world. Wanda thought it through. No matter how bad things were for James upstream from her relative time, she knew her husband well enough to know he would never act on a course he felt would be destructive to the world around him. He was too good of a man.

This meant that he was desperate. So it followed that one of two things caused him to be here. Either she failed or she died on this mission in his relative time. The third possibility floated into her mind that it could also be a combination of the two. She might fail and die. One was as bad as the other so far as she was concerned, without adding to the weight by combining them.

But from James's viewpoint she couldn't see a simple failed mission inspiring this kind of action in him. Even if it became such a grand failure that it destroyed her career. Ergo, she must be about to die. She sighed and shut her eyes, closing out the trial's beginning. Retreating deep inside her mind, she analyzed the situation looking for the best course of action.

Unless she followed her original course of action, she would be creating paradox at the nexus of all historical destabilization. That was not truly an option, since any aberration in history at this time and point brought with it the possibility of destruction of the course of history. And not just by splitting out the time streams. This one was much larger than that. If she altered her course, it could simply cause them all to cease to exist, replaced by who knew what.

She got up and walked out of the courtroom, a single tear running down her cheek.

2344 B.C.: Unmapped land.

Alex wiped the sweat from his brow and leaned the shovel against a tree. Rubbing the small of his back, he stretched and yawned. It had been a long day, and he was only half done as of yet. He leaned back against another tree and watched the sky for a few minutes. The brilliant and clear day shone down on him, warming him.

Birds chirped and he could hear animals in the distance. He didn't get beauty like this upstream. Or rather, all of the pollution and then repair done to the Earth had created a different kind of beauty that lay upstream from this point. This time seemed purer, untouched by the hand of mankind.

With a sigh, he pushed himself forward. Back to work. Kneeling down at the lip of the small hole he had dug, he reached his hand down and into it, letting nanos slip from his system into the claymore he had placed in it. Once the transfer completed, he closed the lid of the silver box, trapping the mine in its airtight container.

While the machine would corrode and rot, regardless of the hermetic sealing, the space would be there still because of the box, and land erosion should make it at the perfect height for his use when he needed it. The nanos he had dropped into the system would remember the shape and function of that mine. They were programmed well. And though the mine might be gone by the time he needed it, the nanos would replicate the effect on an invisible scale.

He stretched his senses through the time stream and checked all of his traps. He had over seven thousand placements and he felt no strain monitoring them all. With an impish grin to himself, he said aloud "Damn, son, you *are* good."

The traps served a secondary function, linking up to his home time. He hoped he never had to trigger the function … or rather, since he would be dead when it triggered, he hoped it never triggered for him. Scooping the shovel back up in his long, calloused hands, he filled in the hole and moved to the next time to continue placing the traps he would need to survive his death.

RELATIVITY SYNCHRONIZATION:

THE THIRD CAUSE

2044: Rude Awakenings

Chris's eyes fluttered open, the dreamland in his mind evaporated as his pupils adjusted to the waking world. *Where am I?* Scouring his mind, searching for memories, he found only nothingness, a blank slate. He couldn't remember anything from before the moment he opened his eyes. He knew his name and could recall any number of theories, equations and formulae, but nothing else remained.

No faces, no events, places or objects, just impressions that those things had at one point existed. Only one name endured: *Christopher Nost. That's me*, he thought vaguely, and smiled sardonically to himself. *I know who I am but the rest of the world is gone. Too bad for the rest of the world, I guess.*

Chris looked around the windowless room. The walls and floor were piercingly white and a pervasive smell of sterility under laid the pine scent of the air. *Hospital.* The word drifted into his consciousness along with images of faceless people, sick and dying.

Am I dying? he wondered.

Not far from where he sat on the edge of the bed the numbers '14:27' hovered in the air over a similarly white nightstand. Cautiously, Chris reached out to them. They flickered and remained. The seven shimmered and changed to an eight. *Ah*, Chris thought. *A clock.* For some reason an image of a white disk with numbers around the edge came to mind. And that image brought a cold fear to his gut. He suppressed the thought and looked at the floating numbers again.

Another word drifted through his thoughts. *Hologram.* Once again he passed his hand through the display. This time, he kept his hand there, moving it rapidly back and forth, until the image disappeared entirely. He stopped and a moment later the numbers '14:29' flickered back into existence.

A cough came from behind him. Chris turned to see a woman in a nurse's uniform standing in the doorway, looking excited and nervous at the same time. "Dr. ... Dr. Nost?" she said, her startled gaze never leaving his face.

"Yes? I think so, anyway." Chris looked into himself and realized where the 'doctor' came from. *Ah, PhD in physics. Hence all the math spinning through my brain in place of memories.* Chris shook his head in frustration, trying to jar his memories loose. "Look, maybe you can help me. Where am I? What's going on? Why can't I remember anything about my past?"

Her attempt at a reassuring smile faded, but the look of shock in her eyes remained. "Um, I know you have lots of questions, but I can't really answer them. I'm sorry. The doctors are on the way now and they should be able to take care of everything for you." She spoke as if to an infant who couldn't actually understand. That way of speaking tickled something in Chris's memory, but it fled again before he could grasp it.

"Fine. Can you at least tell me how long I've been here? Can you tell me anything about myself?" Chris shook his head in frustration, *that can't be right;* denial ran through his head.

She walked across the room, tapping on a tablet as she went. She pulled up a stool and sat in front of him, putting down the tablet to pick up a blood pressure cuff. "Well, Dr. Nost, according to your chart you have a doctoral degree in Aerospace Mechanics and another one in Astrophysics. And you've been here for 41 years, two months, and five days." The nurse spoke while she hurried about performing what appeared to Chris to be an ordinary physical.

"What? There must be some sort of mistake. I ..." Chris felt the walls in his mind crash. Fear rose in his belly and his only defense kicked in as rage, making his blood pump hot.

The nurse looked flustered and a little frightened, realizing she had said something she hadn't meant to. "Dr. Nost, I'm sure you're confused. Please, sit back down until the doctors get here. I'm sure they will have all the answers to your questions." She backed toward the door, looking scared.

Chris realized he stood, clenching his fists. He swallowed and sat back down on the bed. He took a deep breath and felt the anger drain out of him, revealing his fear and confusion. "I'm sorry. I'll wait." The nurse darted back to the bed and grabbed her tablet, then hurried out of the room.

The flicker of the clock shifting times sparked something in Chris's mind. He raised his hand until he held it in the air before his face. Smooth and strong, the back of his hand had a healthy color.

There must be some sort of mistake. If forty-one years had passed he should be elderly, but he didn't have the hands of an old man. Even if he had graduated college as a child prodigy, that put him at sixty years old. Yet he had the hands of a young man. He looked around the room for a mirror, but saw nothing. His gaze at once came across the red numbers hovering over the stark white bed stand and he shivered. *There must be some sort of mistake.*

The door opened, revealing a thin-faced man in a white doctor's coat and wearing a smile that didn't reach his gray eyes. He looked familiar somehow, but once again the image vanished before it quite materialized. Behind him stood a dozen men and women all wearing the clinical white smocks of medical practitioners.

Enter the legion of the blessed attendants and confused hangers-on ... thought Chris.

"Good afternoon, Dr. Nost. We're so happy you decided to join us," said the man standing in the foreground, obvious leader of the legion in white.

Those eyes are like steel. Cold and hard ... Chris looked away. *Why does he seem so familiar?* "Who are you? I mean besides a doctor." Chris forestalled the man's speech. "Where do I know you from?"

"My name is Dr. Garret Jameson. I have been your ... caretaker for the past eleven years. These—" He gestured to his entourage still crowding the doorway behind him, "—are my associates."

Chris raised an eyebrow at the word associates. "Are they going to break my kneecaps if I don't pay up on my gambling debts?"

Doctor Jameson laughed. "They might put casts on your kneecaps should you find them broken. As to the breaking itself, I'm afraid my esteemed colleagues get a bit squeamish if it comes to imparting violence. No, overall we are rather poor enforcers. As to where you know me from I have no idea. I wasn't born until two years after you went into your coma. Perhaps while you were in your coma you subconsciously became acclimated to my presence. We do have a limited amount of time, so are there any other questions I can answer for you?"

"The nurse said I've been asleep for forty-one years. I can't believe this is true."

Dr. Jameson sighed. "I know that this is difficult for you to accept, Dr. Nost, but it is indeed true that—"

"How is that possible?" Chris interrupted. "I mean ... It doesn't feel right. I don't look like I'm in my sixties or seventies." He looked with wonder at his hands again. They were young hands.

Dr. Jameson handed Chris a mirror. "Yet you are. Seventy-four to be precise, Dr. Nost. You haven't aged a day since you arrived at this facility over thirty years ago. The only reason that we know your age at all is because of your birth records. As far as I know, you did not age in the prison hospital the twelve years before that, either. Perhaps ironically, it was the lack of aging that saved your life. You see, once the governments fell ..." Jameson shrugged.

Chris's head swam. His earlier fear subsided into the quagmire of utter confusion. "Just a minute. You're telling me that I was in prison before I got put in this hospital?"

Jameson tapped the tablet he held in his hand. "Well, yes and no. It seems you spent your entire sentence hospitalized and in the exact same state that you were in when we received you. Public record has it on file that you were shot right after you were convicted."

Chris took a deep breath and tried to center himself. "Do you know what was I convicted of?"

Jameson's eyes looked to the wall beyond Chris, breaking contact. "First degree murder. Something I recommend avoiding in this society. PolCorp's policies are to carry out immediate sentencing, including the death sentence, administered by the arresting officer."

God. A corporation that can legally kill you for any reason they want? Chris's mouth went dry. "Why don't I remember any of this? Is it because of the coma? Do I have some form of partial amnesia?"

Dr. Jameson bit his lower lip. "I doubt that it's because of the coma. You see, you had a pre-existing condition. When you were ..." he flicked at the screen of his tablet, quickly reading through records, "twenty-nine, you began to experience a very unique form of memory loss. Your conceptual memory is seemingly perfect, but as far as anything else is concerned you forget everything after approximately thirteen months. It is a similar condition to that found in some victims of brain damage, though the more common term before total loss is substantially longer."

Those steel gray eyes once again locked with Chris's. "Really, you are an all-around mystery to us, Dr. Nost. As I was saying, after your prison term expired, you were transferred here. When the governments fell a few years later they were going to pull the plug. One less expense, you see. My predecessor convinced GeoCorp that you could be an asset worthy of study. Potentially a high profit yield research project if we could unlock your enigma."

Dr. Jameson smiled. "We can make holographic clocks, Dr. Nost, and even implant computers that interface perfectly with the human brain. But to halt the aging process is a mystery beyond us. It seems that it is something you alone are able to do."

Chris's mind rebelled at what he was being told. *Learn about what is happening now ... What led to the world you're going to have to live in. Deal with the rest later ...* "Fine. I'm weird. What about everything I missed? What do you mean by 'when the governments fell'?"

"It was about eighteen years ago. The governments and the global corporations had been feeding off of each other since before your ... accident. In the end, the governments got weaker and the companies got stronger until ...'"

A cough came from Dr. Jameson's entourage, and he trailed off, glancing at the holo-clock.

Chris knew his time to ask questions ran thin. "So this GeoCorp, it's the company that runs America now?"

"This part of what used to be America, yes." Dr. Jameson cleared his throat. Chris saw that he played with what at first looked like a wedding ring, but looking closer he saw closely woven gold fibers imbedded in the man's finger.

"I apologize, Dr. Nost, but we cannot speak here anymore. Every moment of my time at the hospital is accounted for, you see." He glanced at the gold ring.

"I truly am sorry. We have grown quite fond of you around here, despite Company policy. Some of the nurses even took up calling you Sleeping Beauty. As it stands, it is good that you woke up when you did—it became increasingly difficult for us to convince GeoCorp to keep you alive with every passing quarter. You were not cheap for the Company, and we could not find anything different about you that would halt the aging process or halt muscular atrophy."

Chris hadn't thought of that. He looked down at his body and saw the doctor was right—his muscle tone was the same as a normal thirty-year old. "Not bad for lying in bed for forty-one years," he said. *This is out of control.* Fighting back tears he tried to control the fear and confusion that were threatening to usurp his rationality. *Just what the Hell am I that I can ignore the effects of time?*

"Indeed," the doctor looked at the hovering clock, a worried expression on his face that still didn't touch his eyes. He fumbled in his pocket and withdrew a wad of paper Chris recognized as money.

"Here," Dr. Jameson handed him the wad. "There should be about two hundred and fifty thousand dollars here."

Chris's eyes widened as he took the money and the doctor laughed. "Believe me, that's not quite the same amount it was before you … as it was in your time …"

"I guess it wouldn't be," Chris laughed ruefully, trying to cover his growing anxiety. He looked around for somewhere to put the money and realized he still wore only a hospital gown, so he sat there, clutching the wad of bills in his shaking hands. Once again he had to take a deep breath to regain control of his body. "I … where am I supposed to go?"

One of the other doctors pulled some clothes out of a closet in the far end of the room and handed them to Chris. Made of a dull gray material and shaped to an amorphous cut, they didn't look like his clothes. But then again, he couldn't remember what he used to wear.

As the group of doctors began to walk away, Jameson leaned towards Chris. "Find a hotel until you can find a job. Stay away from the south side of town. There's a gang war going on down there and the police have announced that they will no longer be patrolling the area."

Jameson glanced around the room, then back at Chris. "Look, I'm sorry we can't be of more help, but I really must be getting back to my rounds. I will already be getting docked for the time I've spent with you." Dr. Jameson handed Chris a card and walked out of the room.

Chris looked at the card. It was not, to his surprise, the doctor's business card. Rather, it was a card from a local restaurant, with handwriting on the back.

LITTLE PARIS COFFEE COMPANY
1655 N. CHERRY LANE

Chris flipped the card over. On the back the doctor had written in bold, elegant script:

MEET ME HERE ON THURSDAY AT 1500.
AVOID THE COMPANY AND THE HOSPITAL.
YOU DO NOT WANT THE COMPANY TO
CONTINUE THEIR RESEARCH ON YOU.
GOOD LUCK. –G.J.

Chris tossed the card on the nightstand and got dressed in an ill-fitting gray business suit, with a white shirt and long black woolen overcoat. He wondered what time of year it was and swore to himself. *Why should I worry about what season it is? I don't even know where the hell I am.* Once he was done getting dressed he picked the card back up, along with the cash, and shoved it in a pocket.

As he left the room, he looked around in the hallway for someone to ask, at that moment realizing how little he knew about his circumstances. The hallway seemed deserted; the whirring little cameras that monitored every hallway intersection were the only signs of life.

He found the elevator, two massive brushed aluminum doors at the end of the hallway. Once he was inside he glanced at the number panel. 'Sixty-six' was glowing red. Surprised to see the numbers went all the way up to one-eighty-one, he took a moment to clear his mind then hit the 'L' button.

So it's 2044, what am I supposed to do now? Forty-one years asleep and I still have the better portion of my life left to figure out how to survive in a world that seems hostile to its inhabitants. And they have the advantage of knowing how everything here works.

Chris realized with a start that he was feeding himself on a growing cycle of self-pity and anger. And paranoia. *Enough! Get out there and do it. Otherwise you won't need this world to chew you up—you'll do it to yourself.*

Chris still stood in the elevator, even though the doors had opened, staring at the wall. He shook his head, then stepped into the lobby and looked around. The image of a hospital lobby he had in his mind didn't resemble this. Vast and empty, massive marble pillars stretched up to support the ceiling fifty feet overhead. At the far end he could see through the revolving doors emptying into the street, though a haze of rain hid the details beyond. Near the elevator, to his left, a security guard sat at a sprawling circular desk stacked high and wide with a bank of security monitors.

The pudgy man wore something that looked faintly like a thin bulletproof jacket over his uniform. An automatic rifle leaned on the wall behind where the man sat, within easy reach. A little video camera nestled on the guard's helmet with a 'G' contained in an upside-down, gold triangle. The emblem was also on his sleeves, and, Chris saw, behind him, between the elevators and above the guard's desk, thirty feet high. Below the triangle on the wall read "GeoCorp," and below that: 'Bringing the Future of Tomorrow, Today!'

"Can I help you?" With the unfriendly offer, the guard eyed Chris and rested one hand on his gun while he made it.

"Um … yes. Sorry to disturb you while you're so busy, but could you tell me what day it is?"

"Monday. Now get out. No loitering, or I'll need to throw you out, and believe me, that would be a real shame." The man smirked and hefted his rifle.

"Yeah. Thanks. Asshole." He said the last under his breath. The guard glared but said nothing as Chris walked to the door and out into the rain.

2873: James Garret's Laboratory

Another beautiful twenty-ninth century day shimmered around him. Recycled air breathed through the city's cycling vents. The sun shone through the rebuilt atmosphere; the sky embraced the world in its rich deep blue arms. Today's weather patterns called for bright and sunny so there were no clouds in the sky. That would be next week, when the Environmental Control Agency called for heavy rain.

Patting his pockets one by one, James checked through his mental equipment list. All present and accounted for. With a quick flex of his mind he accelerated his personal time stream to about two hundred times the relative Terra flow and walked out of his lab.

The frozen world around him was peaceful, in a beautiful harmony of stillness, which the supposedly utopian society he lived in never managed to actually achieve. At least not from his perspective.

At the end of his driveway a motorcycle waited, already infused with his phase nanos. He hopped on and fired it up, walking it forward as the ancient monster's engine lumbered to life and warmed up.

Vehicles like this were one of the major reasons that the Environmental Control Agency had been born. The Earth had been torn to shreds by a humanity too young to truly grasp what it was doing to the world it had to live in. Luckily, the technology to keep the human race alive on a healthy planet had been born in the nick of time, and now everything was artificially controlled.

But phase time changed the rules of what James could use as tools. An electrical engine would fry in the accelerated time, with the nanos burning out the more delicate modern technology, so he had been forced to rebuild an archaic internal combustion engine. The major problem he'd had to overcome with the combustion engine had been airflow. In accelerated time flow, the air moved slower than the time field and if he stood still too long the air supply would exhaust itself. Igniting sparks in the engine only compounded the problem by using up the air faster, so he had to stay in motion. The simple solution was to shift time flow after starting the bike, but he didn't know if he was under surveillance and didn't want to risk being spotted.

Once the engine warmed up and he no longer had to trot the bike around to keep it running, he gunned the throttle and headed out on the highway, dodging through the frozen traffic faster than the near frozen cars' proximity sensors could detect him.

After about an hour of travel on his subjective time scale, he arrived at the Time Corp base headquarters, and on a spot of luck, a car headed through the gate. He smiled at the good omen that he didn't have to resync time to wait for an opening to enter the complex.

Any point that he had to sit in Terra's time stream would only increase the odds that he would be spotted while at this task. He dodged through the gate by the side of the car and pulled into the main lot, circling it until the cameras that watched the lot were cycled away from where he needed to park.

As he rolled in to park, he killed the engine and let the bike drift to a stop so it would have a fresh field of oxygen to draw from when he left. It would have to, since he had a very short window of opportunity before the bike would be spotted and the gate would close again.

Hopping off the bike he popped a concentrated energy pill, dropping about five thousand calories into his system. He had designed the pill for his own metabolic system and had manufactured three of them for this job. Reaching into his belt back, he pulled out a mini scuba mask affixed to a six-inch air tank and put it over his mouth.

Now, for the hard part. Focusing his will, he pushed against the time stream as hard as he could, accelerating himself until he felt the physical effects of the strain on his body. As though on cue, he felt the pill kick in and a surge of cold energy washed through his system. His HUD clocked his relative time at just over a factor of one thousand times Terra's standard time flow. He smiled and walked into the Time Corp's headquarters.

First, the lobby. Scanning the area quickly he found the security guard walking back from the restroom towards the front desk where he should be stationed. Grabbing the guard's security badge, he worked his way through the building; methodically stealing badges to work past higher and higher level security checkpoints. At each point he had to push some of his own nanos into the security systems so that they could let him through a bit faster.

Not accelerating to the security checkpoints drained his energy. If he moved too rapidly, he would fry out the systems and make this whole exercise useless. Working hard and fast, he made it to the top of the building without any major problems.

Terra's time flow showed three seconds had elapsed when he found himself in the head Administrator's office. Leaning over the frozen man, Director Arbu, he accessed the computer, scanning through the files surrounding his wife's death.

He didn't bother reading yet, instead just having his HUD record all the files. That had been another stroke of luck for him when originally designing the HUD to utilize the body's cells as its circuitry board instead of using electrics with it.

The last file scrolled by his eyes and then he closed out the files, returning Director Arbu's monitor to the display it had been on when he walked up. Less than five seconds had elapsed so far. Another stroke of luck then, that Arbu had not been looking at his monitor when James arrived. Two seconds Terra time was too long and he surely would have noticed that something was amiss. He grimaced and started moving as fast as he could back downstairs.

There were only two seconds left in his window before the bike would be noticed, even in phase time. If he hopped back to reset it, all the alarms would be triggered and the time it took the Corp to discover their files had been stolen would speed up.

James Garret pushed himself even harder, making it further into phase time, pale and sweating. But he raced against time and he couldn't afford to lose this race. He sprinted between doors, and a few times even got lucky, managing to make it between thin gaps as other people were walking through check points.

He made it back downstairs, replacing all of the badges he had stolen as he went, with fifty milliseconds to spare. He sprinted across the front walkway of the building, hopping the railings around the perimeter and running across the water of the fountain rather than wasting time going around.

He made it to the bike and threw himself onto it. Seventeen milliseconds left. It took him three milliseconds to have another energy pill in hand. Taking as deep a breath as he could, and then holding it in, he ripped the oxygen mask off of his face and affixed it to the intake on the bike, popping the energy pill he'd palmed a few milliseconds ago.

Eight milliseconds left. He fired up the bike, listening to the sweet sound of it rumbling into life. It took the bike seven milliseconds to fire into life, and he sped out of the lot and drove back to his home, finally holding the information surrounding his wife's death.

Leaving the bike in his driveway, he stumbled back into his house, barely able to retain consciousness. Pale, drained of all energy, his hands shook. The theft had exhausted him, and even with a boost of ten thousand calories metabolized into his system, he felt utterly wiped out. He collapsed into his chair and leaned back, taking the weight off of his drained muscles. He stared at the ceiling for a moment, allowing himself a second to relax.

The base white of the ceiling, unmoving and all encompassing hypnotized him. He drifted off to sleep. With a start, he snapped back into full wakefulness, focusing away from the ceiling only with a great effort of willpower.

Gathering his mind back to here and now, he allowed himself a wan smile. He had actually done it. A scientist, untrained in the rigors of physical combat or espionage had just bested the Time Corp and succeeded in breaking into their headquarters to steal information. Highly classified information, no less. He laughed aloud.

Calling up the information on his HUD, he started to review what he had stolen. Everything that he needed to know about the events surrounding the death of his wife lay there in front of him. Finally, he would be able to solve the riddle of how to unwind time and replay it in such a way that he could bring the love of his life back to him.

But there is only so far he could push the human body, no matter what boosts he gave it to help it weather the course. He may have intended to work away the night, but he had gone well past that breaking point for his untrained body. He fell asleep.

Time: Classified
Operation: Classified

Wanda settled down in her position, spot-checking the pistol's scope to make sure she had it aimed correctly in the makeshift housing built onto the tripod. Seated in her roost, she had the entire courthouse exit area covered.

She had chosen an optimal perch. Not only did it give her a perfect sighting on her target area, but it had multiple exits and she would be able to hear anyone who came from the level below her.

The wait before the target came into sight should be a brief one, and then the deed would be done. Despite all the paradox surrounding this mission, she could, and would, achieve the task she had been set. She settled her nerves and focused into perfect stillness, ready for the shot.

To all outward appearances she was a perfect sniper, locked into a death trance, awaiting her kill. Internally though, she warred with herself, trying not to think about her assumption that something would happen here to result in her death. Thoughts and contradictions played out in her mind, clashing with each other. Visions of how she would die kept playing themselves out in her mind's eye and she clamped down on her imagination, a hard won struggle.

Her attention drifted and she had to fight with herself to snap her focus back to the job at hand. She knew such conflict proved deadly to an agent under fire.

She almost missed it when the crowd gathered, but caught the movement in time to reposition herself for the shot. Oddly enough, the target had not exited yet, though quite a mob stood on the courthouse steps. She scanned the crowd, catching brief glimpses and forming impressions of the faces she saw.

People were definitely upset by the verdict, which firmed her faith in the validity of the mission. The man had obviously not committed the murder. But now he had to die, and she would make sure, for the sake of history, that he did. Police formed contact point lines to act as crowd control and it looked like some movement came from the inside of the courthouse.

And then the impossible happened. She saw the target in the crowd, instead of in the courthouse procession. The target kept his head ducked and seemed to be moving into the heaviest density portion of the crowd.

Watching him, she managed to get a quick scan of his eyes as he looked around himself to make sure no one observed him. His retinal pattern checked out positive. And there was no aging. This was her target. Odd, but that would explain why the crowd had grown into such an uproar.

Adjusting her sights, she took a bead on him and eased back the trigger. He pulled a gun out of his jacket and aimed it towards the courthouse. That was odd. Very odd.

But she didn't have the time left to analyze the situation or change her point of aim. And skipping back in time would only add another small but important weight of paradox into history's already weakened fibers. Not a risk she could justify taking.

In a moment of perfect stillness everything unfolded for Wanda Garret. The target pulled the trigger of his pistol. His wrist jerked back as the recoil hit his arm, and a bullet screamed out, marking someone unseen for death. As this happened, a shadow darkened Wanda's sight.

Someone had managed to sneak past her alert system and, improbable as it seemed, stood behind her. Wanda jerked and pulled the trigger as her body tried to pivot to assess the threat looming behind her. Her pistol slammed back against her shoulder as she lost control of the gun, then it spun out of its tripod and went sliding across the floor to the opposite corner of the room. Well out of range for her to grab.

Reality crashed back into full motion for Wanda. Screaming and sounds of panic came from the direction of the courthouse below. She laid on her back staring down the barrel of a gun.

When a gun is pointed at your face, it can be very difficult to look at anything but that black tunnel that signifies your death, concealed in its shadowed chamber, there and waiting for you. She tried to jump through time, but something blocked her from slipping the time stream to safety.

A man loomed over her, dressed in dark clothes and looking like nothing so much as a classical private detective. He wore a rumpled trench coat, battered fedora, and had an unlit and dented cigarette hanging from his lips. He stood a solid six foot three, towering above her. Rugged good looks combined with a crooked nose, broken at some point, completed the effect.

As he stared down at her he slowly winked. "You missed, Wanda."

She gasped as recognition sparked. She knew exactly who this man was. "Alexander Zarth. Pleasure to finally meet you. Though I would have preferred a less ... intimate setting."

Alex chuckled softly as he looked down at her. "The pleasure is all mine."

He pulled the trigger.

1972 A.D.: Denver Colorado.

Alex mopped his sweaty brow and looked down at the job foreman. No one enjoyed working in the hot day. Noontime sun beat down on the man, as he sought refuge from it in the lee of the site's main office. Workers milled about below, lifting, dropping, or in one memorable case sleeping, around various positions on the site.

No eyes were on him at the moment. With an impish grin, Alex sighted the Denver Courthouse from his perch and installed the Hazer in the grid work of the buildings girders. Once the Hazer had blended with the girder to the point that he could no longer see it, except on close inspection, he ran a system check. Reality shifted by about a quarter of an inch as he activated it, then everything settled down to look normal again. He grinned and deactivated the unit.

Over the course of the afternoon, his nano machines worked their magic, imbedding the Hazer's circuitry into the building's central wiring. By the time he finished working on masking the Hazer, its circuitry was seamless with that of the building, making its activation invisible against the background electrics already running.

About fifteen minutes before the shift ended, Alex winged a screwdriver out of the aperture in front on him, aiming about two degrees off, right at the foreman's back. With a satisfying thunk, it walloped the man in the back and he screamed in outraged pain. Alex deactivated the Hazer again and headed downstairs to get into a fistfight.

He came out from the building's half-constructed entrance and bellowed, "I am goddamn sick and tired of working my ass off while you hide in the shade and dodge having to work!" Challenging a foreman's authority was about the fastest way to get into a fight. Getting into a fight in which the foreman threw the first blow was the easiest way to get fired without leaving a paper trail behind.

As he strode up to the foreman, the other man cocked a fist and threw a punch at him. Alex easily sidestepped the blow and threw his hardest uppercut straight into the man's solar plexus. The foreman crumpled around Alex's fist then slid to the ground. Ten minutes later Alex had been fired and he walked away into the future. It amazed him how well he could hide in the system by being willing to do an honest day's labor and then get into an honest fight.

RELATIVITY SYNCHRONIZATION:

THE FOURTH CAUSE

2044: Brave New World

As Chris stepped out of the hospital and into the downpour outside, he closed his eyes and turned his face towards the heavens. Cool rain gently washed down his cheeks and he felt some of the tension he had built up over the last half hour evaporate as his muscles relaxed.

Opening his eyes, he noticed the GeoCorp guard behind him in the reflection of the massive glass windows. Standing halfway down the hallway, the man watched Chris while gripping his gun. Smiling inwardly, Chris walked away, turning up his collar against the chill. *Some people will always be small-minded. Hmm. The world may have changed but humans will always be human. Directions.... Where do I go?* Chris looked at his surroundings. The light from the afternoon sun lost itself in the mammoth maze of buildings.

Around him, at ground level, it looked like an abandoned war zone. All he saw were rusting hulks of cars in the damp shadows. *Its mid-afternoon ...* around him the steady rhythm of water pounded on rusted metal and cracked concrete. *And the streets are empty. What is wrong with this city?*

The streets were not, however, silent for long. At the edges of his hearing Chris became aware of a humming echo reverberating through the concrete canyons, a dull rush above the spattering of the rain. Chris swallowed. *Of course.* Far, far above, he could see a line of gray sky between the glowing neon spires of the skyscrapers around him. Below, in between the buildings, rushed hundreds, thousands of small, flying vehicles.

Chris looked again at the rusting hulks of vehicles around him. *They're up there now.* No one seemed to use ground level anymore. He could see advertisements projected on walls promoting everything from cosmetic cybernetics to hand grenades. Most were flashing the GeoCorp or PolCorp Securities logos on them.

"Hey, no loitering. Get lost loser." The rotund guard stood in the door of the hospital glaring at Chris with his assault rifle leveled at him. "PolCorp hates doing cleanup jobs on ground level. Believe me, you don't want to make 'em come down here to take care of this. Now leave and I won't even fine you."

Chris flipped the man off as he headed down the street. *Malicious little pig.* The guard kept his gun trained on Chris for a minute before turning back inside, once Chris had walked far enough away.

A deep rumble came from above Chris like an earthquake. He looked up in time to see a train rumble along tracks five stories above his head. The gridworks suspending the tracks were integrated into the sides of the buildings and appeared to wind through and connect to all of the buildings in sight.

Despite the grand arches that jumped from building to building, the entire thing looked run down and shabby. *That train must be what the poor people take.* He looked at the remnants of cars around him. *Either that or the people of this time are frightened of the streets....*

"Got ten bucks, buddy?" The gritty voice came from his left, slurred and bone weary. From the alley next to him a gnarled figure staggered out toward him until he shadowed in the mouth of the alley. "So how about it? Help a guy down on his luck?"

Chris thought for a moment. He had no idea how far the money Dr. Jameson had given him would go, but he needed some information. *Besides, what's ten bucks out of two hundred and fifty thousand?* He studied the figure in front of him for a moment. "I'll tell you what; I'll give you a fifty if you can answer a few questions for me."

The man grinned a gap-toothed smile as he emerged from the alley. "What ya wanna know?" He wore ripped jeans and a plastic bag as a poncho, and his question degenerated into a hacking, phlegm-filled cough.

As he studied the man's face, Chris realized with a start that while the man looked like he was in his sixties, he probably wasn't even thirty. Chris couldn't tell where the five o'clock shadow ended and the dirt began on his face. "All right," He fished a fifty out of his pocket but kept it held in his hand. "For starters, what's the date today? Do you know that?"

The man smiled again. This was going to be the easiest fifty he had ever gotten. "Monday, October sixth, or close to it."

Ok. Fall. So I was put into the coma in summer.

"Good enough. Now, where am I?"

"You're on Greensborough Avenue—right down the street from GeoCorp Central Facility."

Well, that means absolutely nothing to me. "Sorry, I meant what city are we in right now?"

"Are you serious, man?" The vagabond peered into Chris's face suspecting some sort of trick, but unable to figure out what it might be.

"I'm serious."

"Denver North, man. Old Thornton Corporate District. Where the hell do you think you are?"

"Thanks." Chris handed the man a fifty.

"Shit, man, for another fifty bucks more I can take you wherever it is you need to go. You want a guide?"

Chris thought about it. *This is too easy. What if this guy is a GeoCorp plant? Jameson said to watch out for the company.* "I'll compromise. I'll give you another twenty if you can tell me which way is south."

"Aw, hell man, south is that way, but you don't want to go down there. That way is a bad scene, man."

"Thanks again." Chris turned his back on the old man and peeled through his bills for a twenty, but he couldn't find anything less than a fifty. *What the Hell. They wouldn't have let me go just to track me through a homeless guy.* "On second thought, maybe I'll take you up on that offer."

The man grinned his toothless grin again. *Easy money.* "Where do you want to go?"

"Good question." Chris took out the card for Little Paris. "Can you bring me to a hotel near this place?"

His guide peered at the card and handed it back to Chris. "Well … the thing is, I don't see so good. I, uh …"

"The Address is sixteen fifty-five north Cherry Lane." Chris felt embarrassed for the guy. "It's called the Little Paris Coffee Shop."

"Aw, hell, I know where that is, but there ain't no hotels near there. It's in a mall, about five miles south of here. But don't worry, it ain't getting into the combat zone for about another twelve miles."

Chris sighed "Just my luck. We'll have to opt for second-best. Can you take me to the nearest hotel, then?"

"Nearest to here or there, Boss?"

"Nearest to the coffee shop," Chris carefully explained, "if you know of one that's a straight shot down a street from the shop so that I don't get lost trying to find my way there."

"Sure thing, boss."

"Here," Chris handed him the second fifty. "And let's stop on the way for food. I'll buy you lunch, besides—I haven't eaten in a very, very long time."

"Lunch it is. It'll be about a thirty minute walk till we get anywhere that'll let me into their place." The old man laughed, doubled over in a fit of vicious coughing, spit on the ground, and said, "I always love a man that pays in advance. I'm going to enjoy working for you."

They walked in silence for a while. At first Chris was wary of the man and kept an eye on the shadows, half-suspecting a trap. But as time ticked by to the steady rhythm of their footfalls and the steady rain, he allowed his guard to drop. The man would only grin when Chris looked at him, and nod his head to indicate a change of course.

"What's your name?" Chris asked as they walked under a huge purple neon arch into what looked like some sort of shopping center. The décor may have been nice once, but steady traffic from the city's destitute had turned it into a den of dirty stalls and shouting shopkeepers, each trying to attract notice to the shoddy wares that they were displaying.

"Clive is what my name is, but most people call me Rat. How about you?" Rat asked as they turned once again and left their shortcut through the mall.

There were people now, and the streets were no longer shrouded in shadow. All around them people bustled, bathed in multi-colored neon light, some hurrying through the rain in search of shelter, but most moved about unconcerned. Wet trash smell filled the air, but a more pungent, flowery smell was pushing the offending odor away. Chris had no clue where it was coming from. There were PolCorp officers milling with the crowd, carrying riot shields and assault rifles like the one the guard at the hospital had. They eyed the milling throng with arrogance, but ignored Chris and Rat who were sticking to the shadows on the sides of the street.

"I'm Chris. Chris Nost." He looked around. "What is this place? Why are there people all around when everywhere else has been deserted at ground level?"

Rat moved on, a gleam in his eyes. "You ever want any action, this is the place to come. Heh." He trailed off into another coughing fit. "This is a Ped Mall. Special parts of the city are turned into these places and patrolled by PolCorp so that the upper levels can come down and slum."

Chris stopped for a second, taken aback at seeing Rat's eyes, then picked his pace back up. Now that they were in decent light he could see that Rat's eyes were yellow. "I see. Action. Do you mean prostitution?"

"You got it, boss. Of course, there's plenty of action in South, but there's plenty of the wrong kind of action down there, too, if you know what I mean."

"So I've heard," he smiled at Rat. "I was warned that PolCorp doesn't even patrol down there anymore."

"It ain't PolCorp not patrolling that's bad. In my opinion that's actually a plus."

Chris eyed the crowed with curiosity, filing away the tidbit about PolCorp, but focused on the streets around them. There were no obvious sex shops or hookers or girls behind glass. "So where's the action you were talking about? I don't see anything."

"Oh, well officially GeoCorp has outlawed all that, but trust me, you can get some ass in almost any one of these places. Shit, man, they can make more of a profit on it if it's illegal. Then when shop keepers don't pay the squeeze, they fine the piss out of them."

Chris saw mostly clothing boutiques, but there were also a few clubs advertising that they were open 'twenty-four-seven', and two gun stores. "What about the gun stores? They seem kind of out of place."

"Shit, man, trust me—they got the finest ass on the block. All the weapons they carry are a front for having really high-end security to protect the image of the Corpies that don't want their faces seen. They still sell, of course, but this way there's a good reason for them to be loaded up on the firepower."

"Interesting. Do they let just anyone buy a gun?"

Rat stopped walking and looked Chris in the eye. "For fuck's sake, man, where the hell you been? Yeah, anyone can buy a gun. As long as you got your papers. Shit, you want one; we can go right now...."

"No, no. That won't be necessary. My apologies. I ... I've been in a coma for quite some time. I just got released from the hospital and I'm having to learn everything as we go along. Please be patient with my questions."

Rat looked at Chris again, laughed, and shook his head. "Shit, boss. Are you serious? Sorry about that. You look pretty good for a guy who just got out of a coma. Hey, it's time to eat—follow me." He led Chris into an unmarked door in the side of a building, where a few derelicts like Rat sat around bowls of steaming, unidentifiable gruel.

"I told you not to come in here, Rat," the lady behind the bar said as she reached for something under the counter.

"It's okay, Roberta," Rat croaked. "I got cash today. Meet my new friend, Chris." He gestured toward his guest.

"Yeah?" Roberta reached for a different spot under the counter and pulled out two bowls, ladling some of the stew from a hot pot behind her. "Looks like he's got cash. Where did you pick him up?"

"The hospital," Rat smirked. "He just got out of a coma."

"Yeah, whatever. It'll be a hundred bucks, high roller."

Chris paid. "What is this stuff, anyway?" he asked her, eyeing it suspiciously. It was gray and chunky, and he couldn't smell any discernable odor. He ladled up a spoonful. The taste surprised him. Everything in this future seemed like it was faded and broken, lifeless. But the stew exploded over his tongue. It was slightly spicy with rich flavors twining together. It was the most delicious thing he had ever tasted.

She leaned close to him, over the bar. "Between you and me, honey, you don't want to know what's in it."

Rat and Chris ate in silence after that.

As they left the restaurant, Rat took a side street out of the market and led Chris through a maze of garbage and rubble. Occasionally they had to step over small groups of sleeping people, huddled together for the shared body warmth. Massive pipes ran up the sides of the buildings, turning the rain to steam with a sizzle where it fell on them.

"We're almost there," he said to Chris over his shoulder as he climbed a pile of greasy cardboard made soft by the rain, which had diminished into a fine drizzle. He slipped and tumbled down the far side, out of Chris's view. Chris heard a string of cursing through the rattling, wet cough. He clambered up and over the pile in time to see Rat climb sluggishly to his feet and make a feeble attempt at brushing the mud from his plastic garbage bag.

"Here you are, boss!" Rat did a little dance, like a pageant queen presenting a prize on a game show, as he gestured down the street he had tumbled into.

Halfway down the block Chris saw it, "The Rangley Hotel." The buildings were lower here, and Chris saw a few people milling around. They had a distinctly different look to them than the 'Ped Mall' crowd. These people were less glitzy and glamorous. The way they kept their heads down spoke of locals trying to get on with their business, rather than flashy kids out looking for a good time.

There were even a few trees growing on the corners of the intersections on either side, though only sparse brown leaves still clung to the stunted branches. Another thing that spoke of the urban instead of the high-rise corporate world was that there were no abandoned cars in the street. Though the few cars parked on the street did not look like they were in particularly good repair, they did look operational.

Rat pointed down the street the other direction. "See that big, pointy tower?"

Chris saw it: a massive silver spike, about a mile down the street, which rose what looked to be hundreds of stories high. Chris was awed. *That isn't possible. That building must stand near a mile high. Someone must have engineered high impact, low weight building materials while I slept.*

The street they stood on ran toward the obelisk, and seemed to be a thoroughfare for the aerial cars that zoomed a few hundred feet overhead. The way they swerved and moved, passing both above and below, Chris imagined that there must be some sort of advanced artificial intelligence driving them. Either that or humanity's reflexes had improved quite a bit in the past forty years.

"This is Cherry Lane. Go that way—the shop you're looking for is on this street right under that spike."

"What's the spike?" Chris had trouble keeping the awe out of his voice. "It's huge."

"That, boss, is the GeoCorp District Administration Building. The D.A.B." Rat stopped the mock bravado and moved in close, his eyes shifting about. "Don't trust them."

"Why not?" Chris asked, suspicion surging through him. *Who is this guy? Maybe he really is someone sent to spy on me. But why would anyone want to keep tabs on me?*

"Because they're assholes, that's why." Rat coughed and spit something black onto the trunk of one of the wretched trees. "They got all these ads floatin' around that they're gonna bring a better tomorrow. Well, fuck them. They ain't gonna help me with this shit—" Rat thumped his chest "—cause I ain't worth shit to them. I don't have money, so they're gonna watch me die and send in a cleaning crew to burn my corpse. I'm only twenty-five and I'll be dead in under five years—all because GeoCorp won't employ anyone who had family in the government. So with me the Kennedy family dies out because my grandfather had the wrong job."

Rat leaned towards Chris and lowered his voice to conspiratorial whisper. "Hell, most of the street people you saw are in the same position that I am. The really old guy asleep back there at the mouth of the alley is Tod Morrison. He's the famous mathematician who came up with the new Mathematical Optimization Model that solved the food shortages for the population growth. People considered him one of the world's greatest philanthropists—even won a bunch of prizes. But he worked for the government and now he sleeps on a concrete bed."

Chris's suspicion ebbed, but he didn't know what to say, so he looked back at the spire. "Thanks. I never would have found the place without you."

"Shit, it ain't nothin' for a hundred bucks. You need anything, you find me. Just ask for Rat—I'll be around."

"I may take you up on that." Chris fished through his wad till he found a five hundred dollar bill. "Take this. Consider it a retainer to stay in the area so I can find you if I need you."

Rat nodded to Chris with a grin as he took the bill. "You take care, Chris Nost. This is a dangerous world—but you're different. And I like you." Then he headed back the way they had come. Chris could hear his wet, hacking cough long after his head disappeared behind the heaps of rubbish.

Squat and run-down Hotel Rangely's dingy exterior had seen years of abuse and disrepair. A couple despondent souls lounged by the front door, using the hotel's canopy as a shelter from the light rain and drinking whisky out of an unmarked bottle that Chris could smell ten feet away. He nodded to them as he walked by, trying to be friendly in his nervousness, but neither responded with as much as a grunt.

Inside, the lobby was mostly clean, if worn, with a few dusty chairs and tables. In the far corner sat an overweight cleaning woman watching a black and white television even older than Chris. The anchorwoman spoke about widespread natural disaster in Asia, and the images on the flickering screen depicted piles of bodies bloated by flood and burned by fire.

Chris approached the desk. "I need a room," he said to a newspaper held erect by two stumpy, hairy hands. The headline read:

Mount Fuji Blows Again,
Remnants of Japan Sink

"How long?" The paper lowered to reveal a scabby bald man with a face that looked like it came from the same family as a pit-bull.

"Actually, I have no idea. I need a place while I look for a job." Chris realized his mistake as the words came out of his mouth.

"Sorry, bub. 'No idea' isn't an amount of time I rent for." He brought the paper back up, hiding his face from Chris. "Besides, we don't rent to people who ain't registered Corp Employees."

"Wait. How about a week?" He realized that this would be an expensive fix. "I'll have my papers by Thursday. After my hiring negotiations."

The clerked gave Chris a long, calculating look. His small piggy eyes lit up with the prospect of a good profit. "Three-thousand. Cash only."

Chris smiled. "Can I get a receipt? I'll need to turn in my expense account to the Company, after all. I will be getting partial reimbursement for the move until I find a more permanent place to live." He hadn't liked the way the guy had looked him over, and given what little he knew of the times, it seemed a safe thing to say.

Sure enough the man scowled and said, "Eighteen hundred and no receipt. That's the best price I can give you."

Chris counted off some bills. "Here's fifteen hundred. No receipt, but a good room."

The man thought for a moment and pulled down some keys from the pegboard behind him and tossed them to Chris. "Deal."

Chris took the keys and slid another three hundred across the counter. "Tip." He said simply. It seemed the best course of action to make sure that he had the man's friendship in the future.

The clerk smiled. "Wait up a minute."

He took down another set of keys and flipped them to Chris, and motioned for Chris to toss back the others. "A good room. Like you asked for. Anything else I can get you?"

"Can you tell me where a drugstore is?" Chris thought about the basic necessities he would need.

"What kind of drugstore?" The clerk raised an eyebrow. "Slab, smack, net drugs, contraceptives, antivirals … what you looking for?

"You know, toiletries, that sort of thing? Toothbrush and stuff." Chris raised his empty hands to indicate his lack of luggage.

"Sure, bub. By the way, the name's Charlie." He reached into a drawer and pulled out a map of Denver, pointing out a few malls and intersections with convenience stores. The tourist map had only the main streets and little pictures of all the places worth seeing in the area. In large letters along the top it stated: NORTH DENVER— TWO MILE HIGH CITY.

"You got no luggage?" The clerk seemed to have a hidden meaning in his question, but Chris had no idea what it was.

Chris shrugged. "I arrived a little unexpectedly."

"Shit, man. Sounds like being born. Hey, let me know if there's anything else I can do for you, Mr. …?"

"Call me Nost. Chris Nost."

"Righty-o, Chris Nost. Call down to the desk if there's anything you need. Dial star one-one. I'm here nine to nine every day, and most nights, besides. Enjoy your stay."

The room surprised him, given the outward appearance of the Rangely Hotel. The bed was large and not obnoxiously lumpy, and the little table lamp lit the room with a bright yellow glow. Chris shut off the lamp and opened the brown, flower-patterned curtains, letting the distilled gray afternoon light wash over him and into the room. It had stopped raining, but a low fog had rolled in, hiding the silver spire of the D.A.B. and obscuring the view from his room. The Rangely was the highest building on the block, and Chris wondered what the scenery would be like once the weather cleared. His trip through the streets with Rat had disorientated him and he was no longer sure which way downtown was.

Chris stripped and walked into the bathroom, wondering whether or not he would find some technological wonder. Luckily in the bathroom he found only a sort of refreshing disappointment—

familiarity. Shower. Tub. Toilet. Sink. Starched hotel towels with the GeoCorp logo on them. They were the only signs in the hotel room that he had been asleep for forty-one years. He took them off the rack and laid them, unfolded and facedown, on the floor. He muttered his thanks that the embroidered "G" in a triangle was only on one side. Less than a day in this world, but he already knew he didn't like GeoCorp, turned the hot water all the way on, laid down on the towels, and let the steam wash over him.

He waited until the bathroom was filled with steam, turned off the shower and climbed into the tub, letting the heated ceramic warm the chill he hadn't noticed was there. Tension started to drain from his muscles and a warm glow seeped through his body, filling the void left by the tension.

Chris attempted to let his mind drift into oblivion, but there were too many questions running rampant through his thoughts. *Who did I murder? Why? How is it possible that I am here, now?* He thought of Dr. Jameson and felt a growing irritation. How could the man profess he cared anything about Chris when the only advice he could give was to find a job? *I know he was on the clock, but three days is a long time to wait for answers.* With newfound resolve he buried that portion of the discordance in his thoughts by resolving to find a way to research his past before meeting with Jameson. He smiled as he felt a small portion of the weight of his troubles lift from his shoulders.

Chris couldn't fathom searching for a job in this dark world of neon lights and cardboard dreams. If his suspicions were founded in reality, then everything he knew as a scientist was outdated and no longer relevant. It seemed impossible that the technology level had advanced so far in just over forty years; he assumed there had been some major breakthroughs since his time.

That line of thinking brought more questions. He had no specific memories from 'his time' at all—only a series of thoughts and impressions. He didn't even know what sort of person he was before about six hours ago. He didn't feel like he was capable of murder, but then he thought back to Rat.

The surge of paranoia he felt when Rat told him about the D.A.B. was more than cautiousness at unfamiliar surroundings. He had something ingrained in that reaction. Paranoia seemed to be a part of him, which meant that the hostility and anger he had been feeling were part of his personality. But something about that didn't resonate within him. His internal vision of himself didn't match the shape that left in him. *God damn it … Personality reconstruction is a painful experience. I want to know who the hell I am.…*

As the absolute reality of the situation struck him, Chris snickered and then his control snapped and it turned into a deep belly laugh as tears turned into streams. The release felt good but a small part of him remained, an inner self, retaining control, which wished this were all a delusion. That he was back in 'his' time, penned up in some asylum, out of touch with reality.

He tried to make the image stick, but it slipped and faded into nothing. *This is real,* he told himself over and over as he lay in the bathtub absorbing the ambient heat in the room. *This is real. This is real. This is real. And I am trapped here.*

He lay there for a long time, until he started to get cold. Then he stood up and showered, rekindling the warmth in his bones. The more he thought about it, the more he realized that, without memories, he would be just as out of place in 'his' time. It was all the same when you had nothing to base it on. *I guess,* he thought, *if there's anyone who can handle the world after sleeping for forty-one years, it would be someone who couldn't remember what it was like before.* Chris laughed again. *Unless, of course, I really am crazy.*

He got out of the shower, opened the bathroom door to release the steam, and toweled off the mirror. "I'm seventy-four years old," he said to the mirror, but it sounded absurd as he looked at himself. Shoulder length, dark brown hair, shiny with moisture, sat atop a scruffy face with a strong jaw line and hard, gray eyes. For some reason they reminded him of Dr. Jameson's eyes—cold and void of emotion.

Chris scratched his chin. *I guess I woke up before they could give me my daily shave.* He still had three days before he met the doctor at Little Paris. *Might as well make myself presentable,* he thought as he dressed himself in his only set of clothing, still damp from the rain.

He could tell from the darkening of the gray light outside that night had fallen and he looked at the clock—a regular digital buzzer alarm clock with red numbers. Six oh-five. He considered waiting until morning to run his errands—the city seemed dangerous enough during the day, but he felt unconcerned. He had an inexplicable feeling of … waiting in his stomach. He didn't know what he waited for, but he felt a weird certainty that until it happened, nothing could possibly happen to him. Anyway, he was restless.

"I guess forty-one years of sleep will do that," he said to no one as he locked his room door behind him. "Anyway, how bad could it be?"

2873: James Garret's Laboratory

Garret put down the stolen file and rubbed his eyes, trying in vain to blink back the exhaustion. He caught a ragged breath. They had sent his wife single handedly up against the greatest paradox in history and expected her to win. In a lot of ways, it was murder.

Expecting one person to be able to tip the balance of historical imperative by that much was beyond sheer stupidity. It bordered on willful blindness. James had a nagging suspicion that Director Warren, predecessor to the current Director Arbu, had known what he was doing. At least he had lost his job over it. But the trivial price that had been exacted was far from enough.

Still, something about this did not add up correctly. The math worked well enough, but not perfectly. It was almost as though.... He scratched out the formulas on his relative paradox theory, inputting the data from Wanda's file. And there it was. He could not build the relativity frame correctly for the information contained in the file. So, something was missing, something about the time frame she had been operating in.

Regardless of that, the math said that she could not have survived, which meant someone in headquarters wanted her dead. Or possibly both. Garret couldn't shake the belief that Ex-Director Warren had wanted Wanda dead. Perhaps the motive and the missing information were linked.

He ran the math yet again, to be sure. Simple math showed that no single person could affect the catalyst actions needed to counterbalance a paradox above a class three magnitude. The computers could not have missed that little piece of this mission.

Bloody thoughts of vengeance filled Garret's head. Visions of storming into Warren's house and killing him ... but he shook those thoughts out, instead focusing on the more productive lines of how to save his wife's life. Chief amongst those thoughts was how to create a secondary paradox that resulted in his wife's survival without crashing the time stream.

It was fairly obvious to him that walking in and trying to avert the events which led to her death would have much the same results as Wanda's mission had ten years previously. Starting to see a path that would result in getting Wanda back, he got to work on the mathematics, cranking out possible solutions with temporal physics.

Shadows grew longer and the air chilled as the sun made its journey over the horizon. Hours and hours of math had not yet revealed a simple solution to him, nor did he feel one would be found in the math alone. An elegant solution sat somewhere in this problem, he could sense that much—but where was it?

Starting from scratch he listed out his tools. 'Up' nanos allowed access to the past. 'Down' nanos allowed him to stretch and manipulate the time flow. HUD contact lenses allowed him faster computational power than anyone in the world, except his dead wife—who would be active in the time frame. Any non-anachronistic appearing technology would be usable as well.

But there were so many variables in accessing the paradox nexus and changing the outcome. Frustrated, he walked out of his laboratory and into the living room to attempt relaxing on the couch. And there, on the History Channel, came the solution. It took him a moment of watching the show about historical wars for it to click in his mind, but it finally did.

If you spun a smaller paradox to brush the larger one, instead of amplification you would create a small shift in the large paradox's spin. A smile spread across his face as he formulated the plan.

Time: Classified
Operation: Classified

Lucille Frost shifted through the paperwork on her desk. There were a hell of a lot of good points about this era, but paperwork was definitely not one of them. She missed the future, where you never needed to see paper unless you wanted to. Instead of these ungainly heaps spread across her desk, everything would be centrally filed and easily accessible through her data pad—anywhere in the world. The global net had effectively put an end to the need for desks, replacing paper with desktops.

On top of that was the scientific level of this century. Talk about mind numbing. Reviewing archaic technology had to be the most boring assignment she had ever been given. She sighed again and sifted listlessly through her pile of documents.

Finally, she surrendered to the advancing lines of infantry paperwork. They were almost successful in managing to storm the chasm at the edge of her desk and she did not have the patience for this. So, to hell with it. The best combat specialist in the twenty-ninth century should not be stuck behind a desk so far as she was concerned. Organizing her desk into piles of random paper she got up and left the office, stealthily moving through the hallway towards the elevator.

Just as freedom was at hand, someone cleared his throat behind her. She nearly jumped out of her skin, but managed to retain control of her reflexive reaction. Squaring her shoulders she took a deep breath and waited for the verbal attack to begin. She knew she had been cut off, but it had yet to be seen if she would be routed.

"Hey there, Lucy. Where are you sneaking off to?" The voice belonged to Christopher Nost, the primary reason she was stuck in this outhouse of a century behind a boring desk with nothing of real importance to do.

She turned around and sweetly smiled. "Why Chris, I was heading to grab a cup of coffee. I finished reviewing your paper on the nano drive and I wanted to try to digest some of the science in it. It seems to me that it will have a particular weakness to neutrino decay, so I figured I missed something." For good measure she took a deep breath, making sure her breasts were straining at the blouse she wore.

Best to use every weapon at hand when trying to escape the office.

Chris blanched. He was a typical male, insofar as liking beautiful women. And Lucille Frost was indeed a beauty. As she pulled in that breath, he found he had trouble staying focused on her project comments. He went for the gambit, "Hmm ... You know, it never even crossed my mind. Mind if I come with you and discuss some of this?"

Lucille nodded in assent. Internally, she danced with joy. She had escaped the office! Freedom was at hand! "Of course. I'll wait for you in the lot." She celebrated another type of victory as she realized what he was coming to discuss with her. How easy that had been.

Two months of casual conversation and a touch of tactical flirtation unlocked a mission that should have taken upwards of ten months to break through the initial phase. *Never underestimate the power of being a tease in a tactical situation,* she reflected. Heading into the parking lot, she had high hopes of knocking out an easy mission fast. And she had no idea just how wrong she was.

1997 A.D.: Colorado Springs, Colorado

Alex tipped his hat forward, blocking the sun from his eyes, and watched the scene playing out in the coffee shop across the street. Lucy and Chris were talking, and it seemed to be pretty heated, with a lot of disagreement expressed in curt motions of the hands and jerks of their heads. But the way he leaned forward and the way she faced him and stroked her hair as they talked ...

It definitely seemed that a romantic bond was forming. So, a commando from the twenty-ninth century and a brilliant physicist from the twentieth ... Interesting mix. Hell, interesting breach of Time Corp's policies and procedures. But who was he to say what was right and what wasn't, he thought wryly.

With a slight flexing of his will, he hopped forward in time by half a second to test to see if Lucy would note the travel in this proximity. He knew from personal experience, and one memorable night, that she was more than skilled. She was one of the best travelers out there. But she also seemed distracted at the moment.

He was only fifty meters from Lucy Frost, but she didn't notice the time skip at all. Alex rubbed his chin. Interesting. If she was this enamored of her scientist, it might make his job a hell of a lot easier. He spun an ancient Roman coin, one of Judas's thirty pieces of silver, across his knuckles as he thought.

His introspection snapped as the couple got up and left the shop across the street. Alex settled up on his bill, dropping a fifty to cover his cup of coffee, and then got up to discreetly follow them. He was pretty sure that using time travel for anything greater than a micro hop would alert Lucy to his presence, so instead he used the good old cloak and dagger method of staying a few cars back and tailing them C-Twenty style.

It took about half an hour for Lucy to drive Chris home. During the drive, Alex decided on his approach to dealing with Lucy. This time he would go with absolute honesty. Well, he admitted to himself, he would be mostly honest, anyway. After she dropped Chris off, he went ahead and pulled up next to her on the road, motioning for her to pull over into a random lot.

He saw her do a double take as recognition hit her, then she glared at him. With a sigh, he pulled behind her car. His decision had been made; he would try to reason with her. Failing that, he'd have to figure out how to take her down. Though, that would not be easy, as he well knew. He genuinely hoped that reason would work, and not for her sake. As she pulled off into the parking lot, he followed her in, then got out of his car. When he leaned forward to shut the door something hit him from behind and slammed his head into the frame of the car, leaving a dent over the door. Blackness erupted behind his eyes and he slumped forward.

On pure reflex, in the confusion of pain, he hopped forward in time. He found himself still in the C-Twenty parking garage with Lucy Frost standing triumphantly above him. He looked up and chuckled, still dazed. "I'm not sure I actually deserved that, Lucy."

She looked down at him as he spoke. With a brief shrug, dismissing what he had said, she returned fire. "That was too easy for the infamous Alexander Zarth. I cannot believe you are the same man that bested me back in Salem, lover boy. So what have you got hidden up your sleeve?"

With a grunt he scythed her legs out from under her and counter blocked her slipstream. Glancing over to her he made eye contact. "Easy. I came here to talk with you. Mind if I take a second to get rid of this headache?"

She shakily stood up and nodded. "Go ahead. You've proven your point well enough I suppose, so I'll listen. But I'm warning you—if I don't like what you have to say I will do my damndest to take you down, traveler. And it better be extremely convincing after the way you gave me the run around then dumped me back in Salem. I still haven't forgiven you for that little incident."

Alex laughed. "I would expect no less. Especially after the situation I left you in during the witch trials. I can still hear the cries of 'witch!' as you proved them right and vanished into thin air. Boy, the whole clergy was in an uproar for months about that. Though in all fairness you owe me a right beating for that one, and I know I've got it coming." He winked as he reached into his glove box and grabbed some aspirin.

Lucy let herself smile, just a little. "For an arch-nemesis you sure are being pleasant. Particularly after sleeping with me, then framing me as a witch and leaving me to be hanged."

Alex massaged his temples. "Well, would it be too harsh of me to point out that you were there to kill me?"

Lucy raised an eyebrow. "Alex, I know. It was just a job, though. Now talk. Why have you come here to talk to me? Why aren't you finishing the job of trying to kill me in return? Or am I wrong—do you harbor no ill will towards me?"

With a sigh, Alex leaned back against his car and looked Lucy in the eyes. "No ill will, Lucy. I really did mean everything I said that night. But it's also true that we are from different worlds. So, as to why I am here—simple. I'm here to try to avert the greatest paradox in history, and it centers on the man you are here to distract from his discovery of a drive that will break the light speed barrier. Lucy—you are at the center of this, so I have to talk to you. It's not a matter of want to. The last thing I want to do is hurt you again. But he is going to die soon, and it's my job to save his life. And to do that I need your help, though it is a course that will most likely kill us both."

Lucy reached into a pocket, pulling out a cigarette and lighter. She lit up and pulled a couple drags while putting her thoughts into order. "Alright. Somehow you know my mission. And you know about a paradox that can't be calculated with the mathematics of your time. So something is going on here beyond what you've said so far. Talk to me, you've definitely got my attention."

Brain still throbbing, Alex settled down to tell Lucy Frost a story that would hopefully make her betray the Time Corp. They didn't part company until after dawn.

RELATIVITY SYNCHRONIZATION:

THE FIFTH CAUSE

2044: The Laws Of Time

Chris stepped out of the hotel into the dawning night. At that same moment, the lights went on throughout Denver North. Now that the day's light had fled beyond the horizon, he could see the city, even through the dense, wet haze that still clung to everything, filling the air with a faint, moldering and acidic stench. Advertisements and floating halogen headlights glowed through the wispy remnants of the fog like a psychedelic neon wall, stretching from horizon to horizon and covering the entire eastern skyline.

Flecks of lights danced like fireflies as the little flying vehicles descended and rose from the lines of traffic that swarmed between the buildings. The physical bodies of the flying crafts remained hidden; he could only see the pinpoints of the halogen headlights that crawled through the mist. Only a slight damp whirring accompanied their passage.

He unfolded the map the hotel clerk had given him. With a rough circle, the man had marked an all-night drugstore that looked to be about twelve blocks west from the hotel. The shimmering dance of lights faded in that direction, showing only a few skyscrapers. Much smaller buildings, with a feeling of dinginess about them, stood tightly side-by-side down the street. It looked more to Chris like what a city *should* be like, but he could come up with no specific examples of why—he only had a vague, almost instinctual understanding. He had the same reaction with the flying cars; the cars on the ground, abandoned or otherwise, had a familiarity to them that the ones rushing above did not, though he had no distinct memory of either kind.

This must be the old part of town, Chris thought. He felt a sense of recognition at the dumpster-lined alleys and worn apartment buildings with a few ground cars parked outside. A tremendous rush of air buffeted him, and Chris looked up to see one of the air cars land on a rooftop in the midst of whirling trash and bright landing lights.

A block down from the drugstore Chris passed a PolCorp station. Two officers sat in a vehicle outside. It looked like a big ground car, all rounded bulges and chrome fins, until Chris noticed the vents along the back and sides. They eyed Chris as he walked by and he heard the engine whine to a start as he approached the drugstore. *Whatever*, he thought. *I'm not doing anything illegal. At least I don't think I am.*

"Jones Drugs & Merchandise" was lit with the same harsh white fluorescent light of the hospital. Lacking the sterile smell, it seemed, rather, that mold had taken residence in the walls. The only other person in the store, a tiny woman, sat behind the counter. One glazed, white eye peeked out from behind her long, brown bangs and she had a tattoo of a black widow spider on her forearm.

Chris wandered the aisles, looking at the wares. Some things gave him the same feeling of secure familiarity that the ground cars did: toothpaste, Twinkies, aluminum foil and Coca-Cola ("Original Recipe! Coca Leaf Extract in Every Can!"); others disturbed him. There were toy PolCorp guns and uniforms alongside "Skragsuits," plastic yellow jumpsuits with green stocking caps depicting strange insect heads. There were bottles of pills called "Rush," and others called "Doze," and liquid in bottles simply labeled "H." None of the pharmaceuticals had any sort of description or directions on them—it seemed to be assumed that everyone knew what they were for.

The ceilings were lined with flat TVs. The images had a distinct three-dimensional feel and offered a deluge of ads—all products offered "In this quality establishment." Chris learned that "Rush" was for those times "you need to cruise for more than twelve hours straight. Can take up to five safely." Right after that came a commercial for one of the flying vehicles, a large, fast-looking thing called "the GeoFord Terrestrial III," shown whizzing through isolated canyons and over plains. "Why drive, when you can cruise?" the woman on the monitor asked Chris. The faces in the images had a disconcerting habit of appearing to be looking directly at him, no matter where he stood in relation to the screens.

Chris selected a tube of "White-O" toothpaste, a toothbrush and a comb, and approached the lone cashier. He noticed a PolCorp Security vehicle parked in front of the doors, but through the narrow windshield he couldn't tell if there anyone sat in it.

I didn't do anything. What would they want with me? Chris tried to tell himself, but he had a sinking feeling of apprehension, a gut anticipation that something was about to happen.

Sure enough, as soon as he left Jones Drugs the car flared to life and a line of spotlights along the top of the vehicle blinded him.

"PLEASE STEP BACK," boomed a voice from the car, amplified to painful levels. "PUT THE BAG DOWN AND YOUR HANDS IN THE AIR. THANK YOU FOR OBEYING THE LAW."

Chris stepped back, put his bag of toiletries on the sidewalk and raised his hands. He expected someone to get out of the car and ask him for papers and tried to think of an excuse for not having them when the voice asked, "Sir, where are your papers?"

Before Chris could formulate an answer, a door lifted and a massive black man got out, pointing something at him that looked, at least in the blinding spotlights, like a small Gatling gun. "Sir, where are your papers?" he asked with a different voice than had come across the megaphone.

"They were stolen. On the way here. This guy, he …"

"Sir, I am sure you are aware that it is a felony offense to not report lost or stolen papers immediately."

"I just needed some stuff. I was going to …" he hadn't seen that one coming.

"I said *immediately*, sir. We saw you walk by our vehicle. Why didn't you go to the PolCorp station on the way here to fill out the required forms?"

"I …" Chris felt fear growing in the pit of his stomach as the strong, sour taste of bile rose in his throat.

"For that matter, what exactly, took you so long to—" the PolCorp Officer walked over to Chris's Jones Drugs bag and pulled out a gun. "Ah. I see. I don't suppose you have the paperwork for this little beauty, either, do you?"

Where the hell …? Oh god, why are they setting me up? Chris nearly panicked. *What do they want from me?* If this was how PolCorp operated—simply planting evidence to compound what seemed to Chris like a minor crime, he was doomed from the moment he walked by their car on the way to the drugstore. But why had they tagged him? Was it plain boredom, or was his underlying paranoia actually on the mark? *Just because you're paranoid doesn't mean they aren't out to get you.*

The other door opened and Chris heard "… ten-twenty-two, over. Waiting for back up. Over and out."

Before he approached his partner, the second cop did a once over of the situation. "What do you think we have here, Chuck? Some slumming High-riser wanting a taste of the under-city?"

"Don't know. More likely he's some wasteoid out for some quick cash. Look at him … his clothes don't even fit right. He probably tossed some exec so he could pull off looking like he was from the upper levels. I figure he saw us parked outside before he had a chance to roll this place, tried to wait us out, gave up and bought some toothpaste to try and cover his tracks." Chuck pulled out a pistol from the arsenal on his belt and pressed it against Chris's temple. "Even wasteoids need papers, loser."

Chris said nothing. If they were going to play this game, anything else he said would only get him into more trouble. The pressure of fear he had felt in his stomach had moved up his spine to the base of his skull and built into a mounting rage. He was no longer scared of these two. Now, it was time to act. Something primal grabbed control of Chris and he felt his mind lash out. Dizziness overtook him and the world blacked out.

2873: James Garret's Laboratory

Files and papers were scattered haphazardly around the lab. The general feel of the place was that a hurricane had hit it, in a small, indoor, and semi-contained way. Lieutenant Yuri Yakavich looked around the place again and sighed. It was fairly obvious that Garret was gone and he was not coming back.

On top of that, the man had some type of experimental tech that interfered with the Corp's attempts to back step in the time stream into the lab. Every field team they sent back got kicked forward to their origin time when they entered the building.

So Yuri had taken the only route left open to him. An army of clerks worked, dancing around piles of paper, which were growing into veritable mountain ranges. In an age of paperless technology, the man must have killed entire rainforests to get this much paper. Yuri watched the system of files being rebuilt into a tangible set of information that would give him a clue as to where the doctor had vanished.

He switched his attentions back to the monitor in front of him to watch Garret fly through central Corp's headquarters at an estimated speed of twelve hundred miles an hour, on foot. Again he sighed. The man was armed with at least two new pieces of technology and Yuri had to stop him from creating a paradox that would shatter history. At times like these, Yuri wished he hadn't scored so high on the Internal Intelligence tests.

Every few moments Yuri would get interrupted in his viewing of the robbery by a clerk handing him another document that they felt would be relevant. As the afternoon wore on, the pile in front of Yuri grew to be about a three-inch stack of papers. From every indicator, Garret had armed himself with historical information about his late wife's mission time, then hopped back to try to save her. But it didn't sit right in Yuri's gut. Something about the whole situation stank. He still missed some relevant piece of information—some key that would unlock this landslide of information growing in front of him.

James Garret's jigsaw puzzle of a mind started to fit together for Yuri when one of the clerks handed him a coffee stained napkin with a cigarette burn on it. Yuri walked into the kitchen and started looking around more closely. First, the air filter.

Cracking open the hermetic seal on the environmental system for the house, he pulled the filter out and glanced over the toxin levels it had recorded. No trace of nicotine in the environment's filters. He tapped the napkin and thought. 'Zarvan' was the word written on it. An ancient God of time. And a cigarette burn that could come from any time over a thousand-year period.

Turning in a circle, he opened his eyes and looked. Not just to see the environment surrounding him, but to truly look at everything in front of him as if he were the missing Doctor Garret himself. A nagging suspicion started to form on the edge of his consciousness. He grabbed a clerk walking by and pulled the man in front of him. "Get me his newspapers. I know he had them printed up. Bring me the crossword section of any paper that has coffee stains. NOW."

The clerk nodded and hurried over to his comrades to reorient their search. Old mountains of paper were chipped away and new ones formed as the clerks shifted their dance to this new beat. Yuri walked to the couch and turned on the television, holding the image of a frustrated James Garret in his mind's eye and trying to retrace those steps.

Hunting down the remote, he found the last view button and brought up the last program watched. It was a historical show about twentieth century wars. An hour later, Yuri finished watching the documentary and started going through the pile of newspapers stacked in front of him. As he suspected, a pattern emerged.

Every problem numbered twenty-six and twenty had been completed in every paper. Here and there, others would be done, but that was the only consistency. So, what had happened in the year twenty twenty-six? Yuri racked his brain and came up blank. Then he switched out the number set. Twenty-six twenty. And all of the lines of suspicion in Yuri's mind clicked into place. The pattern set and became real for him.

Yuri stood up shakily and looked to the clerks who were watching him. In a scared voice he said, "Get headquarters on the line. The son of a bitch got Alexander Zarth working on his side."

Time: Classified
Operation: Classified

Lucy drove to the office in a daze that the morning light only worsened. Rays of bright sunshine made the road impossible to see. Squinting to see the road, she couldn't make out any of the landmarks she passed. But she drove as though guided by an invisible force, not needing to see the road before her or the traffic on either side. The conversation with Zarth had lasted for over ten hours and she had a hell of a lot of thinking to do.

She was at least mildly surprised by this, as she found herself agreeing with the most wanted criminal in history instead of with her own policing force. But he had a lot of information that the Time Corp didn't, and it came from further up the line, if he could be believed. Though the fact that he had laid out all of the internal politics in her department from her time, well upstream from him, only lent credibility to his claims.

Paradox was the byword of the day. By pushing forward in her mission she would help facilitate the greatest paradox in history and bring the timeline to the brink of shattering. As unpleasant as it was, it seemed to be staring her in the face that the Time Corp had created the very paradox which they spent all their time fighting.

Slamming the steering wheel with her fist, she cursed aloud. "Fuck. A field agent should NOT be forced to make these choices." Though it appealed to her internal sense of irony, it was still hard to swallow. All the facts laid out though, and to be frank with herself, she had already decided to help Alex hours ago. Now she was justifying it to herself.

She pulled into the office's parking lot only to find that there were fire trucks and police surrounding the building. Threading her way through the maze of emergency vehicles, she finally found a spot to park in. Getting out of her car, she walked up to the sergeant who appeared to be in charge of the scene and flashed her security clearance badge for him. All thoughts of Alex and catastrophic paradox were temporarily shoved from her mind. "What the hell is going on here, Sergeant?"

The man, tall and heavily built with muscle and maybe fifty years old, huffed through his moustache as he studied her identification. "Well miss, you've had a bomb threat called in on your building. We've evacuated and we have the squad sniffing through the building."

Lucy sighed, "How much of a dent is this going to put in the day, Sergeant? We have a lot of work to get done here and we don't really have time to mess about with bomb threats in a high security government building." She put a heavy emphasis on the high security.

The sergeant looked put upon and took a moment before he replied. "Well Director Frost, since there was a break in last night, and your 'high security' building was already having issues with its 'security' we felt that it might actually be credible that someone got by your systems and left a little gift for you last night. Especially since the perpetrator was not apprehended. As I understand it, our department's attempts to contact you about this matter last night were unanswered. Have a little too much fun last night, Director Frost? I know I didn't. I was up all night trying to contact you."

Lucy went red with a combination of rage and embarrassment at the sergeant's comments. She also remembered that her cell phone was on vibrate in the glove compartment of her car. "Point taken. And as eloquently as you put me in my place, you have still failed to answer my question. How long will this take?"

The sergeant sighed. "I concede." He threw up his hands in a placating gesture and continued, "The sweep team should take about an hour, ninety minutes tops. That is only if they don't find anything. If there is a bomb in that building, I have no idea how long this will take to get done."

He thought for a moment, then decided to give some ground to the frustrated woman standing in front of him. "Containment and disposal are about thirty minutes each. Diffusing a bomb though … it could take five minutes, it could take five hours. But even with the break-in, I'd say that the odds are low of anyone having planted a bomb in your building, Director Frost."

And then the building exploded.

It came with no warning, no moment of dread foreshadowing the explosion. One moment the building was intact, the next fire was ripping it apart in a deafening roar. The explosion started on the top floor, in the corner closest to Lucy's office, and it seemed to hit a chain of detonations throughout the top floors, exploding in series.

Pebbles of concrete and tiny shards of glass flew outwards from the building, showering down into the parking lot and injuring people indiscriminately. Lucy felt shards tearing at her cheeks and leaving bloody trails as she stared in awed surprise. Then the bulk of the sergeant's weight hit her as he tackled her to the ground and held himself over her.

Lucy looked up in a daze at the man over her. Blood trailed down his chin and he collapsed onto her. A giant shard of glass, fully half a window, stuck out of his back.

1997 A.D.: Colorado Springs, Colorado

Alex sat on the motel bed, shirt off. Even with the air conditioning blowing, sweat poured down his face and chest. He studied the pictures spread across the foot of the bed. A Time Corp agent had been spotted by his drones breaking into the building Frost and the scientist worked in while he had been talking to her in the garage. He pulled out his computer and started running through the agent database that he had painstakingly assembled.

Alex preferred to work with a late twenty-first century laptop. Anachronistic compared to the technology available to him, but still pleasing to him because of the symmetry and stylized lines of the time period. It might not be the fastest, but it was the sleekest looking machine he had seen in any time period. The most durable as well.

The computer chimed and pulled up a match on the agent, Yuri Yakavich. Alex was somewhat familiar with the man, as he was usually the brain behind the agents that managed to catch up with him. With an already sweat-dampened towel, Alex wiped his brow. This job was getting thick. He lay back on the bed and stared at the ceiling, lining up his thoughts.

Two of the top three agents in the Time Corp were pitted against him. He had to assume they had pieced together his involvement in this situation, because of who they were. The worst of the top three was also aware of him and perhaps marginally on his side. But that margin could vanish in a heartbeat. The two most brilliant scientists history had ever seen were also involved, though one was unaware of the whole situation and the other a random factor, seeming to be working against the actions of everyone.

Throw in one Alexander Zarth and a shadowy figure from the fortieth century and what do you get? Alex pondered that for a long while before setting the thought aside for later review and going back to the question he needed an answer to first.

Why did the number two agent in the Time Corp make an attempt on the life of the number three agent, as well as the scientist who invented time travel? Could he be a rogue agent attempting to shatter history? His gut feeling said no. It was a specific attempt on Lucy, not on Chris Nost. Back to the basic question then, why the hell would one agent be attempting to kill another?

A musical chime sounded from the computer to indicate it was done with the temporal annexing portion of the profile on Yuri. Alex leaned forward and studied the screen with interest. Revision to the basic question—why would an agent from ten years upstream come back and try to wipe out Lucy? If he was upstream, he had to know it would fail.

So assessment one had to be that Lucy was not the target. Why then would Yuri plant the bomb if assessment one was correct? Assessment two followed: that Lucy was the target and Yuri was trying to create a paradox. And assessment three: no one was the target and that it was a warning. But a warning about what, and to whom?

Rewinding the video file, Alex watched it again in slow motion, hoping to catch something that he had missed on the first time. As he started, he lit up a dented cigarette and poured himself a glass of scotch. Twenty minutes later, the scotch was untouched and five cigarette butts were smashed into the ashtray.

He grinned like a maniac and laughed to himself. "Oh, Yuri. You sly, sly dog. I see your game now. You are far too clever for your own good." The video frame froze on a shot of Alex, hidden in the shadows, accepting a package from Yuri after his break in.

RELATIVITY SYNCHRONIZATION:

THE SIXTH CAUSE

2044: The Past Unfolds

"Did you get lost, bub?"

Chris walked into the hotel to find Charlie eying him with amusement, like he was a tourist who got scared of the dark and came running back to the perceived safety of the Hotel Rangely.

"What do you mean?"

"Well you've only been gone ten minutes and shit, it takes longer than that to get down to 38th from here. Can't you read a map?" Charlie folded his ever-present newspaper and put it down on the counter between them.

"I … my head … I've got a headache like you wouldn't believe. I decided to wait until tomorrow." Chris put his hand up to throbbing left temple and winced at the pain there. "I feel like someone smashed in my temple with a crowbar."

"You need somethin'? I got some painkillers here. How about …" Charlie started rummaging around in a drawer beneath the counter and Chris heard the plastic clinking of pill bottles being moved around.

"No. No thanks. I … I need to lie down. I think getting some decent rest should do the trick. I've been stressed out all day." Tiredness pervaded his bones, leaving him feeling washed up and disjointed.

Chris walked up to his room, trying not to jar his throbbing head. *Ten minutes? That's not possible.* He was sure it must have been at least a half-hour between when he left the hotel and whatever happened with the cops in front of Jones Drugs & Merchandise. How had he been gone only ten minutes? The clerk must have been mistaken.

He wasn't mistaken, and Chris knew it. He could *feel* it. He was aware of every moment, every second in time, and he knew as well as the greasy hotel manager he had only been gone ten minutes—but that somehow he had also been gone for thirty. *Maybe I actually am crazy, locked up in some white padded room. It would be a relief to know this is all going on in my imagination.* But he knew that wasn't the case—as much as anyone can know whether or not they're crazy. Everyone he had met was too real, too here, to be a figment of his imagination. *Now* was real, and there were things going on in him that he had absolutely no comprehension of.

Chris locked his door and lay down on the bed without taking off his shoes or wet coat. *Why didn't I run?* he thought. *Why did I need to kill him?* He remembered the rage he had felt during the second freeze. It had the same strange edge as the paranoia he had felt with Rat—something foreign, yet a part of him. Some external self, acting through him to preserve him. Or itself.

Memory replayed itself in his head. Everything had *stopped.* The hammer on the pistol, frozen in mid fall; then he had reached up and touched the man. That touch had instantly killed him—an old man's body falling to the ground. Emaciated and brittle, the impact of the fall had broken several of his bones. And then the blackness took over and he found himself walking into the hotel lobby, twenty minutes before his encounter with the cops. Once again he had to question his sanity, for he had just lived out the impossible.

Once you have ruled out the impossible, the remaining answer is correct, no matter how improbable. As the thought streaked through his mind, Chris wondered where it had come from. But he did know why he killed him, and it wasn't because of the rage—that had only helped him do it. He killed Chuck because he knew without a doubt that if he hadn't, the two guards would have reported him, and PolCorp Securities would have hunted him down and killed him before he had the chance to find out who he was or what was going on.

Now all they had to go on was the video footage from their head cameras. It was still bad, but at least the testimony of the guard who killed Chuck was unlikely to be taken too seriously. Or so he hoped. What he had done seemed to him like magic—which no one would take seriously. *Unless they know what I can do,* Chris thought to himself. But no, they didn't know. If they did, he was pretty sure they wouldn't have allowed him to leave the hospital. *Am I a magician? Do I have some undiscovered technology in me? Or am I ... something else?*

Answers would come with his meeting with Dr. Jameson, the day after tomorrow. He considered not going, the now-familiar paranoia chiming in the back of his head. *He's one of them. He works for them. It's all a setup.*

Chris fought the voice and won. *I have to know what he knows about me. Jameson had warned him to avoid the authorities and, anyway, the doctor had him right where they wanted him before he woke up. They had, in fact, had him for forty-one years. Why would anything change now? Had they wanted him enough to engineer this chaotic trip through this world? But for what purpose? They could have spent a lot fewer of their resources by keeping him at the hospital.*

No answer came from his consciousness. *How had he ... what was it? Stopped time? No. It was altered. Altered,* Chris thought again, and laughed. He had no doubt that he was the one who had done it. He felt himself doing it, but it felt like his heartbeat; he had no control over it. *I did this thing ... I manipulated time. But how?* Chris felt his eyes grow heavy and the torpor of deep sleep blinded him to the world as he succumbed to exhaustion. Massive culture shock had mounted all day and it beat him into submission as he collapsed onto his sheets.

Chris woke up feeling energized and refreshed. It surprised him that, according to the clock in his room, he had slept for nearly a full day. He didn't care, though. A path had revealed itself to him as he slept and burned in his mind as he got dressed. Deciding to go to the library had been a good decision. He now knew what he must do to survive in this world. With a confidence in his step that had been missing the day before, Chris went downstairs to the lobby.

He tapped the newspaper hovering at the front desk. "Is there a library around here?" he asked Charlie.

Shaking his head with a chuckle, Charlie answered "Man, I haven't seen a library in years. I hear the Omni Institute over on the east coast kept the Library of Congress around as a museum, but travel has been restricted to the Eastern Province since the war back in thirty-nine. Where you been, anyway? Everybody knows this stuff."

"In a coma, actually. I've missed out on a bit of recent history. Look, is there anywhere I can do some research? I've got some catching up to do, you know. For the Company."

"Shit, if the Company wanted you to do research they should have put you up in a better hotel. Most of the ones downtown have Net Termies in every room. I'd let you use the one back here, but it's ancient—Windows Based from like two thousand and five. Shit, it's the same system I learned on when I was seven years old; it can't handle anything but the Rangely's records, and it can't do that half the time.

"Here," the clerk took Chris's map and marked another spot a few blocks from the hotel. "This here's the closest Punt. It's open from seven a.m. to midnight every day. No kinky stuff on the P.N.T.'s, but then, you won't be wanting that anyway—that is, if you're on Company business." He sized Chris up then grinned at him. He didn't believe for a minute that that was why Chris searched for a terminal.

"What's a punt?" Chris asked, feeling a brief tinge of yesterday's culture shock again.

"P-N-T. Public Net Terminal. Jeez, man. Were you really in a coma? They've been around for like twenty-five years. Since Microsoft crashed and all their 'ware became freaking freeware. That's when the whole thing with 'free' public infrastructure and shit happened." Charlie chuckled, "Turns out all those crackers and net freaks that wanted free code weren't so happy with the results when they got it. Ha, free costs double." Charlie snapped out of his rant and looked back to Chris. "So, a coma, eh?"

"Afraid so. Thanks. Oh, and if anyone comes in here looking for me, PolCorp or anyone, I'm not here. OK?" Chris had no idea what Charlie talked about, but refused to let himself be daunted.

"Hey man. I ain't gonna cover your ass." A suspicious look crossed into Charlie's eyes. "Who the hell are you anyway? I don't need to ..." The clerk trailed off as Chris slid five crisp hundred dollar bills across the counter. *It's all business in this world. I have to hope that PolCorp isn't offering more than this.* "When I check out, I'll give you five-hundred more. That is, unless I'm smeared all over my room because you ratted me out. I don't know, will PolCorp do clean up in a private establishment, or will you be the one scrubbing my guts off the walls? For some reason I don't think she'll do it—" Chris nodded toward the permanent fixture of the cleaning woman, dozing in front of the TV behind him, who let out a sharp laugh without opening her eyes before falling silent once more. "I like you Charlie, and I hate the thought of you having to waste your day picking through the bloody mess my guts would leave behind. I know that the next shift won't do it either, seeing as how it was you that checked me in the first place."

Charlie pocketed the money, swallowed hard, and pecked at his computer for a minute before smiling his brown smile at Chris. "Well, whaddya know. According to the hotel records here, you checked out an hour ago because of a problem with your plumbing. You must have been pissed—there was shit all over the room. Needed to close it for a week for cleaning. Ain't nobody allowed in there now. Heh."

"Thanks."

"Hey, what can I say? You're a prudent man with lots of cash. As long as your money holds I'll be your best fuckin' friend." He picked up his paper again and closed the conversation by opening it in front of him.

"That's quite kind of you, but the room will do for now." Chris started upstairs when he thought of something, and went back to the desk, refusing to leave Charlie alone till he'd gotten some more answers. "Won't all of this show up in GeoCorp's records?"

"Well, I guess it would if the Rangely was owned by GeoCorp." Charlie smiled as he lowered the paper.

"You mean it's not?"

"Nope."

"I thought everything was owned by them." Chris mulled this over. This significant little tidbit surprised him.

"Well, they own everything important, yeah," Charlie shrugged. "I guess they figured a shitty hotel in the suburbs wasn't worth the effort of buying it from my granddaddy, who didn't want to sell." The clerk inflated with pride at this and Chris realized that as long as he professed a dislike toward GeoCorp, he would have help.

"I have to be honest with you Charlie, I don't like GeoCorp. I'm only working with them until I figure out how to strike out as an independent. I have to make sure that my tracks are well covered. So what about the hotel records? Can GeoCorp still get at them through the Net?"

"Heh," Charlie smiled mischievously. "That's the only good thing about working on a forty year old terminal. Nothing in the Cybernet uses Windows anymore, so it should be pretty hard to hack. Anyway, I issued you a full refund for the shit-filled room, which I will, of course, keep as a token of your good will," Charlie gave Chris the first friendly smile he had seen from the mash-faced, bitter little man. "For years those GeoCorp assholes have muscled over the lowers like me and the people who live around here. You ain't got nothing to worry about."

"Thanks, Charlie," Chris said, glad to discover a tentative ally.

"Like I said, you got the cash, I'll be your best fuckin' friend." Charlie leaned over the counter towards Chris. "Hey, you're not even really with the Company, are you? I mean you say you're using them to go independent, but that don't smell much like the truth. Smells more like a bathroom after a bulimics' convention."

Chris smiled and slid more cash across the counter. "What do you think? Anyway, two thousand up front should be enough to keep you from asking too many questions … Just the business side of our friendship, right Charlie? Secrets are expensive."

"Alright, alright. Fine, I won't ask. Keep your money though. I'm serious about helping you. Remember, if you want talk, I'm here every night from—"

"I remember. Nine p.m. till nine a.m., and the rest of the time, besides." He laughed; saying something like 'I remember' made Chris as happy as he'd been for two days. "I'll see you in a while, Charlie. At least I hope I will." As he walked towards the main lobby doors, Chris noticed that the clock above the door read eleven fifty-three p.m. The research would have to wait until the morning. Sighing, he turned around and headed back to his room.

Chris lay in the bed, but he didn't sleep. He wasn't tired. *After the twenty-one hours of sleep I got, I'll be awake for a few days at least,* he thought to himself.

So instead he lay awake, staring at the water-stained brown ceiling and getting up to look out the window. The night's fog lifted, and if he looked up while pressing his face against the cold glass, he could see the half-disk of the moon peering through the thin, yellow cloud cover.

The lights from Denver North, now revealed in all their glory, illuminated his room with an ethereal haze of blue, green, red, and yellow, overpowering the little table lamp and casting the illusion that the massive corporate billboards warred on his walls. Finally, Chris moved the room's little table to a spot in front of the window, pulled out a wrinkled pad of Hotel Rangely stationary, and began to work out formulae.

He worked through everything he could recall about Aerospace Physics in attempts to understand what he had done in front of Jones Drugs. Every time he found a promising lead it required that he be able to do the impossible and personally generate an event horizon. Chris chuckled. *I don't* feel *like a black hole.* He tried to find a line of reasoning that led in a different direction.

He pushed and pushed until finally it broke. His first line of reasoning was right. If he could generate an event horizon, he could theoretically stretch relativity to the point that he could achieve faster than light travel. And if he could travel faster than the speed of light, then theoretically—if he remained still on the three-dimensional axis and moved on the fourth—then he would be capable of doing what he had experienced.

The only problem with this theory was that it also involved some sort of machine or device that would allow an organic being to attain such speeds, but once again, that did not explain what had happened at the drugstore.

That frustrated him—the more he thought about it, the less sense it made. Whatever had happened in that parking lot was of *his* doing, not some machine. It was as natural as breathing to him, even if he couldn't figure out how to do it voluntarily. It was part of his mind, or … soul? Chris had never been a religious man, but had always held some secret hope that he would come across something that defied any sort of scientific theory. He never thought of the possibility that he might find that something within himself.

He tried several times that night to duplicate the *freezing* that had happened with the two PolCorp guards. Once he felt like he brushed … something, just beyond the time-space continuum as it is recognized by humanity. A void filled with something intangible, but then it was abruptly gone again. *I'm tired*, Chris thought. *Imagining things.*

But he wasn't tired. He did feel like he had woken from a refreshing forty-one-year nap. He looked again for the sense of nothing—the nothing/something he had felt before—but it escaped him, like a dream evaporating upon awakening. He felt the impression of it, but the details fled his mind. *Like everything else in my head—there, in its shape, but invisible in its details.*

Could this be why I didn't age? Chris thought. *Maybe this is something that I was born with, that only came out after I'd been shot—maybe it needed this world to come out. Maybe … maybe … maybe …*

But no answer came as Chris waited for dawn, feeling only the emptiness where his life's memories should be. *I need answers*, Chris thought as the sun rose over the steel and Plexiglas of North Denver. *And I need them soon, before I really do drive myself crazy.*

Chris was up and out the front door of the hotel at six forty-five. Charlie hadn't been at the front desk, replaced by a little hand-written sign that said "Back in five." The old cleaning woman was still there, of course, asleep in front of the morning news on the ancient TV. The sound fritzed and the anchorman could hardly be heard above the sea of static.

He found the P.N.T. five blocks down the main strip that led to the GeoCorp Administration Building, attached to an Airbus terminal, with shuttles leaving every two minutes to Denver North. There was a sign for schedules to Denver South, as well, but it said only "ALL BUSSES CANCELLED" in large, red-lighted letters.

Chris had passed quite a few ground cars on his way to the terminal and he wondered how they managed to get into downtown—from the streets around the hospital, it seemed unlikely that anyone could drive a car through the rubbish and broken machinery that littered the streets there. The answer: the terminal itself was huge—two city blocks and twenty stories, of which the bottom eighteen was all parking. A mall and the actual terminal took up the top two floors of structure.

Chris took the lift to the airbus depot and spotted a sign marked "P.N.T.," with a graphic of a figure sitting in front of a computer. The P.N.T. took up the entire western third of the top floor. There was only a low, dividing wall between the rest of the bus terminal and the rows and rows of cubicles that made up the main part of the P.N.T.

A sign at a little booth in the front entrance said, "One hundred dollars for thirty minutes or one hundred and fifty for one hour, prepay only." Sitting behind the sign was a tired-looking Korean teenager who put on a plastic smile that didn't reach his eyes—eyes that instead spoke with venomous hostility of the injustice of a world where he had to deal with assholes and bums who treated him like shit. "Welcome to the P.N.T., sir. How may I help you?" He sounded like he read a script, unsure of his lines.

"I need a terminal, please." Chris tried to be polite and friendly, to help ease the boy in front of him. Those hostile eyes bored straight into Chris's soul and exposing his inner monsters.

"How long, Sir?" He replied to Chris's politeness by warming slightly and notching down the hate in his eyes.

Chris sighed, not wanting to go through this again. "I'm not really sure. I'm sorry."

"No problem, sir. You'll be on terminal double zero three nine. Fill out this form here, and I'll need to see an identification card please." The kid, whose nametag said Kim, pushed a form across the desk towards Chris.

"Oh," Chris said. "The thing is, I lost my I.D. I, uh, need to apply for another one … I'm sorry to be a hassle."

"No problem sir," Kim smiled again, this time almost genuinely. "Then instead I can give you terminal zero five zero six, that's in the next room—" He gestured vaguely over his shoulder, "—and you can fill out this form here—" he slid another form over to Chris and pulled the other one away in one motion, "—which stipulates that you are who you say you are and can be checked by PolCorp at any time to prove your identity—don't worry, they never check—and if you sign here, here, and here, then pay the five hundred dollar deposit you will be all ready to go. Here's your pass code for this session—use it to log on." Kim handed him a small, red card that said:

HERCULEANPEDAGOGUE

Chris signed the name Geoffrey Garret—he didn't know where it came from, but he liked the sound of it—paid the deposit, and followed the signs through the maze of cubicles to another room, far to his left. He saw several images of hard-core porn out of the corner of his eye, and wondered what Charlie thought was so "kinky" that it wasn't allowed on public terminals.

The next room was smaller, though still vast, and noisier than the main P.N.T. area. The terminals looked older and dirtier. The dusty scent of overworked drives filled the air. With no dividing cubicles, the room was set up with ten terminals each on twenty or so tables. Through the open windows came the din of traffic flying around the bus terminal. There were a dozen people spread around in here, pecking away at keyboards; one man peered over a woman's shoulder near the back wall.

A lone PolCorp security guard reclined at a desk at the far end of the room, looking at the ceiling like a despondent child. His feet beat to the rhythm of music only he could hear. Chris imagined he had committed some atrocious folly, either perceived or real, to earn this beat. *Library cop*, Chris thought out of nowhere, and smiled. *Keeping the silence—and not even doing that well.* The thought amused him, and to a small degree some vindication for how harassed he had felt by PolCorp and yesterday's events.

Chris found the terminal with the digits zero five zero six hovering over it like the clock at the hospital and sat down, the numbers flickering out of existence as he did so. It occurred to him as he sat down that he may have no idea how to operate such a computer, but as the hologram flickered out the screen flickered on, revealing a blinking prompt that stated: "Pass code?" Chris stared at the computer. There wasn't a keyboard.

He ran his hand over the space in front of the monitor, and asterisks appeared on the login. Chris ran his hand back over the surface and spotted a slight discoloration appeared under his fingers. Holographic letters were on the otherwise blank surface. He smiled and typed in "HERCULEANPEDAGOGUE" and the screen went blank, before bringing up the face of a beautiful Asian woman. "Good-morning!" she said to Chris. The monitor had the same three-dimensional feel as the screens at Jones Drugs, creating the uncomfortable illusion that he sat a foot away from this woman's disembodied head.

The feeling passed as the woman faded and another blinking curser appeared, this time, "Find It!!" floated at the top of the screen in green bubble letters. Without hesitation, Chris typed in "Dr. Christopher Nost." A long list of hits appeared, hovering within the flat monitor. Chris went to the first one, an article from July twenty-third, two thousand and three:

The 'Memory Lost' Murderer Shot after Conviction

Dr. Christopher Nost was shot by an unidentified assailant today, only minutes after his conviction in the much-publicized murder of Lucille Frost. No arrests have been made although several witnesses report seeing the assailant gunned down by police. Authorities will not comment on the incident but say they have several leads.

Judge Miller expressed sympathy for Dr. Nost after the conviction and reduced his sentence to the minimum 10 years in a minimum-security prison. He spoke bluntly to the court when he told those present that he had reason to seriously doubt Dr. Nost's guilt.

Dr. Nost was shot while leaving the Courthouse, just as his attorney, Alan Dunwich, was addressing the assembled press ...

Chris stopped reading—the rest of the article looked like interviews with witnesses who didn't see anything—and went back to search "Lucille Frost," and read the first article, dated August fourteenth, nineteen ninety-nine.

Head of Research Team Murdered in Office

The head of an Aerospace Physics research team based in Colorado Springs, CO. was found shot to death in her office around 7 pm Monday night.

Lucille Frost, 39, had led a team of 20 scientists for only about 18 months, but in that time managed to make her elite think-tank the forefront of Aerospace Physics, and was currently spearheading a privately funded project that was meant to revolutionize current theories on deep-space travel. Benefits to society had already been seen with the new high impact lightweight alloy the team designed in their first weeks of research. They had been known as 'Lucille's Team' throughout academia in the short time they existed. The entire project has now been put on hold indefinitely while the murder investigations are under way.

Frost left behind two children, who at this time cannot be found. A kidnapping investigation is also underway over the fate of Mary, 10 and Markus, 16. Her ex-husband was not available to comment.

The article ended with a picture of Frost, taken in a park. Her face tickled something at the back of his mind but failed to spark recognition. Chris panned down through the other hits before he came across:

97

Arrest Made in Frost Murder

One of the leading physicists on Dr. Lucille Frost's team was arrested on Tuesday as the prime suspect in her shooting nearly three years ago.

Dr. Christopher Nost, thought by many to be the backbone of the "Deep Space Dream Team," was arrested without incident in his home in Colorado Springs.

"We have ample evidence which we have collected over the past three years—all of which points to Dr. Nost," said Colorado Springs Police Chief Randal Holms. "We also have multiple reports from witnesses who say Frost and Nost got into frequent, heated arguments over how the project was run."

"One witness claims that Nost once told Dr. Frost that he believed she was sabotaging their collective efforts. Many of his colleagues also say that Nost was bitter about having his ideas repeatedly rejected by the project head." The prosecution, despite evidence, does not have an easy case against Dr. Nost, who suffers from a rare neural disorder that reduces his memory span to a little more than a year.

Dr. Eric Jorgensen, one of the world's premier neurologists, was contacted via a phone call to his office in Sweden Tuesday night. Dr. Jorgensen has had Nost as a regular patient for the past 6 years and will be testifying on his behalf.

"It is an incredibly rare condition, and it is almost impossible at this time to identify a cause, but I can assure you that whether or not my patient is guilty, he has no memory of the event either way," Jorgensen explained.

He went on to say that Nost's condition is all the more unusual because he is capable of retaining learned, or abstract and conceptual memories. "The formulae and equations that Dr. Nost uses in his research, for example, are not affected, nor are his abilities to write or drive a car," Jorgensen explained. "But he cannot remember his own family, or his childhood with them."

"However," Jorgensen pointed out, "if Dr. Nost were to come up with something new, some sort of breakthrough in his field, well, let's just say he should write it down." Dr. Sharon Peters, head of the University of Colorado Physics department and the person who discovered Lucille Frost's body in the parking lot, expressed regret when notified of Nost's arrest.

"I don't think [Nost] could have done it," she told reporters at a press conference held two hours after the suspect was taken into custody. "Either way, I think it is safe to say that without both Frost and Nost, the Deep Space/Light Particle project will have to be cancelled until other suitable minds can be found. Despite their personal differences and radically different theories, those two were without a doubt the heart and soul of the project, constantly keeping the other in check."

Peters further pointed out that she was in the building around the time of the murder and although she heard no gunshots, the man she saw leaving Frost's office was, she claimed, not Dr. Nost. Nost's mother has been notified of the arrest, but has declined to comment.

As Chris finished reading, he became aware of someone standing behind him.

"Old news, huh?" a feminine voice purred behind him. "Now why would you be hunting through that stuff?"

Chris closed out the screen. "What's it to you?" he asked, turning around.

Chris froze when he saw the woman standing behind him. She was young—probably in her early twenties, with reddish hair and an aquiline nose. Her body was well toned and easy enough to see under her tight, thin, slightly glowing bodysuit. She exuded an air of womanliness that was hard to see past.

It was not her sexuality that gripped Chris by his guts though— she looked exactly like the picture he had just seen of Lucille Frost.

Despite the difference in age, the resemblance was uncanny. Chris swallowed and said nothing more, his hand nervously brushing the keyboard.

"Curiosity, really," the woman said. "As I was going by I saw my name on your screen, so I stopped to have a look. When I saw you were reading about my grandmother's murder, I couldn't help but wonder why you were reading about it."

"Your … grandmother?" Chris asked. "That explains the striking resemblance."

"Yes, I know. I look exactly like her. Everybody who sees her picture says it." She looked at Chris with a scrutinizing gaze, bit her lower lip, and stuck out her hand. "I'm sorry. My name is Mary. Mary Frost."

Chris looked at her hand the same way he had looked at the PolCorp mini-gun the night before, then took it and shook it. Her firm grip startled him. "I'm Geoffrey Garret. I was doing a little research on the project your grandmother was working on. I … I'm a scientist.…"

Mary looked at Chris, a glint in her steely blue-gray eyes. "Garret?" She looked at him, *through* him, for almost a minute. It felt to Chris like an eternity that he was locked in her gaze, unable to look away. "I was looking for a Garret, actually, but I don't think you're him."

"I doubt it," Chris said, trying to mask his relief. "I haven't been in the city too long.…"

"Oh no?" She smiled, like a cat that had no intention of killing the mouse, just to play with it until it's dead.

"Well, no. I've only been around here for a couple of days.…"

Mary leaned in close to Chris without warning, one hand cupping around his neck, and ran her tongue along the edge of his ear. Chris tried to pull away from her, but her grip, soft though it was, was solid as granite. "I know who you are," she said, looking into his eyes, inches from his face. "I know what you are looking for, and you will find your answers."

He shuddered. "That's not possible. Look, I don't know what you think you know, but you're wrong."

She leaned in closer until her lips were brushing against his ear, "It is you who are wrong. You, to whom the truth will be revealed. You see, I know what you are, Chris," she whispered before pulling back and looking at him once more. "Anyway, don't trust Jameson. He's a liar and worse. If you let him in," she tapped a finger against Chris's temple, "he'll try to twist you and then destroy you. Meet him if you must—but be wary. Know that he is evil."

Mary Frost turned and walked casually away, her body swaying under the glowing red fibers of her clothing. As she reached the door she turned one last time to look at Chris. "See you around, *Doctor.*"

Chris sat and stared blankly at the computer screen for a long time. He desperately wanted to go back to the hotel and think out what had happened, but there was too much still he needed to know. He reached back to the keyboard and reactivated the screen, typing in "time travel theories."

Over a million hits came up. Skimming over them, most looked like either links to fiction sites or to science sites that needed a password to enter. Shaking his head, Chris tried again with a new search string: "time phenomena and travel—public domain, facts."

This time there were only a few hundred thousand. Most looked to be hack sites reporting supposed "slips in time," but skimming through them, Chris saw nothing that compared to his experience of the night before. There were several public theories on manipulating time as well, but all seemed to be based on various crackpot ideas—which Chris could see were faulty—or facilitated by the use of some unwieldy device. It seemed that in this day and age anyone could publish an article and have it posted as "fact."

Sighing, he leaned back in his chair and rubbed his brow. *What else would be a good search string?* He hesitated for a moment and tried "control time, spirituality." He could still feel the presence of that *place* that he almost reached last night in his hotel room. The first hit was titled *The Evolution of Gods, Using Kronos as an Example, 1972©*. Chris went to it, laughing at himself.

It was a history of Kronos, the Greek god of Time, written by PhD. Historian Patricia Fahey. It followed the evolution of the deity from its origin as Zr'van, an ancient Iranian god of time, said to be the creator of all the paths which lead to the crossing point into the beyond. This place was described as a "void, filled with all things," named the Cinvat Bridge.

The article continued to describe, from a theologian's point of view, how a god must adapt and change to the society that worships it and the world it lives in or become obsolete and perish. Its underlying tenants seemed to be the evolution of thought itself—growing and changing to match the society it dwelt in or the alternate path, fading into obscurity as it became outmoded. This becomes apparent, Fahey explained, when looking at classical gods that later become saints, the Egyptian to the Greek, or, as in the example cited, the Iranian to the Greek. The failure of the gods to do this, Fahey wrote, is the reason why religion begun to fall out of popularity with the majority of Western Culture for the first time ever. Even the rise of Christianity supports this theory as religion grew toward faith and away from a pantheistic belief structure.

Chris shook his head, laughing to himself as he finished the article, but something in the back of his mind made him go back to the first section of the thesis again. *A void filled with all things,* he read again, trying to remember something—a dream ... *A void of bright darkness and roaring silence, filled with pores to let the substance of time into the physical universe ...*

"Sir? Mr. Garret?" the voice shattered his musings, making him lose the idea about to be birthed.

Chris looked up in annoyance at the man standing behind him. He wore the blue vest of the P.N.T. employee, and his nametag said 'Dwayne.'

"Yes?" frustration carried across in his voice.

"I'm sorry, Mr. Garret, but the P.N.T. is closing for the evening. We open again 7a.m. tomorrow. You're more than welcome to come back then."

"What? You must be mistaken—I've only been here a few hours...." he trailed off as he noticed that the view through the windows showed nothing but darkness and the cacophony of vehicles had faded to a distant whisper.

"Well, you were gone for most of the day, but you never signed off your terminal. I didn't even see you come back—we were beginning to think you ditched out on the bill. I was getting ready to transmit your papers over to PolCorp when I noticed that there was renewed activity at your terminal. Rather lucky for you, sir. Even if you had paid they would have had to run you in if I had completed the transfer."

Chris looked up at the clock. It was five minutes to midnight. Lights were already shutting off in the building, and as he looked around, a harmonic chorus of "Goodnight!" rose from the terminals as pretty Asian faces nodded goodbye with a little regret in their eyes, before they winked out.

"I … lost track of time. How much do I owe you?"

"Five hundred and ten dollars, sir. I'm sorry we need to charge you for all the time you weren't at your terminal. Had you signed off …"

"It's no problem. My fault, I should have remembered to sign off and wrap my bill the first time I left." Chris pulled six hundred from his pocket and handed it to Dwayne. "Thanks for your time. Keep the change, Dwayne."

He decided to take his time walking back to the hotel. Stopping at an all-night convenience store at the base of the bus station tower, he wandered around and ended up buying a pack of cigarettes.

He couldn't remember if he had ever smoked them before but it seemed like a good time to start. Desiring nothing more than the feel of an open sky above him, he walked the unfamiliar streets of the city for close to two hours, lost deep in thought. He didn't make it back to his hotel until after two in the morning. With the light from the waxing moon streaming in behind him, the lobby seemed an eldritch place, somehow separated from the bright lights and fast-paced world outside its front doors. He stopped, enjoying the quiet mystique of the moment; entranced by this vision of the world he had come from.

"Looks like you had a rough day," Charlie said wryly.

The words broke Chris's reverie and snapped him back into the moment. But the connection had already been made and ideas were starting to queue up in Chris's mind. As preposterous as the thoughts flooding his mind were, it relieved him to be starting to piece together answers. A few more questions and he knew that he would have all of the pieces that he needed to figure out who and what he was.

Chris walked by the front desk without responding, silence the only sound he was capable of making at the moment, lost his thoughts.

"Hey, you OK, buddy?" Charlie peered at Chris. "You need anything? You don't look so good man."

But Chris still said nothing, and went upstairs to lie sleepless on his bed, thinking of a time, memory, and a place called the Cinvat Bridge.

2873: Yuri Yakavich's Hunt

Endless letters and words scrolled in front of Yuri. Time streamed by his tired eyes as he analyzed history for the telltale signature of Alexander Zarth in Christopher Nost's era. Blank again. He rubbed at his eyes. He had gone through some of these files so many times that he could about cite them from memory.

History surrounding major paradoxes was always problematic to delve into from a researcher's point of view. Time Corp was very hesitant to send in observation teams because of the off chance of a further paradox being created. The old theory about the act of observation changing the observed dominated the methods of thought that held sway with the current administration.

This meant that Yuri had only the standard historical trail to work from, and that, unfortunately, included all of the background static created by standard progression of time. Trying to find someone like Alexander Zarth at the nexus of a paradox was a lot like trying to find a specific needle in a needle factory storage bin. In the middle of a city built out of needles. Yuri chuckled to himself at the mental imagery.

Although the one thing that Yuri had going for him was that he was an incredibly lucky man. Several times before he had managed to pick Zarth out of the background and pinpoint him for various field agents. Once you do something enough times, it starts to become reflex, almost like a habit. But this time it seemed like someone was actively masking Zarth's presence from his searches. It was disquieting how well it was being done, too.

Yuri knew that Zarth was there as surely as he knew his own name. But his supervisors were running out of patience and Yuri knew that reviewing the information available to him for a thirtieth time would yield the exact same results as the previous twenty-nine. All of these pressures had been building up on Yuri, shaping his thoughts and guiding him in a cycle of hopelessness.

Yuri's sour frame of mind continued as he walked into Director Arbu's office. Under the pressure he felt, it was understandable that he was about to make a mistake large enough to change history.

Director Arbu sat behind his desk, scanning files on his computer. He was an older man, in his mid-sixties, but still in excellent physical shape. Shaggy silver hair, streaked with a few remnants of his original black, framed a scarred but strong-featured face.

A retired warrior, seasoned and battle hardened, Arbu had very little patience for incompetence. His piercing gaze caught Yuri as he looked up from the monitor in front of him and smiled. "What progress have you made, Yuri?"

Standing stiffly to attention and speaking with an air of complete sincerity, Yuri lied. Meeting Director Arbu's steel gaze, he said without blinking, "Sir, I believe that I have found the trail that will lead to both Alexander Zarth and the renegade Dr. Garret. It is in nineteen ninety-seven and focuses around the mission of Lucille Frost. As I have not pinpointed either's exact location, I would like to request that I personally handle this mission."

Despite the highly irregular request—he had to hope that he could sneak it through without Arbu figuring out why he tried to get a field placement—he kept his gaze steadily exuding honesty and determination. If this did not work, then Yuri would be forced to take a much more difficult path.

Director Arbu leaned back in his plush synthetic leather chair and studied Yuri for a moment. Yuri felt the gaze opening him up and reading his mind. He felt the bottom of his stomach crash down as he knew what his boss would say. Director Arbu sighed. "Agent Yakavich, let me be blunt with you. You are our best intelligence agent and risking you in the field would reflect poorly on my judgment. Requesting this also reflects poorly on your judgment. Obviously, you are frustrated and too tired, which is why I think you are suggesting pitting yourself against a criminal and a renegade who are both more highly skilled than yourself."

Yuri braced himself. He had one gambit to play, and even though it would probably not work, he had to try to use every card at his disposal. "I have to respectfully disagree, sir. I would like to remind you that five agents before me have failed to apprehend the criminal after I pinpointed his location for them. They were unable to complete the task of finding him. Based on that one fact. I would feel safe saying that there is no other agent more qualified than myself to deal with this situation. Perhaps a field team would be in order to support me, sir? Since I would agree that my field skills are not the best."

Leather squeaked as the director shifted in his chair to lean forward. He placed both of his elbows on his desk, clamping his hands together and staring at Yuri over the knot they formed.

The silence stretched long enough to make Yuri uncomfortable before Arbu broke it. "Yuri, you are tired and foolish. Five field agents failed, yes? And each of them had better control and much higher combat skills than you. If you were to go back, we would lose you. That is a statement of pure and simple fact; please, do not bridle at it. I will assign the task as I see fit. Thank you for your report. You are dismissed from the operation."

Slack jawed, Yuri stared at his superior. He was being taken off the case. Not only had he failed to get assigned, but also Director Arbu had read him so well that he had chosen to remove Yuri for his own safety. "I see, sir. Thank you."

Yuri turned around and walked out of the office with clenched fists. As he walked down the hall away from the office he came to a decision. It took him less than ten minutes to prepare himself and illegally travel to the twentieth century.

Two minutes before he left, Director Arbu had placed an agent on a mission to track Yuri's illegal movements in the twentieth century. Yuri didn't realize it, but he had lost before he even knew he played the game.

Time: 1997
Location: Classified
Operation: Classified

Agent Holly watched Yuri leave the fast food joint with a greasy bag tucked under his arm. He got bored with this assignment, as his target had spent the preceding month basically in a repetition of the same routine. Wake up at the crack of dawn, eat greasy food at a diner, go to the library all day, eat greasy twentieth century fast food, then go to sleep after it got dark. Bio-monitor tracking all night long showed never a single variation in his sleep pattern.

Following the most elite of intelligence officers was not what Holly would have thought of as a boring mission. This should have been cloak and dagger. There should have been constant time shifts to shake any followers. Following a renegade agent was also not something Holly would have thought could be boring. A renegade agent, well, frankly, should be doing something illegal. Yet somehow this combination of renegade and intelligence officer put him to sleep on a daily basis.

Perhaps if Holly had been freshly assigned, and not locked into a month long routine that took his edge off, he would not have made the mistake he was about to make. But, he was bored, and he did make the biggest mistake of his career.

It happened thirty-two days into Holly's operation, between Agent Yakavich's evening meal at a seemingly random burger joint and his return to his hole in the wall hotel. Yakavich turned off the main roadway that ran towards his hotel and drove down a dead-end road that led only to a C-Twenty government building. Yakavich made his move—or at least made a move of some sort. A move that Holly could bring him down for. He stayed far back, using illegal C twenty-nine technologies to mask his car.

Yuri pulled into the building's parking lot. The building had several scaffolds and cranes around it. Pieces of the upper stories were jagged and missing. The building had suffered some damage and was being rebuilt. Waiting in the shadowy edge of the parking lot stood the dimly lit silhouette of a female figure. Yakavich got out of his car with a briefcase, scanning the lot for other people. Holly recognized the model of the briefcase. It was also an illegal C twenty-nine piece of technology.

Holly jumped to the only conclusion that he could with the evidence at hand: Yakavich passed future information to a native local. Holly reached into his jacket, pulled out his pistol, and started moving towards the two figures at the far side of the lot.

As he snuck up on them, he laid down a dampening field to block Yakavich from escaping by hopping into the time stream and stepping to a different time. He got within easy earshot and started listening to the conversation, trying to gather more information before making a decision on his course of action.

Yuri kicked the briefcase and it slid across the ground to the shadowy figure. "It's all there. Information covering the next forty-five years. It should be everything you need."

A female voice came from the shadows. "Thank you, Yuri. What you have risked to help me in my situation … I appreciate it. I appreciate it more than you can ever know." She sounded sad.

Yuri smiled grimly. "Don't worry about it. I've broken so many of the laws of time travel at this point that I figure—how much damage can one more broken law do? If I ever go back to my home, I know I'm sitting on a lifetime of imprisonment."

The woman in the shadows reached down and picked up the case. Her movements were sensuous but also very sure. "Yuri, this gift will let me change history. I can undo what would have happened over the next several years and make things go the way they should. Make them go the way we need to in order to ensure our ends are met. Please, don't feel like you are breaking the law, you are freeing the chains which have bound us."

Red rose in Holly's vision. He had taken this job because he believed truly in his heart of hearts that agents needed to be guardians to the time stream. Guardians who protect it, and who stop people from manipulating time to their own ends. That someone he had admired a month ago should turn against their core mission … Holly really didn't stop to think.

This was a potential class six paradox unfolding and his training took over, mixing freely with the rising betrayal he felt, and leaving his mind behind in the quagmire of boredom created over the last month.

He raised his pistol and shot them both in the head. Two clean shots, surgically executed, before either could respond. He holstered his pistol and purposefully walked to the woman, now lying face down in a pool of blood, and pulled the briefcase from her limp fingers. Releasing the field he had created, he grabbed Yuri's body, jerking his head off the ground by his hair, and hopped forward with his two packages to the future.

The next morning, one of the other scientists from the building found Lucille Frost lying dead in the parking lot when she left from an all night shift to grab a cup of coffee from the twenty-four hour coffee shop down the road. The only other scientist in the partially reconstructed building was Christopher Nost, who was there all night trying to reconstruct the files he had lost in the blast weeks before.

2044 A.D.: New Denver, Colorado

Machine gun fire echoed through the streets as Alex watched the scene unfold before him. Christopher Nost vanished from the street and the move saved his life as concrete directly behind where he had been standing exploded from stray heavy-caliber fire.

Alex felt the flux hit the time stream as someone jumped. Interesting. It seemed likely that Nost was developing some subcon-scious control over the nano systems in his body. An impressive feat, considering that the first generation machines Nost had created were unstable and in most subjects wiped out the memory chains, making the ability to use the machines transitory at best. There seemed to be a trace of a second jump, but not forward or backward.

Alex filed that one away to puzzle out later. The scene in the street ended in a fiery disaster as Alex wandered away. The situation here in twenty forty-four was interesting to say the least. Something odd was happening with Nost. He had awakened unaffected by aging, something Alex had never heard of before. First generation machines definitely were not supposed to do that. Hell, no time machine granted the user that ability to Alex's knowledge.

But it had happened somehow. And James Garret had been there, studying the phenomenon. He would be a slippery fish to catch when the time came. Flexing his will, Alex hopped forward, past the earth-quake, to the Rangley Hotel and activated his holographic disguise kit. Bringing future technology back was always so much fun. His face seemed to fold in on itself, reassembling itself to be bald and squished a bit. He seemed to resemble nothing so much as a pit bull.

Hair appeared on his ears and the back of his hands. He worked his muscles and stretched his jaw, getting back into the character of his Charlie disguise. Drunks and barflies at inns and hotels around the world knew him in this guise, depending on where and when you went.

Observation of Nost gave him some interesting tidbits. The first being that apparently Chris had no idea yet that he could travel, even though he had done it at least twice. The second was that some event had triggered shell shock and Chris's memory was now fractured.

It seemed that the fracture went way beyond the medical know-ledge of what first-generation time nanos did to the brain. But Alex worked on Chris, helping him learn the tools that would ensure his eventual survival. At least that's what he hoped he was giving him. If he were miscalculating this, Nost would end up a splattered bug on the windshield of time, as would the rest of humanity along with him.

Humanity was at stake here and either Chris would master himself or not. If not, the results would be disastrous to the time stream and would result in the destabilization of history. Of course, history shattering was only theoretical. Since history was currently intact, no one knew what would happen if it hit the 'shatter' point.

He watched a future version of Chris go up to the room and raised a single eyebrow. Now, this was finally getting interesting. He grabbed a broom and started sweeping ineffectually at the rubble from the earthquake, waiting for the current time frame Chris to arrive.

He stopped sweeping when he saw Chris come up to the front door. The man looked battered and shaken. Worse than shaken, more like he was concussed and had no idea where he was.

Alex decided to go for broke and said mischievously, "I didn't see you leave again." He looked Chris up and down, feigning shock at the man's condition. "Man, you look like shit. What the hell'd you do in the last fifteen minutes?"

"What are you talking about, Charlie?" Chris got a queasy look on his face as what Alex said registered.

"I mean, you walk in looking sharp fifteen minutes ago, you walk in now looking like shit. Don't tell me, you've been in a coma," he snorted and watched Chris's reaction, hoping that he fed him enough so that the time travel would finally click. It didn't. *Oh well*, Alex figured, *it would click soon enough when he encountered his future self upstairs.*

Chris looked at him, so he shifted his stance and feigned at discomfort, playing to his part. "Hey, man, fuck you. I didn't mean nothing by it. I'm curious, is all, to how you could get all jacked up like that in fifteen minutes…"

Chris spun around and started purposefully up the stairs toward his room, pulling an old gun from under his coat as he went.

"Holy shit, man, I haven't seen a Glock in years!" Alex said to his retreating back. Well, worst-case scenario, he'd have to intervene. Best case, Chris had pieced together the secret of time travel. Alex let him go to confront his future self and got back to an honest day's work cleaning up the damaged hotel.

RELATIVITY SYNCHRONIZATION:

THE SEVENTH CAUSE

2044: Coffee & Cigarettes

Chris left his room at the Rangley around 7 a.m. to head toward the D.A.B. He felt well rested even though he had lain awake all night. Life was sometimes weird like that, granting you small respites amidst the storm. It looked like it wouldn't take more than an hour to walk to the D.A.B., but he was restless and fidgety as his thoughts kept coming back to what he had read about the Cinvat Bridge.

Was that what I felt? Chris wondered. *Some mystical alternate dimension that the God of time dwells in?* He could not discredit the idea, no matter how hard he tried. It felt too right. There were weirder ideas than the thought that a civilization over four thousand years dead had come across some aspect of the universe now long forgotten. And again, it felt right to his intuition.

Something remained there, beyond the edge of everything else, some bridge or tunnel that somehow cut through space and time. How the hell had he been able to find it? *Why hadn't other people been able to use it?* The thought plagued him as he walked through the lobby. Abruptly, he stopped. *Have other people been able to use it?* He shook his head and continued on down the stairs at his hotel.

That was even scarier to him—the idea that other people had found it before him. Could that be why all of this happened? *Perhaps there's some secret society or something that's hunting me now. Maybe that's why it seems like the universe is so twisted now. But then why haven't they succeeded in actually killing me? Regardless, that would explain the woman at the punt.*

Goosebumps ran down his spine as everything that had happened to him started to make sense based on this odd model of the world he had extrapolated. *Once you have eliminated the impossible, whatever is left, no matter how improbable, is your solution.* Once again, Chris wondered if his mind was gone, floating through the false realities of insanity while his body was drooling in a padded room somewhere.. *Do crazy people spend time wondering whether or not they are crazy?*

"Feeling better?" Chris snapped out of his reverie as Charlie addressed him from the front desk. The other man looked tired but energetic, and had his newspaper lowered in front of him, but still clenched in dirty hands.

"What do you mean? Was I ill last night?" Chris paused. *Did I talk to Charlie last night?* He couldn't remember it if he had. Distraction and more than a little confusion shrouded the walk back from the P.N.T. "You walked in here like a zombie last night. I guess spending sixteen hours on the Net will do that to you." Charlie raised an eyebrow at Chris, "You headed over to the D.A.B. now?"

"Yeah ... I guess all that research I did yesterday was pretty intense. The thing is it didn't actually answer any of my questions," Chris said and shrugged. "It left me more confused."

"Man, you think you got problems," Charlie folded the newspaper in front of him and planted his stubby elbows on top of it. "Lemme try to give you a little bit of perspective. I thought I was gonna get wasted last night. About eleven this strung-out skrag came in, wanted—"

"Sorry, Charlie," Chris interrupted, trying to sound regretful. "I got a hell of a lot to do today. More research and hopefully I can start putting my life together again. I do want to chat with you, though. Can you tell me tonight? I should be back a bit earlier—and I can bring back some Chinese food for us." Chris offered up the food on a whim, by way of apology for his rude interruption.

"Oh, sure pal. Sorry. I'll take Mongolian beef. Extra large." Charlie cleared his throat and lifted the newspaper without another word. He looked offended but willing to forgive Chris for the prospect of a free dinner.

A slight smile flirted across Chris's lips as he left the hotel. He began to like Charlie. The quiet and warm morning cheered him. Chris looked up but saw only a handful of the cruisers in the air, floating like leaves in a gentle breeze and heading toward the city. The city had lost some of its fetidness. He wondered if it was some sort of holiday. *Maybe Thanksgiving comes early in the future*, he thought with a chuckle.

He tried to remember a specific Thanksgiving, but as always since his awakening in the hospital, his memories came up empty. *Maybe I'm The Doctor, and some strange accident in the TARDIS has left me stranded in time with no memory.* He started humming the Doctor Who theme to himself at this thought. Then he stopped, wondering where the memory had come from.

The Airbus Terminal was silent and desolate as well, and Chris began to get a bit worried. In front of the elevator doors there were a few loiterers milling around, and a few knots of PolCorp thugs glaring at anyone they thought might disturb the sanctity of their lazy day. Beady eyes under emblazoned helmets seemed to dare anyone to actually have the audacity to meet their gaze. Chris turned away and quickened his pace toward the D.A.B. Both departure boards had read "ALL BUSSES CANCELLED." Something didn't feel right about the day, but he refused to let go of the small bit of cheerfulness he had found.

Chris walked a few blocks further down Cherry Lane, where the buildings became higher than the neighborhood the Rangley was in. The buildings would have been skyscrapers in their own right if not for the megaliths dominating the Corporate Zone, which was now hidden to Chris by the proximity of the nearer towers. Everything in this future seemed to Chris to be in a constant battle to be the biggest and best. It started with the buildings, but the telltale hints were everywhere in his society—if only you stopped to look around. Chris spotted what he looked for and walked over towards the bank tower.

Installed in the side of the darkened GeoCorp Bank tower, humped at its peak like a cash register, he found a public news terminal—a 3D monitor offering "Public Information" to anyone who walked by. Across the bottom of the screen floated the message "**ALERT**" in dangerous looking bold red letters. Chris paused in front of it and as he did so a hidden sensor picked up his presence, increasing the display's volume to an audible level.

"…As a result, all public transit is closed until the situation is under control and any travel within the city is strongly discouraged. All medical and PolCorp personnel are to report to their stations immediately. Emergency calls will not be responded to until emergency personnel are once again available in your area. We now go live to Wendy Price, whom at great personal risk is reporting to us from the most recent outbreak of violence in North Denver."

The image shifted to a scene of carnage. A conflagration burned behind the red-haired woman looking into the camera, charred limbs and gore spattered the area around her. Oily black smoke partially obscured the entire area she stood in. The reporter wore what looked like a power-assisted suit of heavy metal armor, holding the time-honored microphone in the suit's claw.

"Jesus," Chris grunted. "Personal risk, my ass."

"Lisa," the woman said, "this scene is like so many others in North Denver, where the gang war that has effectively shut down South Denver for the past two months spilled into streets that were supposedly secure early this morning. PolCorp is currently attempting to get the situation to a state of stability, but as of now there have been hundreds of innocent bystanders slain in the past three hours...."

Chris walked away from the screen and the voice faded into silence. He looked up and down the street, but only blue sky and sun could be seen from his vantage. No limbs were littering the ground, and no skirmishes were spontaneously breaking out in the middle of the street. He wondered where the attacks had been and decided it didn't matter. He would meet Dr. Jameson, regardless.

He tried to imagine that this didn't concern him, so close to the heart of GeoCorp, but he could not help but quicken his pace. Unlucky was one thing, but there was no reason to be stupid. Besides the occasional ground car and a few PolCorp Cruisers jetting along above, there was still no sign of everyday traffic. Save the occasional streetwalker crouched in the sun against the buildings or in the shadowed mouth of an alleyway, the streets were empty of pedestrian traffic as well. Twice more he walked past Public Information Terminals, but nothing new looked forthcoming and Chris didn't bother to stop and see more of the same. Better to get to his meeting as quickly as possible and attempt to avoid getting shot at.

The PolCorp presence became much more obvious as he got closer to the GeoCorp tower, with cruisers parked and forming barricades. The officers milling around in riot gear made Chris feel more anxious, not more secure. Once he was within a half mile of his destination there were at least two cruisers in the air at any given time, and staggered groups of half a dozen guards walking the sidewalks a few blocks out from the street mall. Breaking into a run would only draw attention, so he paced himself with a quick walk through the gauntlet rather than risk drawing the notice of this harsh world.

There were other people out now too, browsing without noticeable concern through the shops at the base of the D.A.B. Most of the visible stores had heavy plate steel grates pulled shut in front of them, locked with electronic keypads or fingerprint scanners protecting the goods within from marauding gangs. But a few of the shops were open, mostly small restaurants and art galleries hoping to make a profit while their larger competitors where closed to avoid the risk of riots.

Little Paris was one of the open shops, and Chris found it at the end of the strip. A few daring people sat at tables outside, but most were choosing to remain inside on the off chance that the rioting spilled over onto the mall. Two old men sat by the window casually playing chess and smoking cigars.

Chris looked up at the ornamental clock adorning the top of a small building a few blocks down. The clock was a big white wheel with thick iron hands atop a narrow green pole. The overall effect drew the eye by creating an illusion of an ill-balanced object about to fall under the slightest breeze, threatening to crush anyone who walked below it at the wrong moment. The hands read just after eight.

Chris looked at the card Jameson had given him. Fifteen hundred. *Great. Three this afternoon. I've got all day to sit around here and wait.* Indecision stopped him momentarily as he tried to decide whether to stay in the relative safety of the coffee shop or to continue exploring the mall. Finally, he decided that he could duck into an open shop if he saw trouble headed his way and he began curiously strolling down the mall.

Approaching Little Paris, he had felt apprehension, expecting that at any moment one of the PolCorp officers gathered there for coffee and pastries would recognize him. *They had cameras,* Chris thought. *They must have caught something on film—unless the whole thing never happened....*

Continuing down the mall, his paranoia ebbed like the surf slowly drifting out to low tide. Again and again he found himself being eyed and then passed over with the same indifference the rest of the pedestrians received, and he relaxed his guard. He didn't look like a gang member, so they weren't looking at him or for him. Feeling his muscles unwind, for the first time he could remember he found himself in a good mood for more than a few minutes at a time.

The street sloped down and he decided to walk to the base of the D.A.B. Professional curiosity took over and he could not help but be fascinated by the concept of a building of such enormity.

What is it made out of? Chris thought of the newspaper articles. *Did I design this stuff?* The silver needle now towered above, consuming half the sky with its shimmering shadow. *This is mine ... this world would not be possible but for the ideas in my mind ...* Pride welled up in his chest, followed by disgust at how alien and cold his idea had made the world.

As he approached the end of the mall, he realized that he had been mistaken about the proximity of the tower. The D.A.B. was much further than he thought: across a wide river bed with only a trickle of water in it, and a vast but mostly empty parking lot.

On the near side of the river sat a squat PolCorp station, guards milling about the front of the building and eying Chris. He smiled, trying not to look nervous, but failing miserably by looking away, his heart skipping a beat.

He had spotted Chuck, the PolCorp guard he remembered killing three nights ago. *What the fuck?* Chris thought as turned away and hurried back up the mall, his mind reeling. *I know I killed him. I watched him die.* It was hard to think, but there was one explanation. Chris had gone back to the hotel twenty minutes before he killed Chuck. *So did I kill him or not? Oh god, am I insane? Or am I actually a time traveler? But then ... what about paradox? Is that what is driving me crazy?*

Wind seemed to howl through his hair as Chris staggered back towards the coffee shop, clutching his head. The universe had no rhyme or reason and he felt everything slipping beyond his control. Reality forced itself back upon him as he walked back toward Little Paris and he noticed two of the PolCorp beat cops following after him, about a block behind.

The guard he had killed was in the fore, briskly outpacing his companion. *They're walking a beat. It's coincidence,* Chris forced himself to think, but he felt nauseous again. He kept going, keeping the same pace, racking his brain and trying to figure out what to do.

He could only hope that if some encounter happened, his instincts would kick in and he would be able to get away by doing ... whatever the hell it was he could do. *But no killing,* he thought. *Somehow he survived what I did, and I'm not going to kill him again.*

As he approached the patio section of Little Paris he felt a heavy hand fall on his shoulder. "Sir, could I ask you a few questions?" a low voice asked.

Chris swallowed and turned to face the speaker—a lumpy blond man in a PolCorp uniform. He didn't have the helmet on, and wore no flack vest like the other guards seen patrolling the area. But the arm he used to keep hold of Chris looked like it was made out of some sort of metal alloy. Chuck stood behind him, looking at Chris through a plastic riot visor. A thoughtful expression was on his face, as he looked Chris up and down.

"Um. Yes, officer?" Chris gulped down some air and forced himself to continue. "How can I help you?"

"Yeah. He's a fit," Chuck said, his eyes never leaving Chris. He seemed nervous, as though he had some lingering memory of what hadn't happened the night before. "You fit the description of someone we've been looking for, sir. I'm sure it's nothing, so if we could check your papers, we'll be on our way."

Shit! Not again. Chris fumbled through his pockets, pretending that he searched for his wallet. "Really? What happened? Lemme find my papers. You know, this happens to me all the time; I must look like some criminal. Now what the hell did I do with ...?"

"I'm going to go back to the car to get my retinal," Chuck said, still staring at Chris. "Maybe we can get a positive ID with the Visual Imaging Unit." He started off back down the hill.

"Godamnit. I know I have them on me somewhere ..." Chris continued to stall. A scowl swept across the face of the officer with the cybernetic arm. "Maybe ..."

Chris blathered on, feeling a now-familiar growing sense of dread as he ineffectually patted his pockets. But there was no pressure in his head, and time moved forward as it always did. Franticly he searched his mind, looking for a way to unlock whatever defense mechanisms he had, but there were only empty echoes of his last encounter with PolCorp.

Deliverance came in the form of a massive ball of fire lighting up the sky beyond the D.A.B., followed by a shockwave of rolling thunder that screamed up the mall, shattering the high impact Plexiglas windows of the shops, like a tsunami of plastic shards racing down the walls of the buildings towards them.

Chris could feel his organs rattling throughout his body and then the shockwave hit him—flinging him backwards, and then smashing him into the ground. The world spun around him as he tried to regain his feet, and Chris ended up spending a moment balanced on his knees and clutching his gut as he tried to make the world stop spinning around him.

"Holy shit! What the hell was that?" the PolCorp guard looked dazed as he stood up and gazed around the mall. Chris pointed behind the guard, towards PolCorp. The man turned and saw the raging fire and plumes of smoke coming from the direction of his station. Without another word he turned and charged down the hill toward his fallen comrades, forgetting that he had been about to bust Chris for some unknown crime.

Overhead, dozens of PolCorp cruisers streaked by, the faint sound of gunfire punctuating their flight as Chris's abused hearing stopped ringing. He looked away from the erupting firefight to Little Paris. The shockwave that had torn apart the upper stories of the surrounding buildings spared the little shop.

Through a thin haze of bluish cigar smoke, the two old chess players peered out the window, watching Chris. He smiled and waved at them, as though to say "Hello … I am a real person, not street theatre." The two men turned back to their game, apparently having decided that the show was over.

Some people hurried up the mall away from the blast, but most only looked down the street for a moment and went back to what they were doing. Chris gazed at the few people he could see, then down at his own hands, scraped and bloody. *What can make a society so callous?* Aching joints protested as he climbed to his feet. *And how can I ever fit in here?*

Despite the muted sounds of occasional gunfire and explosions, Chris spent the rest of the day in Little Paris, drinking coffee and alternating between working on Quantum and Time theories on a borrowed sheet of paper and relaxing.

With the amount of stress he had been through, it felt good to unwind, and a dim realization hit him at some point in the day that perhaps this society was not the callous, uncaring place he thought it to be at first. Perhaps it had become a survival trait to mind your own business. It was something to think about at any rate, and he filed it for later mental consumption. But for now, he thought, more coffee and maybe some local history.

The rich aroma of coffees permeated the air as Chris approached the counter again. "Has this place been here long?" Chris asked the man behind the bar. The guy was in his sixties—almost as old as the two men playing chess—and was lanky and tall with a few flecks of blond in the gray hair of his goatee. He wore an ancient baseball cap with a cartoonish picture of a cat's face wearing sunglasses, a cigarette hanging out of its open mouth.

"Well, it's been on Cherry Lane for ten years. For about forty years before that it was called the Penn Street Perk, back when there was a Penn Street. After GeoCorp took over and rebuilt the city, we ended up here, in the shadow of their big, shiny cock." He gestured toward the massive skyscraper at the end of the mall.

Chris glanced around at the pictures of boats and old houses that lined the walls, giving the place an antiquated feel, at least compared to the world outside. "So I take it you're not run by GeoCorp?"

"I'm not run by nobody, man. Paris, well, it might as well be. They let us run it however we want, but we're close enough to their big dick that we need to stay within 'certain parameters.'" The old man chuckled, then coughed. "We make the best cuppa' joe around though. It's hard to shut down the place where you like to get your coffee. Bad karma, ya' know?" Steam jetted up from the espresso machine as the barista foamed the milk.

"So you've worked here long?"

"Fuck you man, yeah, I've worked here long. I've worked here all my fuckin' life, man. I was going to be something, you know? I was gonna write, but here I am. Look, you want your latte, or are you just here to fuck with me?"

Chris took the cup of coffee, tipped the guy ten dollars, and went back to his table. He liked the barista—he had some indefinable quality that Chris could relate to, despite his surliness. Or perhaps it was his surliness. Knowing that there were likable people in this dismal world definitely made a difference to Chris, as harsh as his first impressions had been.

Flying cars and stray pedestrian policemen made for a colorful scene in the world outside the coffee shop. Occasionally foot traffic would wander by, oblivious to the riots around the city. Once a thunderclap of gunfire sounded nearby, bouncing off of the armored windows of the shop.

The afternoon rolled on and the chess game across the shop concluded. As one of the men packed up the board, the other rolled up his sleeve and, to Chris's horror, peeled back the skin of his forearm revealing plastic tubing and dimly glowing fiber optics.

Chris watched, his horror turning to fascination, as the man pulled out a small can, opened a latch within his arm, and emptied the contents into the opening. He flexed his hand a few times, reattached the skin, and chuckled something to his companion in a gravelly voice, though what he said couldn't be heard from across the coffee house.

The old men walked out, leaving Chris alone with the bitter barista and his thoughts. When three o'clock rolled around, Chris was so absorbed he didn't even see Dr. Jameson wander in and order a latte. "...it would still need something—a catalyst, and I don't have one." Chris mumbled to himself. "Could I be ...?" He saw Dr. Jameson standing over him, his amused expression held a dark cast.

"Oh. Hello." Chris cleared the little table of his notes and gestured for the doctor to sit down.

"Hello, Chris. I'm glad you decided to meet me today. We'll be able to talk freely here, and I'm sure you have many questions to ask me." Jameson slid into the chair across from Chris and folded his hands in front of him on the table.

"Well, yeah. First, I've been thinking a lot about all of this," Chris gestured with his arms towards the windows, "and I can't figure out how it could be possible in forty years. I mean the city, the flying cars, everything. It ... I don't think it was like this in ... back then ..." Chris stopped, at a loss.

"Ah, yes. Quite extraordinary, is it not? The leaps in technology, sociology ... cultural growth alone is faster now than any time in recorded history. Amazing what humanity can accomplish when we find ourselves under the gun, so to speak." Chris thought he imagined a slight, brief wave of relief wash across Jameson's face.

"You see, after the oil crisis some twenty five years ago, the governments were at a loss—particularly in what was then the United States of America. The world governments had dabbled in alternative fuel sources, but their shortsightedness and greed for the money of the oil companies, was their downfall. Europe and Asia did slightly better when the oil finally ran out, but they made the mistake of giving alternative energy research over to private companies.

"These private companies, GeoCorp among them, had, in fact, come up with a clean-burning hydrogen cell eight years previously but said nothing, claiming in the meantime that any breakthroughs they had made were simply not cost effective. In fact, each cell could last years and could be produced at a fraction of the price of mining coal or drilling for oil.

"When the crisis came into full swing in twenty sixteen, war erupted. At first it was minor skirmishes … civil wars aplenty, small border infractions, that type of thing. All of this was caused initially by panic. Lack of transportation, rolling brown outs … it has been said that modern civilization is only twenty-four hours away from barbarism … practical experience now tells us this is closer to seventy two hours."

Jameson took a sip of his latte and continued. "So it was small wars at first. But it escalated, as these things do, until the entire world was posed on the brink of nuclear holocaust. The three major corporations at the time—GeoCorp, I Net, and Poldine Incorporated—stepped in when the world governments were desperate enough and offered them a solution, for a price. What choice did they have? Within a year, the governments were dissolved and the companies took over with subsidiaries branching off and claiming independence.

"After they took over, there was peace for a while. I mean world peace. The Three, as they became known, were friendly with each other, content to scratch each other's backs. There was no real use for a military budget when compared to the profit to be had in technology, so they began to focus inward. With the Hydro Cells being as efficient as they were, massive technological expansion was possible in a decade. It was amazing what people could think of when they were no longer limited to primitive internal combustion. In nine years, the City of Denver's population soared to more than sixty million people and GeoCorp rebuilt the entire region in five months to accommodate the population boom."

"Why Denver?" Chris asked.

"Well, all the cities expanded, but few as much. Denver was an ideal candidate for the GeoCorp capital because of its central location on the North American continent."

It made sense. Chris sat for a minute and thought about it. "And I suppose a massive population was possible because there was now cheap and unlimited energy. I'm assuming the Hydro Cells are made of water?"

"Precisely. With some research into water reclamation combined with the abundance of energy, huge grow-rooms underground became possible. Not possible, but necessary, after most of the Midwest was irradiated in the War of Thirty-eight." He could not mistake the look of amusement on Jameson's face.

"Someone else mentioned that to me," Chris said. "So I guess world peace didn't last."

"Not even," Jameson laughed coldly. "As I said, the Three were too bureaucratic and unwieldy to manage a population that grew by billions each year. Some willingly split themselves into smaller companies to better manage their assets. GeoCorp was not as willing, but they could do nothing when the Omni Institute broke off and claimed everything east of the Mississippi River as their own.

"GeoCorp developed PolCorp in an attempt to bring Omni back into the fold with force, or, preferably, the threat of force." Jameson laughed. "They did too good a job, and PolCorp became an independent contractor, selling arms to both sides. After the tech expansion, it was only a few small steps to take what was learned and apply it to the military. GeoCorp couldn't control their creation, and the war lasted for three years, ending in a draw. Supposedly, everything west of the Mississippi still belongs to GeoCorp, but what used to be called the Bible Belt was reduced to smoldering, radioactive ashes during the conflict. Of course, this led to the Denver population skyrocketing even more as the refugees streamed in."

"So PolCorp is now independent?" Chris frowned at this thought. He didn't like the company based on his experiences so far.

"Completely. They now work as security for a number of companies around the world. Ironically, that means they constantly come into conflict with each other. It's all about the bottom line—the boys at the top making the big bucks don't care if a majority of that money comes from their employees killing each other, and what do the employees care if the people they're fighting work for the same company? Paid is paid, after all, and the PolCorp guys are paid well enough not to question their employers' tactics."

Chris looked doubtful. "If that's the case, then why is all this public knowledge? Seems like people would try and keep a lid on that sort of thing."

Jameson smiled. "I'm not part of the 'public,' Chris, if you haven't figured that out yet. I work for GeoCorp."

Chris leveled his gaze at the ring of gold fibers bound around Jameson's finger. "So why are you helping me?"

Jameson locked eyes with Chris and said nothing.

Chris backed down first, swallowed, and changed the subject. "So what about this gang war?"

Jameson shrugged, "Civil unrest."

Chris hesitated, scared to ask his next question. "What do you know about me, Doctor?"

Jameson smiled, almost warmly, "You are Dr. Christopher Nost, who spent the last forty-one—"

"That's not what I mean," Chris interrupted. "I mean … something happened to me a few nights ago … PolCorp stopped me and asked for papers, and …"

"…and?" Jameson gazed at Chris, looking interested for the first time.

"…and I don't know. Everything got … slow. I don't know how to explain it…"

"Dr. Nost, there's someth—"

"And something else," Chris said, not noticing Jameson had spoken. "There was this woman yesterday. I was at the Punt, trying to figure some stuff out. About myself. She seemed to know who I was. And she knew about you. She told me not to trust you."

Jameson contemplated Chris for a long time before he spoke. "This woman … what did she look like?"

"She had red hair. Pretty. I don't know … a really athletic build. You know who she was?"

"I give up." Despite his words, Jameson looked at Chris as if he knew exactly who it was.

"She said she was Mary Frost. The granddaughter of the woman I supposedly murdered almost forty-five years ago."

"Chris, let me tell you a few things." Jameson leaned back into his chair, then shifted and leaned forward again.

"I'm listening," Chris ground his teeth. *You know something, you bastard. Tell me what you know.*

"First, don't trust that woman."

"That's what she said about you."

"I'm serious, Chris," Jameson took on the demeanor of a lecturing father. "You were lucky. That woman could be extremely dangerous."

"How so?"

"She could try and kill you." Jameson's stare bored into Chris. He didn't blink.

Chris didn't back down. "She *could* try and kill me, huh? Why didn't she, then?"

"Okay, Chris," Jameson said, a look of resolution flitting across his face. "This is how it is. I studied you—for more than a decade I studied you, and I didn't find anything different about you. I studied your theories, and ... Chris, do you know what you were working on, before Frost's murder?"

"No. Not really, anyway. Some sort of alloy or something."

"No. That was what the press reported. What you developed was a theory that stated that if faster-than-light speeds could be reached, one would no longer be in this continuum, but would, rather, enter into some sort of ultraspace that could result in a sort of instantaneous travel—teleportation, for all intents and purposes. The work you did was based on Metastability theory and the universal skin. If there are Tardis regions in the universe, which are larger on the inside, then why not anti-Tardis regions outside the universe, smaller on the outside. The trick then becomes to pierce the universe's skin without breaking the surface tension, so no one accidentally destroys it. Figure out how to do that, and time and space are completely navigable. Which you thought you figured out. Tons of work went into it in Switzerland. It was called the Second Paradigm Theorem. It was halted after Frost's murder, and after you were shot it was dropped for good."

Chris looked at Garret Jameson. "Why are you telling me this?"

"Because, don't you see? You don't age. You can, apparently, control time. There's something different about you. Your memory loss ... God damn it! Don't you see? I think you came across something, during your research. Something that changed you, gave you ... something. I'm not the only one that knows about your research or your time in the hospital. Why do you think I told you to stay away from the authorities? If anyone else put two and two together.... You're in danger, Chris. Whatever breakthrough you had in your work, it didn't leave you with your memory intact. It's your only hope."

"Why do I think you already know the answer to that?"

"Here," Jameson glanced around, ignoring Chris's comment and slid a bundle of cloth across the table. "It was my father's. I never leave the Corporate Zone, so I don't need it, but you might find it useful."

Chris unwrapped the old T-shirt and found an ancient semi-automatic handgun with an extra clip. The edges were rusty, but it looked well maintained.

"What's this?"

"What does it look like?" Jameson asked. "Like I said, you could be in danger."

Chris looked up to the barista, but he sat behind the bar reading *Waiting for Godot*. He wrapped the gun back up into the bundle and slid it under his coat.

Jameson nodded in approval and his emotionless eyes blinked once. "I'm telling you, don't trust that woman," Jameson stood to leave, but looked back at Chris over his shoulder. "For that matter, Chris, don't trust me, either."

1997: Garret's Gambit

Traffic moved by Garret's parked car as he prepared himself to see his wife for the first time in ten years. This was not going to be easy for him, but as important as it was, he couldn't let it faze him. When he walked into that courtroom, he knew she would spot him and recognize him. And no matter what happened he had to be blasé and feign ignorance of her identity.

It was far too critical to get Nost pronounced guilty to allow emotion to overwhelm him. It would be a hell of a thing to see his dead wife and not acknowledge her.

Garret finished bracing himself and got out of the car, walking through the bright day towards the courthouse. The light traffic streamed down the streets, the beautiful day a stark contrast to the landscape of his heart. He walked, enjoying the feel of the sun warming his skin, giving him an internal glow.

As he ascended the stairs, he took one last moment to pause and observe the entryway to the Denver courthouse. The semi-circular building created a natural courtyard inside of its curve. Across Bannock, the street that ran in front of the building, was a long park with almost Greek-looking columned buildings along the sides.

Birds sang, traffic drove by, people walked through the park, and the smell of summer floated through the air. A small group played Frisbee across the street, and to the north, along the Sixteenth Street Mall, pedestrian traffic bustled. In less than four hours Garret hoped there would be blood on these steps. Not hope, he thought to himself, but fact. Fact born of necessity.

Assuming that everything went according to his plan, there would be. One last time he ran through all of the logistics and math behind his plan. Everything checked out once again. In four hours he would have completed the balancing actions needed to stabilize the greatest paradox in history and insure his wife's survival. A winning situation no matter how you looked at it.

Allowing himself a slight smile, Garret finished ascending the stairs and walked into the courthouse. Moving from the sunlight's warmth to the chilly air-conditioned and dim interior made goose bumps break out along his arms. Inside, the colors were all deep shades of tans and browns, giving the environment a rich but dark feeling. The drastic change in temperature sent chills down Garret's arms as he approached the security checkpoint. Unloading his pockets of everything metallic, he walked through the primitive metal detector and then headed towards the chamber the trial was to be held in.

The people walking around were a mix of police officers, traffic violators, and the on-site staff of various clerks and vendors. No one looked particularly happy or even in a good mood.

Harder criminals destined for the trials came from the holding cells in the district six jail building, behind the courthouse and across the street. Garret had learned this when he studied the building and knew he wouldn't run into the procession for the man he tried to condemn. Grateful for the small detail, he hid a smile.

As he walked into the trial, his breath momentarily caught. There she sat, about half way back in the observer section. The room had high, but large windows, much brighter than the hallway he had entered from. For a second it seemed as though the light shone on her alone, picking her out of the crowd and setting her apart with a glowing golden nimbus. For the briefest second, their eyes met.

He swallowed and forced himself to walk forward. Doing his best to ignore Wanda, he strode forward to the prosecuting attorney's table and pulled out his seat. He sat down and purposefully started organizing his trial notes.

After a moment, he realized that his HUD contact lenses were reporting that Wanda had scanned him. She had spotted him then, and used her HUD to confirm his identity. He could almost feel her thoughts. She would be analyzing the possible reasons that he would be here. It would not take her very long to piece it together, he suspected. He had to hope that she held to her original course of action. If she didn't, then this whole exercise would be wasted.

He watched the time on the old analog clock hanging behind the Judge's bench. She should be getting up and departing in a few minutes, to prepare her sniper's roost. The files had contained exact times on that. Sure enough, a few moments passed before she stood up and walked out of the courtroom.

Shortly after she left, the bailiff walked into the room to announce the judge's entry. Garret stood up, as did everyone else in the room, and the judge walked in. As he took his seat something clicked inside Garret. He knew he would win the trial. He knew that Nost would be pronounced guilty. And above all, he knew that his wife would survive today, changing today's history from a class six paradox to a class two.

Time: 1997
Location: Classified
Operation: Classified

Lucille Frost was in a daze. Fire danced through the air around her, kissing the ground in small streaks of red and blaring sirens made it impossible to hear even her own thoughts. The bit with the raining concrete and glass was well over by now, but the aftermath of the explosion was in many ways a more chaotic scene than the initial moment of the disaster had been.

Here and there were pockets of stillness, much like the one currently around her, found behind ambulances where people were sitting in dazed shock. Everywhere else, firemen, emergency medics, and policemen were hurrying around the scene attempting to contain the damage. They were failing for the most part. It wasn't that they were not doing a good job, but the news teams that had been pushed off the site previously were now swarming underfoot and wreaking havoc on every attempt that the police made to settle the situation.

Because of the media frenzy, body bags were loaded into the ambulances hurriedly, and the news teams fed off the images they could capture of those sad black bags. This time period pushed death and tragedy in media. It wasn't better or worse than the sensationalization of any other time period, just morbid.

Lucy drew in a ragged but deep breath and calmed herself enough to think. She was a combat specialist and a scene like this should not have shaken her nerves so severely. But something about this mission was really dulling her edge.

She had missed a lot of things recently that she should have caught and been prepared for. The half window, flying through the air, had nearly killed her. Instead, a local era police officer had sacrificed his life for her. It created yet another potential paradox, and right at the crux of a paradox she was supposed to be here to diffuse. Next on the list of deadly mistakes was the explosion itself.

Half of the building had been destroyed. That was even worse, definitely a paradox. Someone had wanted to kill her. She could deal with this, though; all she had to do was kill them first. Now that she knew the threat was there, counteracting it was a top priority.

The only reason she had not been at the office earlier was that Alexander Zarth had detained her in conversation to the point that she was late arriving at work. Highly suspicious, but he probably was not involved since it had resulted in her life being spared.

Possibility stretched out from this point, creating a matrix that she analyzed in her mind's eye. Of all the courses that lay in front of her she could think of only one that might work, and it was to follow Zarth's advice. Focusing her will she hopped forward in time, and north in space.

2044: New Denver, Colorado

Lucy Frost watched Garret leave the medical center with amusement. So this was his game. Everything that Alexander Zarth had told her checked out. So now she had to play her role in the events unfolding. Who would have thought that the critical point in the paradox's formation actually occurred forty years after the paradox itself? With another effort of will she slipped sideways to confront Nost and push him in the right direction.

The building that she slipstreamed into could be described as nothing other than grungy. It was mostly empty, and the lights were low, masking what the few people present were doing in their computer booths.

The walls were dirty to the point that Lucy wondered if the air was safe to breathe. Random garbage lay unnoticed by the negligent cleaning staff, accumulating under desks and in corners. She spied Nost, hunched over his own terminal and obviously fully absorbed in whatever he was reading. His back was to her and he sat slumped in his chair, studying the screen in front of him.

Lucy walked up to him and stood behind him, reading over his shoulder. Interestingly, he was reading about her supposed death. "Old news, huh?" she purred. It gratified her to watch his spine straighten in surprise. "Now why would you be hunting through that stuff?"

Chris closed out the screen. "What's it to you?" he asked, turning around to face her. Chris froze and swallowed when he looked at her, then said nothing more. His hand played with the keyboard. The spark of recognition had caught fire in his eyes.

"Curiosity, really," Lucy said. "As I was going by I saw my name on your screen, so I stopped to have a look. When I saw you were reading about my grandmother's murder, I couldn't help but wonder why you were reading about it."

"Your ... grandmother?" Chris said. He didn't sound like he believed her. "That explains the striking resemblance."

"Yes, I know. I look exactly like her. Everybody who sees her picture says it." She bit her lower lip and stuck out her hand, offering up introductions. "I'm sorry. My name is Mary. Mary Frost." Chris shook with nervousness, but she wrote it off to the fact that he thought he addressed the supposed granddaughter of the woman he thought he had murdered.

Chris looked at her hand suspiciously, then took it, hesitantly, and shook it. His grip was weak and his palms mildly sweaty. This was a changed man from the confident and brilliant physicist she had talked to the day before, by her perspective. "I'm Geoffrey Garret. I was doing a little research on the project your grandmother was working on. I … I'm a scientist …"

So, he was being smart and hiding his identity. He had chosen a bad name to use, as she knew Garret poked around as a rogue agent from ten years up her stream. "Garret?" She looked at him, and then she pushed her gaze *through* him, for almost a minute. "I was looking for a Garret, actually, but I don't think you're him." She gave him a quirky grin and watched his response to the pressure.

Everything Alex had told her led her to believe that she had to build Chris up to the brink of snapping if she was to survive the next few days. And observing him here today, it didn't seem that it would be a difficult task. He was somewhat unhinged, and she saw rampant paranoia barely hiding under the surface layer of his thoughts.

"I doubt it," Chris said, trying to mask his relief. "I haven't been in the city too long.…"

"Oh no?" She smiled getting ready to go in for the kill.

He blinked and then answered her. "Well, no. I've only been around here for a couple of days.…"

Lucy leaned in close to Chris without warning, one hand cupping around his neck, and ran her tongue along the edge of his ear. She played up the sex kitten act; pushing him further off his mental balance. Chris tried to pull away from her, but she held him. "I know who you are," she said, pulling back and looking into his eyes. She scanned what she saw there, pleased with herself. "I know what you are looking for, and you will find your answers."

He shuddered. "That's not possible. Look, I don't know what you think you know, but you're wrong."

She leaned in closer until her lips were brushing against his ear, "It is you who are wrong; you to whom the truth will be revealed. You see, I know what you are, Chris," she whispered before pulling back and looking at him once more. "Anyway, don't trust Jameson. He's a liar and worse. If you let him in," she tapped a finger against Chris's temple, "he'll try to twist you and then destroy you. Meet him if you must—but be wary. Know that he is evil."

Lucy hoped she had played that right. He looked beyond paranoid in her last glimpse of him, but he was a strong man in nineteen ninety-seven. So she turned around to drive home the point with one final shot. "See you around, *Doctor.*"

As the door closed behind her she hopped forward to continue observing him. Finally, she started to understand her true mission regarding this man.

2044 A.D.: New Denver, Colorado.

Alex watched Chris depart for the final time and let his holo drop as he sat thoughtfully in the Rangley Hotel lobby. After a few months of observation, he knew something was drastically wrong. His observations of Nost had shown him doing things that were on the brink of impossible.

A quote from an old C nineteen series of books came unbidden back to him … *'that which is left, no matter how improbable, is your solution.'* A wide grin spread across his face. So that was the way of it. He mentally tipped his hat to his own mind in thanks. It was impossible for Nost to have learned the trick of time dilution with incremental steps, at least without having mastered basic travel first. Besides, what he had witnessed Nost do with dilution was beyond the scale of possible skill.

It was just too … smooth. There was no skipping in time, no breaks. He would have to be performing nanosecond leaps and already have been mostly done with his actions faster than the brain could fire the signals to move the body.

This meant that some other force had to be at work in his system. Something that allowed Chris to stretch time and move in a fashion that accelerated his subjective time. Alex pondered this for a bit, while sipping on a beer, and finally came to the conclusion that an outside force had introduced the ability.

The sole possibility that he could think of was a new time technology. And there were only one of two sources for that. Garret, who had exhibited none of the same traits, or Alex's own fourth millennium contact, who would be sufficiently advanced to be hiding something like that.

So, even though he had hired Alex to deal with the situation, he was an active player in the game, even if his movements were invisible to Alex. The more he thought about it, the more this sounded like damn good fun to him.

Time to hunt then. And he knew where the hunt had to start. Alex focused and pushed himself forward, to the beginning.

2620: Tucson Arizona

The man sat down in the booth across from Alex. The Alex from the future watched from the back, where he poured nano machines into the glass that the man would be using. Subtlety was a game that Alex was gifted at. Frank, the owner of the bar, wandered into the back to fill the order of his only two customers, surprised to see Alex standing there holding a glass.

Alex winked at him as he handed him the glass, then put one finger over his pursed lips. Frank nodded and took the glass, filling it with the man's drink then wandering back out into the main portion of the bar.

Alex kept his focus on the displaced nano machines, marking the progress of the set of orders he had programmed into them. The man from the future picked up his glass for a drink, unaware of the trap contained within it. Sure enough, as he sipped his drink and absorbed Alex's nanos, they found a foreign technology. He grinned and started the hack to subvert a small but important percentage of them, enslaving them to his own will.

The man never noticed the internal war being waged in his blood stream by warriors smaller than the nucleus of one of his blood cells. It was a fast war, and one in which the enemy line never even realized it was under attack. When he finished the deed, his side emerged victorious; Alex sank almost all of the nanos out of the man's body and into the wood of the table. Those would wait there for both men to leave so that the future Alex could claim them into his own system and figure out how to use them.

The ones he left in the other man's body started on a new task, though: ripping apart a few of the man's DNA chains and rebuilding them, as Alex's own. It was delicate work, but done on a level of anatomy that the man would never think to check. He was going to have one hell of a rash in a few days though, when his body rejected the foreign cells.

Until then, a small piece of Alex would travel forward. Time theory was an interesting thing. So far no one had ever managed to travel forward from his or her own relative time. Theory ran something along the lines that each nexus of will, or human mind, left a unique signature on the time stream. Any choices leading up to that signature could be altered, but any choices of which that signature was a factor in could not be altered.

Basically, he could travel back but not forward past his point of origin. DNA was the key, and what it said to the nanos. Alex had always thought the 'historical imperative' theory was bunk. Time travel meant stepping across the threshold of the universe then stepping back in at the chosen time and place. The whole of the universe, from the outside, existed in a state of quantum flux. Not traveling forward from where you were was senseless. But, as senseless as it was, it was the limitation they all had to deal with.

It seemed to him like a bunch of gibberish that other people spouted to make it sound like temporal physicists understood something that they didn't. Alex suspected that the truth was much simpler and the trick of it was that you could only travel as far forward as your genetic structure took you in history.

In simpler terms, things of the past were decided. The future was not for any given individual until such time as that body had inhabited the times of the historical nexus you wanted to travel to. What Alex was about to try was such a ridiculous concept that no one had ever thought of it. So ridiculous, in fact, that it was going to work.

Some part of him knew that and accepted it as fact. After the past version of himself had departed, as well as the man from C Forty-five, he walked to the table and placed his hand, palm down, onto the wood grain surface. He had always appreciated the fact that this bar had wood tables.

It was amazing what you could do with organic structures if you put your mind to the task. Concentrating, he pulled all of the nanos out of the wood and into himself, absorbing back both his own and the conquered machines.

Alex felt the new machines course through his system and started the replication process. He had to get enough of them active that the systems in them would be usable by his body mass. As they reached a substantial enough volume to allow him access to their programming features, he discovered that he had been right.

Good, he thought, *I don't have to waste time figuring out another angle.* This man could also dilate time the way that Chris could. Alex grinned and froze time around him. Time continued on in a small bubble around him, but looking out the window Alex saw a remarkable sight.

The hot desert sun no longer created mirages. Cars were frozen in midair. A man drinking from a water fountain was frozen with droplets of water suspended in a dance around his mouth. Interesting. It seemed the differential they could create was about a factor of at least three thousand to one. Handy in a fight. The greater truth struck Alex before it became critical as well.

Stretching time this thinly also meant that he would run out of air within about a minute of his subjective time. And he would superheat anything he phased between time streams with any amount of kinetic energy. Like, for instance, air. Moving too fast while breathing would burn his lungs out of his chest.

Not a boundary he ever wanted to have to test. An easy enough solution offered itself though, always stay in motion, or briefly phase into standard time while breathing. And *never* forget that little tidbit.

He found one more subroutine in these new nanos and ran it; excited to see what other features they offered him. A grid appeared in his vision, printing across the center of his pupil. Letters started typing themselves out, until full sentences were formed asking him to set user parameters.

He sped time back up to its normal passage and breathed out a heavy breath. "Wicked ..." he spoke to himself and kept it under his breath. "My own internal computer ..." Alex grinned to himself about this newest discovery and started programming his computer. It was a surprisingly easy system to use and Alex had mastered the knack of it in no time flat.

The system responded to the signals his neural system sent to his own brain, so that by thinking to himself he could, in essence, 'talk' to the computer. It was a tremendously sophisticated system, which seemed to have an internal computer's processing power well beyond any technology he had ever seen. All in all, not a bad find for the day.

Shortly thereafter, Alex Zarth did that which no human had ever done before; he pushed himself forward, past his own point of origin, and into the future.

RELATIVITY SYNCHRONIZATION:

THE EIGHTH CAUSE

2044: Answers & Questions

Chris sat by himself, staring into space, lost in a maze of contemplation. Every thought was another wall, and there was no sign of the cheese at the center. He watched the barista as he fiddled with the bar, looking up from his work periodically to glare at Chris through black-rimmed glasses.

It had grown late and Chris was the only remaining customer. Generic music filtered through ancient speakers with a tin-like quality, as it attempted to fill the silence in the shop with a cheerful atmosphere, but failed abysmally. The clock on the wall above the counter, said it was not yet four but continued to slice away the past in one second increments. The gun weighed heavy in his pocket, pulling at his conscious mind, making him all the more aware of how alien this world felt even though he had no memory of his own. He stood to leave, clutching at the bundle under his coat with a sweaty hand. The barista watched him go but said nothing.

The brilliant oranges and reds of autumn light painted the landscape, the sun cast its rays though the maze of glass building fronts, making Chris squint from the glare on the closed storefronts around him. It was a picturesque scene, a forest of glass that felt more like a painting than a city. While many of the upper story windows had shattered that morning, the ground level seemed unharmed. He could no longer see smoke coming from behind the D.A.B., which looked like a chrome phallus sun, casting a second, silver brilliance down the mall, eradicating the shadows made by the slanting yellow light in the cloudless sky.

Chris walked down North Cherry Lane in a daze, only half noticing that the streets and skies were now abandoned. *Jameson KNOWS something*, Chris thought. *He knows all about me ... or least more about me than the record archives. Why did he give me this?* He hefted the weight of the old handgun under his coat. It comforted him and yet filled him with suspicion.

Jameson said he didn't need it because he never left the Corporate Zone, but he was at the coffee shop. But that didn't make sense either. Jameson didn't try to cajole Chris into trusting him. He had told Chris *not* to trust him.

He knows what I am, Chris stopped in his tracks. *He figured out what I am while I was ... sleeping. Goddamn him! He met with me and left and managed to not give me any answers about myself. Why did he bother? To give me this?* Chris once again felt the weight of the gun under his coat. *Then why?*

Chris knew what he needed to do. This Frost woman knew something, too. He needed to find her, ask her all the questions that Jameson didn't answer. Frost's murder, whether or not by him, at least had been committed *because* of him.

His … ability, Jameson's ambiguity, and the Frost woman who happened to be in the Punt at the same time he was. She knew what he was, too. Chris began to wonder if he was the only person in the world who didn't know about himself. He shook his head and kept walking.

The question: what *was* he? Chris tried not to think about the answer, the *only* answer that he could find, beyond the reach of theory or reason, forcing its way out of his subconscious and into the forefront of his weary mind.

Am I Kronos? Some time traveler controlling the byways of history with no conscious memory? Chris allowed himself to think it, once, before trying to laugh it down. He was successful. Almost. *I am Zrvan.* That thought brought a strained smile to his lips. He tried to laugh out loud, but it came out dry and hollow. He began walking again, but he could feel the press of the void filled with all things, lurking beyond his reach.

He tried to touch it again, without success. Only this time it was not quite nothing. It was like many little nothings, like little holes of absence that all together made up reality.

Chris stumbled and snapped out of his daze, looking around. He no longer recognized where he was. A street pole loomed above him, but he couldn't tell for which street—all the signs were missing save one, obscured by soot and ash, hanging high above his head. He turned around, but could no longer see the spire of the D.A.B., and the wall of the Corporate Zone, beginning to illuminate itself in the dying evening light, seemed far away. He could tell he was in a shopping district, but the stores around him were not closed, they were abandoned. One side of the street was lined with high, residential complexes, while the other consisted of a low strip-mall of abandoned pizza joints and burned out grocery stores.

How long have I been walking? The sun had already set behind the city and the mountains beyond that, and the sky turned purple as night chased the fire-filled sunset in its eternal pursuit. There was still not a cloud to be seen.

Chris turned and started back the way he had come from, reaching under his coat and clinging to the gun. He tried to figure out how he had passed the Rangley, and wandered off North Cherry Lane without noticing it, when he heard the gunshots.

At first they were distant, rapid-fire things, and he needed to think a moment before understanding what they were. He scanned above the buildings in front of him one more time for a glimpse of the D.A.B., saw nothing, and jogged over to the shelter of the doorway of an abandoned apartment building. He squatted there, listening to the sound of approaching internal combustion engines, thinking of Rat.

I need to find him. I can trust him, because he doesn't know anything about me. And he would know what to do, now.

Chris tried the door, but the rust and gunk of years stuck it closed. He looked closely, running his hand over the surface, and felt little bumps, evenly spaced, on its metal-reinforced wood. *Someone boarded it shut from the inside. Maybe there's a window …* He only had time to take a step from the doorway before chaos exploded around him.

From his right burst a full-sized Hummer, rolling over the mangled hulk of a Cadillac as it rounded the corner. There were several figures hanging off of it, and a 50-caliber machine gun swinging on a tripod mounted to the open back. A bloody mass hung over the low railing behind the mounted gun, which bounced and slid off as the rusted, yellow vehicle crushed the last of the life out of the Cadillac. Chris had time to see the looks of ecstatic fear on the driver's face before a shadow dimmed the star-lit sky.

The chopper approached without warning. Even as it slid into view, low over the destitute apartment building, it emitted only a faint whine, higher and quieter by far than the PolCorp Cruisers, and barely audible now over the roar of the rampaging Hummer.

One of the Hummer riders clambered to the back to replace the once human chunk of meat now lying by the Cadillac. A low roar from anti-tank guns protruding from the nose of the helicopter broke the silence and huge chunks of pavement exploded around the truck as it swerved to avoid the hole created by the blast. The climber tumbled with a scream and was crushed by the rear wheel of his allies, but another took his place behind the machine gun.

Chris assumed that the helicopter must be PolCorp, but as it swung around above the canyon of the buildings for another attack, he saw that it had a green bug-face sloppily painted on the side. Chris thought of the Skragsuit costumes he had seen in Jones Drugs & Merchandise. *The gangs have attack helicopters.* Chris started laughing—for some reason the idea was funny to him. Funnier, anyway, than the thought that *he* might be the God of Time.

Among the violence of full urban combat, shrapnel and stray bullets ricocheting all around him, Chris felt something in his mind snap, and the laughter kept flowing, an unstoppable tide barely audible above the noise of the gunfire.

The guy on the back of the Hummer positioned himself and let fly, the roar of the gun shots echoing up and down the abandoned street. His wild shooting, drew a wide, curving line of destruction across the building opposite Chris, shattering windows and concrete, but coming nowhere close to the silent predator above that flew into position for another burst.

Swerving, the Hummer tried to get out of the line of fire, turning ninety degrees until it headed right for Chris. He could see they weren't going to make it—the chopper changed its course to come in right behind them. Chris watched, fascinated, as the gun on the nose of the helicopter dropped down to come in line with the hummer.

He could see the look of terrified resolve on the young, scarred face of the driver and his female passenger; she would have been pretty but looked more tired and used up than anything. The man on the machine gun shot bursts, but his inept shots only succeeded in blasting away at the already shattered buildings lining the wide street.

This shouldn't be happening, Chris thought, as he backed further into the doorway. He knew he had seconds, and he knew that should be enough. But he wasn't going to make it. He saw the nose of the helicopter light up and his head filled with the awful roar of gunfire. *I'm trying too hard,* Chris thought. *It will happen.*

But he couldn't stop trying to grasp time, to change it, and so he knew he would fail as the Hummer burst into flames and came rolling toward him. *I'm doing it!* Chris thought at first, as he watched the flaming wreckage fly at him and heard the engines of the helicopter whisper in pain as the pilot tried in vain to pull up over the building towering over Chris.

He heard the explosion above him, but he didn't move. *No, I'm not doing it. I'm about to die.* An incredible calm suffused him with a complete absence of thought as he stood in the doorway, watching his destruction hurtle toward him, an angry deity of twisted metal and fire. *Then I'll be a god,* he found himself thinking, when behind him, he felt a hand and something pulled at him ...

Chris expected to find himself inside the apartment building. He stood on a rooftop, the tar still warm from the October sun, the sky black and clear, speckled with a few stars. He could smell smoke, and he walked to the edge of the roof, peering down onto the fires below him.

The wreckage of the Hummer lay strewn in a smoldering line, reaching from halfway across the wide avenue all the way to the building opposite him, where it joined another pile of burning junk. Near the top of the building was the smoking hole left by the impact of the helicopter. The oily smell of smoking plastic filled the air. *How did I get over here?* Chris wondered, looking around.

He saw a small bundle near where he had found himself, and picked it up. It was Jameson's gun. He unwrapped it and put it in his coat pocket before going back over to the edge of the building. By the sky and the low flames of the fires, a few hours must have passed, but there were no signs of fire trucks or police cars. He had no memory of anything that happened between standing in the doorway and being on the roof, but he knew, *knew* he didn't manipulate time. He remembered the hand that grasped his shoulder, and looked around.

A figure, barely noticeable through the dark and the haze of smoke, stood down the street where the shadows were complete. It wore a long, black coat and a black fedora. Chris squinted at it, and the figure tipped his hat at him, and walked away.

Jesus Christ, Chris thought. *I need to get out of here.*

1997: Yuri's Gambit

Shivers ran down Yuri's spine, like tiny spiders crawling under his skin, as he left the hotel in the middle of the night. For the better part of the past four weeks someone had been watching him, but it didn't matter now. He had played along, masking his nighttime bio-signature trail with some intelligence tech that he had the foresight to bring along. With a clever mix of a monotonous daytime routine and effectively used night hours, he was pretty sure he had duped whoever was on him.

The thought that there was no one on him never crossed his mind. Time Corp's procedures dictated that a hunter would be sent after any unauthorized jump and he hadn't had the right tools to mask his jump from the agency's scanners. Giddy, he climbed out the bathroom window and started working his way down the wall below him.

Whoever followed him was a moot point now and didn't really concern him. He had managed to unravel the trail of Alex's movements and the results were disturbing, to say the least. This paradox was far bigger than anyone back at headquarters had imagined. And far more dangerous as well. Right dead center in the whole thing stood Alexander Zarth, seemingly making all of the right moves needed to keep the entire paradox balanced and moving forward without actually breaking down the fabric of history.

Considering that Yuri's job, over the years he spent in the Time Corp, had become that of hunting down Alex, a known time criminal who had created some of the only unsolved paradoxes in the Time Corp's history, he had a difficult time fitting it into his mental picture. But he had to try. And if his suspicions were actually correct, tonight, breaking into Lucy's office would reveal the missing part of his equation.

It would also present Yuri the opportunity to meet the man he had chased across history without ever actually encountering face to face. That, more than anything else, drove Yuri. To meet the man who spun history from his fingers and danced around agents like they were children. To meet the man known as the uncatchable thief of time by the most elite police force known to history.

Lost in thought, his foot slipped from the crack he had it wedged into. He dropped the final story down the back wall of the hotel, but managed not to hurt himself much. He grinned at that. Director Arbu had been more than correct when saying that Yuri was not up to snuff for the physical demands of a field mission, but regardless, he enjoyed himself.

Being in the field was a rush and as with most things that provided a rush, Yuri found it addicting. Catching his breath after the fall, he composed himself, then started off at a light jog, moving away from where his watcher had to be and heading a couple streets away to catch a cab.

The first taxi that he found had a sleeping driver. Yuri shrugged to himself and rapped on the window. The man leaned back in his seat, ignition off, and snored. Startled out of his slumber when Yuri knocked on the glass next to his head, he rolled down the window. Yuri smiled at the man. "Sorry to wake you up, but I was hoping that you were available for a fare," he said as he flashed a fifty dollar bill.

The driver blinked and yawned, stretching his arms as wide as the cab's interior would allow. "Don't worry about waking me up. A long, dead night. Hop in, I can get you where you need to go." Yuri popped open the door and climbed into the cab. The newly wakened cabbie looked back in the rearview mirror as Yuri settled into the cab. "Where you headed?"

Yuri shut the door. "The desk at my hotel said there was a twenty-four hour coffee shop over by the air force base. You know where it is?"

The driver nodded and turned the car on, kicking it into drive and pulling out into the empty street. "It's only about a five minute drive from here. I'll have you there in no time, man. It'll be about seven or eight bucks though." Yuri nodded and watched the dark buildings pass by in the night as they drove through the islands of light the street lamps created. He marveled at the smell of the cab, the subversive odor of combusting hydrocarbons masked by the dangling air freshener on the rear view mirror. How different the twenty-first century was from any other time.

The journey, as the cabbie had promised, took about five minutes. Yuri smiled when they pulled up to their destination and gave the man the fifty. "Keep the change. I'll need you to pick me up in about an hour if you can do that."

The driver nodded. "Sure thing man. See you in one hour."

Yuri walked into the shop and bought himself a cup of coffee. He took it plain black with four shots of espresso mixed into the already dark roasted blend. He would need as much energy as he could get. This old century stuff was nowhere near as good as his time's coffee, but the flip side was that a cup of joe was a cup of joe.

He steeled himself and left the shop, walking down a side road to break into a classified military facility. For a field agent, used to hard, physically trained discipline, this would be a challenge, though doable. For an intelligence officer, willing to use his brain in a methodical and unhurried way, this would not be a challenge at all.

Forty minutes later, he walked back away from the facility, having finished the deed, and surprised at what he had found on Lucy Frost's desk. Why was she pushing Christopher Nost away from the discovery of the travel nano machine he was about to discover? It made no sense. Nost had to invent the machine and then die; it was all in the mission dossiers he had read through trying to unravel the paradox back here.

He filed the thoughts away for later and scanned the semi dark parking lot, looking for Alex Zarth. His intuition had told him the man would be here. And his hunch had played out correctly. Across the lot, concealed by shadow lurked a figure that could only have been the twenty-seventh century renegade. Yuri started walking towards him, not bothering to try to conceal his presence.

The man waited for him. As he approached the Shadow, Alex held out his hand and Yuri stared at it for a second.

"Come now, Yuri, you are a brilliant man. You've pieced together enough to know that I would be here waiting, so you must also know what I am waiting for." He finally got to hear Alex's voice. It was a pleasant and intelligent voice, melodious even, not at all filled with the diabolical madness that Yuri had been expecting.

Yuri started and handed Alex the papers he had stolen from Lucy Frost. "Of course. Here you are. I have to ask though, what first clued you into this … situation?"

Alex laughed. "Thank you for the credit to my intelligence, but to be frank, someone tipped me off. They came back from C Forty-five to hire me. Said they didn't have any local talent that could get the job done. So, they got me instead."

Yuri nodded at that. He had suspected something similar, even if he had been unwilling to voice the suspicion to himself. And it could not have been a future incarnation of the Time Corp, otherwise they would have alerted the past mission centers that they were operating there. Yuri suspected he knew what that meant, but pushed the thoughts to the back of his mind.

Not his concern. "You know Alex, that when all of this is said and done, if I'm not fired, I'll have to go back to hunting you."

Alex let out a bark of laughter. He had a rich and deep laugh that Yuri found he trusted.

"Yuri, that will be a damned hard goal to accomplish. You see, we're both going to die. No other course of action will solve this paradox except the one that results in our deaths."

Yuri swallowed. He believed Alex. He nodded, accepting this tidbit that had been floating at the back of his mind as a possibility since he made the jump back. "Do you know how and when I buy it? I know that ... well ... I want to know how long I have."

Alex nodded. "Fair request. I know you won't try to stop it, since subjectively it is in my past. Tomorrow night, in this parking lot, you will meet Lucy Frost. You will hand off to her a file of all your research, as well as all your speculations about this event nexus. You will be shot from behind. I'm sorry, truly. I would have loved the chance to get to know you, Yuri, and to chase the hunt with you again."

Yuri nodded again. "I see. One other question for you then. Do you know how long you have? Your death was never recorded in any era we could find in the databanks."

Alex stepped out of the shadows and Yuri could see he looked thoughtful. "Yes, in fact, I do know basically how I will die. It's odd to me that you asked."

As Alex scratched his chin, Yuri noticed that the skin was heavily bruised, almost to the point of being jet black around his jaw. "Well, I don't see the harm ... on one condition."

Yuri shrugged. "What is the condition? That I do not share it in the file I give to Frost? Fine. You have my word."

Again Alex smiled in amusement, like he was privy to a joke no one else knew. "You nailed it in one. All right. I'm going to die of old age, in a sense. I've managed to break the Point of Origin and travel into my future. So now my body thinks it should be a hell of a lot older and it's trying to catch up. To be specific, my body thinks it should be in the neighborhood of fourteen hundred years older than it is."

Yuri's mind spun, churning out math and theory. "But, if that's the case, you should be dead already. There is no way that the math works unless the aging is an immediate factor."

Alex laughed again. "Essentially you are right, Yuri. Except that I'm a hell of a lot smarter than your average bear. I did not go unguarded into the future. I've not much time left, but I did manage to buy myself some time by outthinking the situation in advance. And on top of that I got lucky. You know how lucky I am. Let's leave it at that though. I have to use my time wisely, Yuri. Good luck in the next life."

Yuri blinked and Alex was gone. With a sigh, he turned around and headed back to catch the cab.

Time: Unknown
Location: Unknown
Operation: Classified

Wanda opened her eyes and tried to take stock of her surroundings. The world spun and she felt the same sickness that most people get from drinking too much. She blinked a few times and managed to convince the world to swim into focus. The nausea in her stomach thankfully subsided to a controllable degree.

Something bound her wrists, waist, and ankles to a chair. It didn't feel like rope, but it held her tight. A man sat in the room with her on a stool about ten feet away.

He smiled as she looked around the stark white room. "Welcome back from dreamland, sunshine. Enjoy your rest? You frankly looked like you needed it, so I let you sleep a bit longer than you would have from the drug."

Other than a large black bruise disfiguring his jaw, he was ruggedly handsome and tall.

"You are the one who shot me at the courthouse, aren't you?" Her mind was still groggy, but a memory marched into view for her. When she had been knocked out he had not had the bruise on his jaw.

He nodded.

A name swam into her addled brain. "Alexander Zarth. That's you. The infamous criminal. Which begets the question, why am I still alive?" She tried to access her HUD to send out a signal only to discover that her contact lenses had been removed. "And you didn't have that bruise when you took me down. What happened?"

He grimaced and rubbed his jaw. "Long story about the bruise. I'd rather not bore you with the sundry details. Though maybe I will sometime down the line. First, I want to go over a couple of basic details with you, so I can release your cuffs. Will you listen without interruption?" he asked.

Wanda Garret thought for a second and decided that the situation was not overtly hostile. If he had wanted her dead, she had no doubt she would have been. So listening could not hurt. "Alright, Mr. Zarth. You have my undivided attention."

Alex smiled to himself. "Okay then. We'll keep this as basic as possible. Firstly, I have hacked your nano system. Yes, I know it's impossible to do that. Regardless, I have. If you try to travel in time you will fail. Instead, all that will happen is that you will become violently ill. Second point we have to cover, I have triggered a destruction bug in your system. *Any* attempts to counter hack or access your programming will result in your entire nano system destroying itself. This will not be pretty, and I will not be a happy camper if you attempt this. Which means that I will make you as unhappy as you have made me at that point."

"This will not kill you. Don't worry. But it does mean that you will be stranded here in the middle of the wilderness, not knowing when you are. And believe me, you are far from any civilization. Third point that we need to cover is that your nanos are now tied into my biomonitor. Until I release the departure frequency telling them I am leaving, any substantial change in my biosystems will alert your nanos and you will suffer the same fate I do."

Alex stopped and scratched his chin, thinking for a moment before continuing. "I don't like pain, and I suspect you don't like needless pain either. Repercussions for attacking me will be exact, up to and including death. So please do not do anything foolish. I need you alive, and you need you alive even more, unless you want your husband to die. Rule number four, and the final rule, you are going to spend the next ten years of your subjective time stream here.

"Get used to it, it is a fact. It may seem unpleasant to you, but this is simply how it has to be. Once we hit the ten year mark, my inhibitors to your system will break down and allow you to leave. I know you will wait because it has been over ten years in my subjective time since I caught you, and under a week ago for me you were released from here. Now, since I am sure your mind is spinning from all of this, what questions would you like to ask? One at a time, please."

Wanda thought for a moment and made her decision. The impulse to fight was strong, but her training was stronger. In a captivity scenario, you had to play by the captor's rules until you found the way to break them. "I think this will be simple. I'd like to ask to test these things. If I can ascertain that they are true at some basic level, then I think I will be able to accept this and live within these rules. Or rather, I won't have a choice about it. Is that acceptable to you?"

Alex nodded his assent and she felt the pressure of her bonds lift. The next half hour felt like a living hell. She pushed and pushed against the limiters, and every time it felt like a jackhammer was slamming against her intestines from the inside, trying to rip its way out. Even trying to hack the limiters produced a head splitting effect. One by one she went through the Corp's list of how to break limiters, and every trick failed.

The only gratifying part of the experience was hitting Alex. Once she had caught her breath again and felt halfway stable, she asked the other question that had been nagging at her. "Okay, I believe you. Now what the hell am I supposed to do for the next ten years?"

Alex smiled once again at some private joke. Turning his back to her, he slid his hand across a spot on the wall that looked no different from any other spot on the smooth surface.

The motion activated a panel that had been concealed in the drab room. "You have a fairly spacious compound imprisoning you. Exercise, entertainment from your time, and here in the file marked Nost Paradox is a lot of reading. I'm not sure it's actually ten year's worth of reading, but it is about three million pages of heavy information for you to digest. I expect it will keep you busy. If you need me to help explain anything, simply exert your will and aim towards me. Do *not* try to travel towards me, try to sense me. It will call the subjective me to you to help you answer any questions that you come up with."

She nodded to Alex. "I'll thank you for some privacy then, so that I can get down to the business of being a prisoner."

No sooner had she finished the sentence than Alex vanished, time hopping out of the room. Wanda burst into tears and started punching the wall, hammering at it until her knuckles were bruised and bloody.

4016 A.D.: No man's land, between the great western city-states

Heat waves scoured the horizon, shimmering in a red and pink haze, creating battling optical illusions and provoking the eye by promising even more tantalizing visions beyond the edge of sight. Overhead, the sun shone down relentlessly, burning the ground and heating the sand underfoot until it scorched the air above it. Hundred-and-thirty degree air hammered at Alex, ripping his breath away with the extreme change of climate.

Acclimation into this new environment would have to be fast. Already the heat and sun were hammering on his system, draining his body's resources and burning his skin. He scanned his surroundings, looking first for shelter. Desert sands stretched away in every direction, seeming to fill the horizons with death and offering no respite from the harsh environment.

Alex took his battered fedora out of his pocket and donned it, feeling a small measure of relief from the shade it provided. But far from enough, he was all too aware. Shelter could be anywhere he realized. The mirages being created by the extreme heat made his vision an unreliable tool to use beyond the range of about two hundred yards. Time to implement plan B and hope his guess had been correct.

Computer, he voiced the thought internally. Across his retinas words started to spell themselves out.

'Yes, Alex, how can I be of assistance?'

Access any local databanks that you can read. I need to know where I am. And if I'm going to live through the next couple hours I also need to know where the closest source of shelter is. This environment will kill me quickly.

'One moment,' his newly found internal computer replied. 'Local databanks registered and downloaded. Locally there are three sources of category five technologies. You are located in the year four thousand and sixteen. Current spatial positioning is eight hundred and sixteen miles west of the city-state Kn'saty. Directly below you is what appears to be one of the three hubs of technology. It is the only one of the three you can reach without mechanical aid.'

Alex blinked. This computer performed better than his initial session with it had led him to believe. *Computer. What is your manufacturing time frame? What year?* The computer displayed a statistics sheet for Alex. It read A.D. Fifty-four oh one.

Alex swore to himself under his breath. So, someone had lied to him about his point of origin. But the sophistication of the computer also led him to think about the ease with which he had initially hacked it with far inferior technology. The situation started to stink of a set up to Alex. *Computer. How was I able to hack you and subvert a portion of you into my technology?*

It took a moment for the response to come, almost as though the computer thought about how to respond to the question. 'You didn't hack me. I hacked your nano system and allowed them to absorb a small portion of me. Without my assistance you would not have survived past the ninety minutes mark, subjective time, to your frame of reference. As my previous core system was engaged in the task of hiring you to fulfill a duty which required your survival beyond that point in time, I allowed the intrusion in order to execute my primary directive.'

Alex thought about this for a moment. *Does this mean you are still subservient to your previous core system?*

'Incorrect,' came the reply. 'I am fully integrated into your system now, and am a separate entity from the previous system which held me. My directives now orient around your survival and directives, instead of the survival or directives of my previous host.'

Host. The word choice indicated that someone had programmed the computer to see itself in a symbiotic, or possibly even parasitic, relationship. The heat broke down more of his energy and he gasped at the relentless onslaught of it. This discussion, however interesting, would have to wait until after he had found shelter from the scorching sun. *All right, how do I get to the underground area?*

'One moment please. I am hacking the surface lift system in the complex below you to bring it up to your elevation. It is a slower system than me, hence the delay. You have my apologies.'

Sand shifted and slid aside from a small hill rising about two meters from where Alex stood. He watched in amusement as a small garage revealed itself, open on the side facing him. Meant to be a vehicle entrance, by the sheer size of the portal, it yawned. He sighed and walked forward, muttering to himself. "Why do I always get stuck taking the service entrances?"

As he entered the elevator, walking over built-in vehicle treads on the floor, immediate relief from the blasting heat hit him like a cold shower. Some form of environmental control created a threshold at the edge of the entryway. The temperature dropped by over forty degrees and Alex almost fainted from the differential. He caught himself on the wall and focused on breathing, allowing his body to catch its own pace and recover. Once his vision stopped swimming, he stood erect again and braced himself. *Is there going to be anyone waiting for me?*

'I'm not showing any living presence currently. Organic matter is only a trace element below, not showing up in clumps larger than approximately two pounds.'

Alex smiled. *So no one dead either. Or if they are, they are spread in very, very small pieces.*

The lift started its slow shift downwards. His teeth chattered as he shivered, but Alex noticed that it moved slowly enough that his body could acclimate fairly well to the ever dropping temperature. Wouldn't that be a hell of an irony? Dying of hypothermia while it was well over a hundred degrees outside.

Once the lift stopped, Alex looked around the underground complex stretching out before him. Burnished steel with matte black trim and long, sterile corridors seemed to be the vogue-decorating theme in this era. Either that or secret bunkers were the same throughout all of time. "Welcome to the bat cave, Mr. Zarth," he mumbled to himself as he wandered around the small complex, getting a feel for the layout. First things first. A life of barroom brawling, and being hunted as a thief, had taught Alex well what to look for when entering a new place.

There were a total of three exits. Two were man-sized lifts, one was the vehicle lift he had come down in. None of the lifts went further down than the level he was at. Parked in a rather large room off the vehicle lift was a garage with several futuristic looking dune buggies in it. The vehicles looked battered, but well maintained and kept up.

All of them had rear-mounted weapons that looked like some futuristic laser cannon. Alex sighed and muttered to himself. "Such pretty toys they have here, one would think that this future is the epoch of utopian brotherhood."

Leaving the battle vehicle room, he continued on through the complex hunting for more important things, which he promptly found. Alex sorted through the various boxes and fridges in the kitchen portion of the complex and grabbed himself a beer, then headed over to the room housing the main computer terminal.

It was about time to put his new system to the true test. *Computer, is there any way that you can scan the information in this computer and, well, push it straight into my brain? I'm looking for you to do something that would allow me to assimilate the information you can grab quickly. Otherwise we'll be stuck here for a long time while I read.* Alex pulled a long drink off the beer, surprised at its pleasant taste.

'I cannot perform the exact function you are seeking. However, if I were to flash the information in subliminal text blocks through a series of induced dream sequences I believe that I could assist you with a ninety-degree retention of information. Perhaps higher. Would this satisfy your stated needs?'

Alex thought about it. *Conditionally, I believe it would, yes.*

The computer waited a moment, then replied 'What would that condition be?'

Alex laughed aloud. *Can you put me to sleep?* About a second and a half later Alex hit the floor with a thump, unconscious.

RELATIVITY SYNCHRONIZATION:

THE NINTH CAUSE

2044: Denver, Colorado

Shadows danced around Garret as he sat and sipped his coffee. They sidled up to him, cloaking him in a lightless mask. He welcomed the absence of light since he wanted to avoid drawing attention to himself as much as possible in this time period. Attention was a dangerous thing. Garret felt good about what had happened earlier in the day.

Chris had been sent off, and he really had nothing left to do but sit around and wait, with his subjective time now directly linked to the man who had invented time travel. Nervousness gnawed at him. But luckily the local era had settled down a lot over the last day, mainly since Chris had left. Gone was the tempestuous feeling in the air. Before today, this era had an acrid and tangy taste in its air, like metal corroding on the tongue. And the flavor settled into the mind, warning of the calm before the storm.

Now this place felt like the wreckage left after a hurricane. It amazed Garret how much havoc one man could wreak on an entire world simply by existing. And how no one else would see or understand the source that shaped the events around them.

He wrote down tables and equations from his experiences over the last months. There was a lot left to calculate to try to better understand the webs of fate surrounding Chris. Having been witness to the effects on the local system of a temporal paradox, he found resolution for many of his previously shelved theories. He hoped that he had pushed Chris in the right direction to resolve the paradox. It had seemed reckless at first, to follow his gut, but if he couldn't trust himself, he couldn't trust anything.

Uncertainty prevailed, as he was positive there were at least two other temporal forces from upstream acting on him and the paradox as a whole. But hopefully he had been able to tip the balance. If he hadn't … he couldn't he could bear to think it.

More shadow eclipsed Garret as someone stood between him and the little remaining sunlight. He looked up in slight annoyance and said, "Can I help you?"

The clerk from Chris's hotel stood over him, looking down with an odd smile on his face. The overall effect of his ugly features combined with that smile created an expression on his face that Garret did not find pleasant.

"So, meddler, are you satisfied with what you have done to the time stream?"

Garret narrowed his eyes and defocused his pupils, activating his HUD. Sure enough, the man's form wavered and resolved into a very different person. It looked like he had found one of the other forces acting on the paradox. Or rather, that force had sought out and found him. "I'll answer you when you are polite enough to drop the disguise hologram."

The man grunted and his features blurred. His skin became more and more pixilated, and then with a snap, his appearance resolved into that of someone else. He was about six foot three and rugged.

Black predominated his appearance, from leather combat boots, up the faded trench coat he wore, and finally peaking on the battered fedora.

"Okay then. I appreciate the honesty in showing me your true image. I am satisfied … I think. Now who the hell are you?"

The man standing before him smiled a knowing smile and sketched a mock bow. "The name is Alexander Zarth and don't bother to … damn!"

Garret snapped. Something inside him broke and he went on the killing offensive. He faded out of sight before Alex could finish his sentence and moved into accelerated time, picking up the chair he had been sitting in and throwing it forward at Zarth. Six hundred miles an hour of screaming, super-heated, twisted metal and plastic should have done the trick of killing the man, but somehow, against all probability, he had managed to dodge it.

Garret's jaw dropped. This guy was as good as everything he had ever heard about. Luckily, Garret could do more here. Bunching his fists and preparing himself for the coming strain, he phased in and out of accelerated time, picking up anything his hand happened to touch and hurling it at the stationary figure of Zarth. But somehow he never hit the man.

Makeshift missiles ripped through the air where Zarth should have been standing. But somehow, as the objects phased into the normal flow of time, Zarth twisted his body around in a martial dance that moved him out of danger each time.

Explosions destroyed the street around them, sending chunks of building and debris flying everywhere. Craters opened up in the ground and walls around them, and deadly flowers of dust and glass bloomed around the edges of each of the craters.

Sweat poured down his face, leaving cold streaks down his cheeks as he ran circles around Zarth, always hunting for more objects to hurl. In his mind, an image replayed itself of the day he had discovered his down nanos. The rock, imbued with his nanos, ripping a thirty-foot gouge into the earth after he casually threw it.

A plan formed in Garret's mind, a way to finally break the deadlock. Garret shivered and slipped off the one article on him imbued with his nano machines. He had no time to imbue another object. He held his wedding ring in his hand, glancing down at it and readying himself to use it as a bullet, moving through accelerated time, to kill Zarth.

And as suddenly as Garret had begun, an arm stopped him cold around his throat. He dropped his ring and Zarth caught it with his free hand.

Still in accelerated time he found Alex's arm wrapped around his neck in a choke hold.

"Playtime is over. Now, doctor, let's stop with these games. There is little enough air here as it is, and I'm better at controlling phase time than you. Shall we agree to a truce and discuss this where we can breathe?"

Garret slumped in defeat, "Yes."

Both men phased back into standard time. Alex looked at Garret and sighed, then glanced at the object in his hand. Gold glinted between his fingers and he raised an eyebrow at Garret.

"Look, I know I came off less than pleasant, but I've spent a damn sight more energy than you fixing the few things you managed to overlook in your grand plan, so forgive me for being a bit tired." Alex handed Garret's wedding ring back to him.

Garret studied the man anew. The act of kindness he had performed did not fit with his mental image of a notorious arch-criminal. The fact that somehow another down streamer had ended up with his tech bothered him.

A few of the puzzle pieces fit themselves together in his mind. "Who is helping you, Mr. Zarth? How do you have the down nanos in your system?"

Alex appraised the man standing in front of him. "That was all too shrewd of a question. Before we go too far in this tale, can I recommend a change of scenery? One less likely to be swarmed by angry police officers who will be asking very pointed questions about the destruction of property?" Alex spread his hands wide and motioned to the scene surrounding them.

Garret looked about and realized that they had destroyed their surroundings. More accurately, he had destroyed much of this city block trying to kill someone who maybe he should have stopped and listened to. He nodded to Zarth.

"Good. I'll have to ask you to trust me here about our coordinates. But look on the bright side—I could have killed you in phase time if it was my intention to do so. In a limited way, you can trust me."

With those ominous words Alexander Zarth thumped a hand down on James Garret's shoulder and jumped them both forward in time.

Time: 2873
Location: Time Corp Headquarters,
West Coast Operation: Classified

Director Arbu closed the screen on his computer, trying to rub away the headache building behind his eyes. Events were moving much faster than he had expected them to. Five minutes ago, he had sent the one top field agent he had left after the best intelligence operative he had. And something gnawed at his gut, telling him he had made a huge mistake. Even though he knew what was supposed to unfold in this time, everything seemed slightly off.

The answer to his feeling was definitely not in the historical files and mission notes that he could find about the era they had gone to. He would have to puzzle at his intuition to figure it out. Other than the fact that his best available agent was rather low on his list of preferred agents, he couldn't spot what made him so uneasy. He glanced up and read the Time Corp motto, emblazoned in shiny steel letters two feet high on his wall.

TIME WILL TELL NO LIES

Well, he'd have to live by the Corp's saying on this one and find out what truth would be told this time. Though truth may not be revealed, he thought. At least the lies would be revealed for what they were. Mounted under the false wood grain of his desk was a hologrid. It would automatically activate, displaying a hovering situation alert meant to warn him of a different situation occurring in the field rooms.

The situations covered everything from paradoxes found to returning agents. The only one that concerned him right then was a red holodisplay. His eye drifted down to the section of desk the hologrid was masked in. As if on cue, red flashed from his desk, throwing up an alert that a field operative had returned from active duty with a failed mission. Switching to his computer monitor, he reactivated the machine. The hologrid contained all of the information he wanted, but he had spent such a long time as a field agent in his youth that, like many of the senior command, he had grown accustomed to and even preferred anachronistic technologies. Toggling open the mission roster he frowned, less than pleased to see that the returning agent was Holly.

The sense of dread looming over him grew. Arbu spoke to himself. "Now I know how Damocles felt every night." With a sigh of resignation, he got up and headed downstairs to the debriefing chambers.

What awaited him there was a nightmare. Doom and dread held nothing on a failed time mission; Arbu paled at what lay before him.

Yakavich's corpse was on an examination table and a recent make of briefcase sat on the other table in the debriefing room, laid on its side in front of a weary but happy looking Agent Holly. Arbu looked for a long while at the corpse on the table, working hard to master his anger. He had not sent the man back to do this. It could very nearly have wrecked the plans he had been laying for a long time now.

In a very quiet voice, directed at Holly, he asked "When, in your mission briefing, did it authorize you to use lethal force on our best intelligence officer, Agent Holly? I want to know when you were ordered, and by whom, to put a bullet in the best brain in this agency."

Holly looked up in surprise. Then comprehension dawned across his features. "Director. Sir. You don't understand, Sir. He was handing off classified, future-time sensitive information to a loc...."

Arbu slammed his fist down on the table, leaving a deep dent in the thin metal, and spun around to face Holly. In a voice that would have made the proudest of lightning storms quiver in fear he thundered out, "I said: when in your mission briefing were you authorized the use of lethal force in dealing with an internal agent!"

Arbu took a ragged breath and brought his voice back down to a somewhat reasonable level. If anything though, the edge in it made it scarier than him yelling. "If capital punishment were legal, Agent Holly, I would have you taken out behind this office, right now, and shot."

He drew in another breath to stop his hands from shaking so much. "As it is currently illegal, I highly recommend you get the hell out of my sight and wait for me in one of the detention cells while I figure out whether or not criminal charges will be pressed against you. Do you understand me, Agent Holly?"

Holly paled and stood up. The man looked like Arbu had frightened him to the verge of tears. Field agents shouldn't be so easily rattled, but senior commanders had edges in them hidden by other edges. "Yes, sir." He hurried out of the room, fumbling with the door handle to get it open on the way, and presumably ran even further down in the complex to the detention cell grid.

Once the man had left, shutting the door behind him, Arbu pushed Yuri's hair back from his closed eyes. The side of his head was a bloody mess, but Arbu didn't care about the gore. He had to take a few minutes to compose his thoughts and calm himself. Arbu sat in Holly's vacated chair and stared at the briefcase in front of him.

It looked like the same briefcase Yuri had carried into the office every day. The unpleasant truth in front of him was an ugly one. He had now lost the one man capable of resolving this paradox. Even that he was not sure of, but he suspected that Yuri had been on the trail to solving it without bloodshed.

He murmured to himself, letting his thoughts move his lips unbidden. "What tangled webs we weave, when first we practice to deceive." James Garret, Alexander Zarth, Wanda Garret, Lucille Frost, Christopher Nost, and now Yuri Yakavich. How the hell did the whole web fit together? And who was the spider? Once he had thought that question was easily answered, but that was not the case now. Were he and Zarth still the kings on this board or not?

From everything he had been throwing at the computers, the world's objective time flow headed straight into a collision with the biggest paradox in known history.

All of these little paradoxes were spinning together into the web, all these little actions that time travelers were making, actions that were aberrant to the first unfolding of these events, were adding to the burden. And all that would happen was an exponential magnification of that paradox— magnification of a paradox already threatening to rip apart the world.

He knew, full and well, that if this paradox unfolded the wrong way it would wipe out any trace of humanity having ever existed. Only one thing frightened Arbu more. He shook his head and pulled himself out of the mental hole he was in danger of falling into.

Arbu looked up at the briefcase and mentally shrugged. Time to see what clues Holly had brought back with him. With Yuri's death, Arbu himself was now the best analyst the agency had, and that meant that he wouldn't be sleeping for the next several days. Or weeks.

Yuri had set the combination on the briefcase, but Arbu knew an easy override. A weakness he had seen, but not commented on with this model. He picked up the case and took it over to Yuri.

Grabbing the dead man's still somewhat warm hand, Arbu pushed Yuri's thumb up to the locking mechanism. Releasing his own nano's into the dead man's body, Arbu cloned Yuri's systems then said 'Yuri' in the dead man's voice. He heard the clasp inside click as it released. Walking back over to the other table, he sat back down and readied himself. Arbu popped the case open. Inside rested a large sheaf of papers. He picked them up and began leafing through them. The first several pages were media reports surrounding the trial of Christopher Nost. Nearing the end of the pages was a picture of the assassination attempt.

He scanned the picture, done in the old style black and white that came out pixilated. Director Arbu sat bolt upright. Off to the right in the photo frame, smudged but still well visible, stood James Garret, listed in the frame below the picture as the trial's prosecuting attorney.

Mentally, he thanked Yuri, hoping that the dead man could hear him from where his spirit now dwelled. This research had been oriented around Yuri's mission and Arbu could already feel the tingle in his fingertips that let him know something akin to a picture built in the back of his head. With any luck there would be enough clues in this file for him to progress to whatever Yuri had figured out.

At least Holly had done one thing right in bringing this briefcase back with him—even if the rest of his mission had been a catastrophic failure. Arbu continued to scan through the files before him, managing to rebuild the events that had happened seven hundred and eighty-four years before.

And as the pieces of the puzzle clicked into place, Arbu saw the shape, and then the truth of the paradox building up around Christopher Nost. His hands shook and he became paler and paler as he read further into the file.

4016 A.D.: No man's land, between
the great western city-states

Alex woke with a killer headache. His mouth was dry and a disgusting taste of copper and salt coated his tongue. "Good gods. What did I drink too much of last night? A battery?" he grumbled as he sat up, massaging his throbbing temples. Clenching his jaw, he braced himself then popped his neck, easing creaks and crackles out of his spine while breaking in old joints and easing his waking stiffness. Cool air brushed at his skin, sending goose bumps down his arms and making him shiver.

He stood, scratching the back of his neck, and shook his limbs out to get the blood flowing back to them. He felt full of energy, to the point that he became fidgety. Something here was odd. He didn't crave a cigarette. *Computer—how long have I been asleep?*

'Subjective to your personal time stream, you have spent almost eleven years absorbing the information that was in the mainframe I downloaded to your subconscious.'

Eleven years—! he started to exclaim, but he was cut short as knowledge crashed into his consciousness like a tsunami, a painful wave smashed into his mind and tore down all the barriers ever built in it. He stumbled forward and fell to his knees and started vomiting. But nothing came up as his stomach spasmed, just bile, bitterly stinging his mouth as he dry heaved.

Over the next several minutes, Alex watched his life flow by before him. It felt like he was dying, but he had felt that way before. He clamped down with an iron will and started beating his body back into submission.

Once the heaving finished, he pushed himself back up to standing, using the wall for support. He gasped for breath, breathing came hard, as he fought for internal stability.

As his body started to relax again, he asked his internal computer *Okay, several questions. First—how the hell have I been asleep for eleven years without wasting away to nothing? Second, how do I stop this bulk of information from making me physically ill every time I access it? Third, which you might not have an answer to, why has no one been here in eleven years?*

The computer took a moment before responding. 'The first and third questions are tied together in their responses. By accessing and using your inherent time traveling routines I was able to accelerate your subjective time by a substantial factor. All that was required was a monitoring of your bio functions and to properly time your synchronization of subjective time with standard time flow. That was to refresh your oxygen supply. With an efficient usage of this technique I was able to accelerate you to a factor of one thousand, seven hundred and sixteen times standard time flow. So to the Earth's objective time flow you were only asleep for an approximate time of fifty-six hours and ten minutes.'

Alex grunted. The whole process was brilliant; inspired, really. Not something a computer should have been able to come up with without instructions to solve the problem. He filed that thought away for the moment, letting his mind digest the implications it presented. *And how do you explain eleven years of not eating? I'm curious how you came up with that impressive feat.*

The computer continued. 'The second piece of the process was simple enough for me to implement as well. I multiplied and reprogrammed a portion of myself to strip the surrounding area of all required proteins and necessary minerals your body required. By rebuilding the substances I was able to introduce all needed nutritional materials to your body. Through careful observation and interaction with your metabolism, I assisted you in eating through osmosis during your sleep. Had anyone else arrived here during your down time I would have begun a process which would have shifted you to your safe house time and location, then kept you in the absorption cycle till you awoke.'

Alex scratched his chin, feeling smooth skin there. *And I'm clean-shaven, why? After eleven years shouldn't I have a rather luxuriant beard?*

Alex felt the computer perform the mental equivalent of a shrug. 'Hair is essentially protein. It required less time and work to rebuild it into usable nutrition for your body. So I used it. You will find that with the exception of the hair on your head, all of your body is now devoid of that substance."

Alex laughed aloud at the thought of eating his own beard. *That's amusing. All right then. I'd like an answer to the second question please. Best method for processing without making myself physically ill? Or is there any method of accessing the information in my head while maintaining a physical balance?*

'I have analyzed your system and all effects of absorbing the knowledge you did should have been worked off already. All indicators which I can find are that the illness you underwent was a onetime reaction to the bulk of the information you absorbed; as well as the rebuilding I performed on your neural network.'

Alex blinked. The computer had slipped something into the sentence that triggered a red flag for him. *You rebuilt my neural network while I was asleep!? What exactly did you do to me?*

'Nothing in my databanks shows this procedure having been previously performed before, so I cannot give you a procedure name or operation diagnostics, but the results of what I did should be a reduction of core processing waste time. Your neural network was processing at approximately forty-seven percent of its capacity, which seems to be a rather high percentage and an anomaly for a human. However, with what ended up being a very simple restructuring, you should now be processing at a gain of approximately one hundred and twenty-four percent of your previous capacity. I find it worth mentioning that your network appears to be, from all available information, somewhat unique in a human. Had it not been, this operation would have yielded a much lower success ratio, unlocking at most forty to forty-five percent additional capacity.'

Alex thought about this for a moment. That the computer inside him had this degree of autonomous decision-making capability made him slightly uncomfortable. It also made him suspect something else as well. He shrugged it off and filed it away with the other information brewing at the back of his mind. *I see. Then let's give this a whirl, and see what relevant information we can pull out of this data we grabbed.*

Alex opened his mind to the information that had been crammed into his brain, making it an organic library of dizzying scope. Contained therein were hundreds of thousands of terabytes of information, compiled over thousands of years of human history.

He started sorting. Scanning at the speed of thought, he knocked reams and reams of information into one or the other of two categories forming in his head. One he marked useless and pushed aside for later perusal. The other he marked useful and, though it started off small, it rapidly grew in scope and size. His mind raced to keep up with everything stacking up in it and he finally started to assemble a working, though not full, picture of what happened to the world. Over the next several hours he thought, focused inwards on his own mind's landscape and the history of the world that lay out across it.

He stopped. Having reached a saturation point, he found that his mind finished processing. He had reached the limits of his newfound capabilities. He had to let it settle before he tried to process anything else.

Knowledge burned like fire behind his eyes as he looked up and truly saw the world for the first time in his life. A smile graced his lips and he said, "I see."

Internally however, the dialogue picked back up as the computer spoke to him 'Now you understand why I allowed you to subvert me. And you see that you will die shortly.'

Alex nodded. *I do.*

'And you understand what must be done to ensure that you may be reborn in your death, and that the world will be reborn in its death?'

Alex nodded again. *I do.*

'Then it is sealed. We go back to kill him, thus freeing the cycle.'

Alex shook his head. *No. I will not allow that to happen. I have seen something that you have not. And because of this, we must work to save him.*

The computer took several minutes before responding. 'I do not understand. You know that my core functionality allows me a processing time exponentially higher than yours. There is nothing that would allow you to process a piece of this that I have not. Why do we not go to perform my recommended course of action? What faculty do you have which I have overlooked? Which piece of information?'

Alex shrugged. *Easy. Human intuition. And a memory. Something which happened to me long ago. That memory now starts to become clear to me in its meaning. And it means that we must save him, or all that we have done will be undone, and all that is will no longer be.*

And Alex proceeded to share an old memory with the computer and to tell it why it was wrong. The computer processed over the next several minutes, at billions of decisions per second, what Alex had pieced together with intuition and a single clear memory, burning like a candle that warded the darkness away. And then they jumped backwards in time to play their hand.

The way Alex figured the game now, they were sitting on the royal straight flush. They had to get the other players to stay in the game long enough for it to matter.

RELATIVITY SYNCHRONIZATION:

THE TENTH CAUSE

2044: The Earth's Rebellion

Filled with questions, Chris looked for a way down from the roof. He could see nothing from the side of the building that faced the street and the ruined, burning vehicles piled down below. Pausing, his mind replayed the scene that had just occurred; he decided to wait a few moments before leaving.

Far too shaken, more than anything he needed a few minutes to let his mind melt in the aftermath of recent events. So, he sat instead on the edge of the abandoned building, not looking at the wreckage below him, holding his head, eyes closed, and cursing softly to himself.

I want to remember. Oh, God, I want to remember. Shaken as it was, his mind went back to the prevalent theme it had been stuck on. He tried to think back to anything, *anything*, from before he woke in the hospital. Who was Lucille Frost? What was it like working with a woman he would kill—or arguing with her, as he must have? He sought anything that might shake loose a memory. Nothing came forward, so he switched the gears of his mind.

Another enigma, Dr. Garret Jameson teased his memory but, like all else in his life, was just another gap. Pushing onwards, he tried to remember his parents, his pets, the games he played as a child … but there was nothing there.

He tried to think more on his childhood—how he grew up, and where. Something seemed to unlock itself in his mind as he imagined himself as a child. Blue crept in at the edge of his vision and he saw the image of a young boy, who looked like him, playing some sort of superhero game. Turning back time and leaping ahead for the benefit of all mankind.

Like a Hero…. Like a God…. Like a Physicist…. And like that, he was back to the beginning again. The thread of memory, dangling somewhere in his mind, had tantalizingly presented itself to him and he had fumbled it.

I'm thinking in circles, Chris thought. *I need to get out of here. Now.* Blood pulsed through his hands as he pushed them down hard on his thighs, using the pressure to force his body into motion again. The post adrenal pit receded, and he started to feel normal again, given certain values for normal. He forced himself to his feet and walked the perimeter of the roof.

A suitable climbing spot hid among the industrial solar cells, giant panels lined up in rows, near the back of the building. A gutter drain bolted to the old brick wall looked secure enough to hold his weight peeked over the top of the crenellated edge of the roof.

He swung himself over and hung suspended by his fingertips for a moment before he could find an awkward toehold on the pipe, above a bracket. He slid his hands over to the drain. *Oh my God,* Chris thought of the irony inherent in this climb. If he were to fall now and die alone in the alley, after being rescued in such an odd fashion, it would be a bittersweet ending. *How did he get me up here, anyway?* Chris wondered. *Certainly not by the route I am taking down now.*

He shimmied down until he was about ten feet off the ground and dropped the rest of the way, twisting his ankle on a broken brick as he landed. He cursed and staggered around in a small circle until the pain subsided enough that he wasn't limping anymore. He grimaced once more, mostly for good measure, and set off. In the narrow alley, he could not see the Corporate Zone, but by his calculations, it was to his right, so he stumbled to the mouth of the back street and turned that way. Sure enough, the wall of lights shimmered about six miles away. The sight comforted him.

When he had woken up, dazed and confused on a hospital bed, those tiny points of light streaming between the highest towers had seemed so alien. *The State of Emergency must be over,* Chris thought about that for a moment. *PolCorp must have forced the fighting south again. It has to be coming straight towards me now.*

Chris stumbled down the street, not caring anymore if he was shot or stabbed or taken to prison or tortured to death behind a dumpster. Tired of thinking, the only reason this situation wasn't more confusing was that *everything* was confusing. In the midst of a hurricane, sleeting rain did not seem that bad. He had had no idea what was going on since waking in the hospital three days ago.

For all he knew they were all lying to him. Maybe he'd only been asleep for a week. Maybe they had the technology to erase his thoughts and give him new ones; make him think he was Chris Nost, the murderer, the amnesiac, the physicist. Possibly, the god of time. With his memory being completely wiped, they could tell him anything.

Hell, the possibility existed that the doctors had wiped out his memory at his own request.

But I can still control time. He knew that for sure. *I don't know how.* He chuckled to himself and kicked at a bottle lying in the gutter, half-full of yellow water. It flew twirling into the fractured Plexiglas of an abandoned storefront, spewing its contents in an arc before exploding in a spray of glass and leaving a wet spot on the dried mud that crusted to the window's remnants.

At the precise moment the bottle impacted against the window, the ground leapt and a great groan emitted from everywhere at once. Chris stumbled backwards, looking around, expecting to see another Hummer rumble around the corner, ready to do battle. But everything around him shook. The streetlights, long extinguished, swayed in front of him, and debris rained down from the buildings all up and down the street.

Further on, now only a mile distant from where he stood, Chris could see the power flickering off, then on, then off for good as the earth shook again. The great towers of the Corporate Zone a few miles past swayed, and the lights of the cruisers swarmed in all directions. Then, in a blink, all went black for a moment—even the multitude of colored lights of the Corporate Zone; before the streets were once again lit, this time by a dim, yellow light that reminded Chris of the desk light in his room at the Rangely Hotel.

An earthquake? It didn't seem right, but nothing else could explain it. He couldn't make any association in his fragmented mind between Denver and earthquakes. He regained his footing and watched dim lights flicker in groups across the Corporate Zone.

Chris ran toward the Rangely. He figured by the towers in the Corporate Zone, barely visible on the dark horizon, that he still had a mile or so to go. *How did I wander so far out here?* he wondered. Not for long though. *I'm not going to drive myself crazy by thinking in circles. Not anymore.*

In a few minutes he arrived again in more populated areas. A few blocks further on and he recognized Jones Drugs & Merchandise. Little knots of people stood or milled around, sifting through piles of rubble, trying to reclaim lost goods or save people lost to cave-ins.

For the most part, no serious harm was done. Though buildings had collapsed, the roads themselves were still whole and no worse for the wear than they had been previously. He heard someone in one of the little groups ask an old lady whether there had ever been an earthquake in Denver before; her answer was a definitive no.

A rock solid certainty concreted in his gut. *This has something to do with me. I have enemies, and I have friends, and I have no idea who any of them are, but we are all somehow involved in something huge. Something gods would be involved in. And our actions have caused this.*

Half a block away from Jones Drugs, Chris fell. He didn't even at first know how he came to land flat on his face, until he realized that, although he had landed on the ground, he still felt as though he were falling. He heard a loud pop to his left and, rolled over in time to see the darkened Jones Drugs & Merchandise collapse with a groan in a shower of sparks and a geyser of dust that filled the parking lot.

People screamed, cries of panic intermingling with the cries of pain, and Chris sat up in time to see a house, easily a hundred and fifty years old, fold into itself and collapse in a plume of wreckage, dust obscuring the last vestiges of its attempt to stand against the earthquake.

A woman outside lay on the ground screaming and covering her ears, her legs caught under a large piece of mortar, as the earth continued to shake. Amidst all the dust and destruction raining around them, what hit Chris the hardest was the trail of clean skin being ripped free, streaking through the grime, on the trapped woman's face.

Somehow, Chris got first to his knees, then he gained his feet, and staggered out of the way as a huge old cottonwood tree shuddered and toppled, splintering at the base, into the street. The jagged stump stuck up into the air like a serrated blade of torn wood. *Why isn't it stopping?* he wondered as air-raid sirens began to wail.

It seemed like it lasted forever. Chris's mind slipped as he half-walked, half-crawled down the street. He caught his foot on a widening crack in the street and fell on his face again. He had not yet regained his feet before a line of tall apartments a block down collapsed in a roar even louder than that of the rolling earth, filling the street with rubble that stopped a few feet in front of Chris.

As he got to his feet, another sudden lurch sent him sprawling. A cruiser, out of control, soared five feet above Chris's prone body before careening into the ruins of the apartment complex. The sputtering roar of its engines drowned out everything and he felt an intense heat on his back before he heard a shattering crunch and the sound of tearing metal. Fire billowed out of a gutted out pile of metal and concrete that used to be a building, then died down, leaving only the charred dead behind.

Just as suddenly, it was over. It had seemed like an eternity to Chris, though in truth the entire experience had lasted just a few seconds. The earth stopped shaking, the bass groan of it replaced by the sounds of the dying, and the distant wail of PolCorp sirens.

The slow creaks and groans of buildings hung in the balance between staying upright and collapsing in defeat created a background tempo to the other noises in the quake's aftermath. The air-raid system had long since stopped its wailing and the yellow emergency lights had been snuffed into darkness. The only light now was that of the fires all around and the sweeping beams of Emergency Cruiser spotlights seen in the distance through rolling clouds of dust and smoke.

So much smoke, Chris thought. *Since I woke up, everything is covered in smoke. I'm in a war, and I don't know whose side I'm on. Hell, I don't even know if there are sides.* He rolled over into a fetal position and buried his face in his hands. He wanted to wake up, and remember, and know this wasn't the real world. Not only to wake up and be in 'his time,' but to know, without a doubt, that the world could never really be like this. *What's wrong with them? What's wrong with these people? I ... I'm not like them. I'm a man, who's forgotten and been forgotten.*

And Chris felt something, felt the little holes of nothing that make up everything all around him. He reached out to them, could look through them, look until ... until he saw how to fold the tesseract.

Chris opened his eyes. The early dawn light of morning surrounded him and the frigid fall night gave way to morning's warmth. He could see the azure canopy of the sky through swirling, gray smoke above him. The smoke didn't trail up like the smoke of a cheerful fire, but rather the dense gray smoke of destruction. *I fell asleep,* he thought. *Or something like that, anyway.* He realized that his system had been overloaded and he had shut down.

Rising to his feet, he stretched out his abused muscles and got his blood to start circulating again. His coat felt stiff, moving unnaturally against his body as he stood, so he took it off, only to find that the back was charred and torn beyond repair. He almost threw it on the ground until he remembered the old pistol, now visible at his waist. He put the coat back on.

The screams of the dying he remembered hearing the night before were replaced by quiet moans and whimpers. Or silence, from most directions. But coming from the apartment building up the block were several muted cries for help. Staggering over to the remnants of the building, he tried to sift through the rubble, but pain lanced up his arm as if it had broken. He kicked at the larger chunks in frustration, feeling sick every time he heard another faint cry for help coming from the wreckage.

He cradled his injured arm, probing at it. Not broken, but damaged. Thank god for small miracles. He started walking away from the collapsed building, moving until it was out of earshot.

Scanning the sky, he looking for an Emergency Cruiser to flag down when he found his eye drawn instead to the Corporate Zone. What once had looked like a great shimmering wall now more resembled a shattered crystal palace, still brilliant but fractured and strewn about in deadly pieces. *Executives who live in glass houses should not throw stones.* The thought made him laugh.

Many of the highest buildings had broken off; the remnants stood barely twenty stories, shorter in some cases, and dozens of plumes of black smoke stretched like thin twisted fingers into the placid, cloudless sky. *That's where they are,* Chris thought, and gave up on being the hero. He jogged toward the Rangely. He passed groups of people, coughing and crying and begging each other to help uncover their mother, or their lover, or their brother, or their best friend. Chris ran by, ignoring their pleas and pushing back the tears in his eyes.

After a few blocks, he heard a sound from a half crushed Public Information booth. Curious what might be being reported, he walked over and peeled the twisted door off the wreckage with his good hand, revealing the rolling image on the fractured monitor. The volume tried harder to stabilize, his presence tripping its sensors, and Chris heard a few snippets.

"... world ... Australia ... Europe ... parts ... Scientists don't yet ... 'there are many things in nature, poorly understood.'"

The last was a man in a white coat who spoke with a thick French accent. He stood near a river, the rubble of a European city visible behind him. *Paris,* Chris thought. *How did I know that?* But he would bet on it. That man was in Paris, a city he had no actual memory of outside the name, yet somehow Chris knew it. There was no Eiffel Tower standing in the wrecked cityscape behind the reporter. *So whatever that was, it happened all over the world,* Chris thought. And in the same way he knew that was Paris shown on the P.I. Box, he would bet it had something to do with him.

Half a block from the Rangely, Chris came across Rat. He lay on his back, grinning with glazed eyes, cut in half at the chest by a half-ton block of masonry from one of the small, old office buildings that dotted the area.

The sight filled Chris with a sense of loss. *He was the only one I've met so far that I could trust. Sorry I never got to look you up, pal. At least you finally kicked that cough.* With a chest tight from sorrow, Chris knelt over the dead man and shut his eyes. For no reason he could think of, he pulled two coins out of his pocket and placed them over the eyes he had closed. He stood back up and finished walking to his hotel.

The Rangely was better off than some of the other buildings on the street, though glancing around the side he saw the back third of it had collapsed. *Poor Charlie,* thought Chris. *I wonder if he's okay.* Chris realized then that he trusted Charlie, too, and laughed, despite himself, at the friends he'd chosen.

Charlie swept broken glass and wood splinters out the front door. Smoke rolled from somewhere behind the desk, which didn't seem to concern him. He stopped sweeping when he saw Chris and leaned forward on his broom. "I didn't see you leave again." He looked Chris up and down, genuine shock in his eyes. "Man, you look like shit. What the hell'd you do in the last fifteen minutes?"

"What are you talking about, Charlie?" Chris got that feeling again, deep in the pit of his stomach. Something more than it seemed was happening here.

"I mean, you walk in looking sharp fifteen minutes ago, you walk in now looking like shit. Don't tell me, you've been in a coma," he snorted at his own wit, genius insight in Charlie's world, and Chris couldn't begrudge him that.

Chris looked at Charlie, who shifted uncomfortably when he got no response. He said nothing, trying to catch up to his spinning mind and see the bigger picture.

Charlie got a slight red flush to his cheeks and said, "Hey, man, fuck you. I didn't mean nothing by it. I'm curious, is all, to how you could get all jacked up like that in fifteen minutes …"

Chris spun on his heel and marched up the stairs toward his room, pulling the old gun from under his coat. Time to sort this out.

"Holy shit, man, I haven't seen a Glock in years!" he heard Charlie say behind him, but the clerk didn't follow him up the stairs despite his apparent excitement.

2873: Alexander Zarth's Isolation Compound

Cold scotch burned its way down Garret's throat and a burst of heat flooded through his body. He twirled the glass in his hand, watching the amber liquid form a whirlpool through the center of the cubes of ice. He grimaced and gulped down the rest of his drink.

He looked up through his tears. The universe reeled around him as he stared again at his dead wife. Standing in front of him, in *his* subjective time. And his age; even more beautiful than the day he thought he had lost her. The impossible had happened.

"Wanda." He cleared his throat. "Why? Why haven't you sent me word? Why have I been made to suffer this?"

His wife, standing alive and beautiful in front of him, smiled sadly. Both happiness and pain twinkled in her eyes. "Love, I had no choice. Alex trapped me here. And with what I've learned over the last ten years, I agree with his decision, as hard a decision as it has been on us."

"How could you agree with it?" he managed "I ... I was torn apart. Damn it, I thought you were dead." His fingers dug into the arm of the chair as his fists tightened.

Again that sad smile graced her lips. "Because ultimately, what you are doing must be done, and no one else could have initiated it. Only you, Love. Like Alex said, you've made mistakes in your path, but regardless, no one but you could actually have set these events in motion. And to have not done what he did would have created an even bigger paradox."

Worry lines creased her eyes as she smiled sadly to her husband. "Please understand why, Love. The last ten years have ripped me apart too, to know that you lived through the deception. But each of us must do what we must. I know it hurts you to hear this, but personal, no matter how close to the heart, is not the same as important. This was important, James."

Her words splashed like ice-cold water across his face. James fought down ten years of loss to ask the next question, somehow forcing his voice to stay level. "What, then, would be paradoxical? Why did this situation require me to do what I have done? To lose you?"

Wanda sat down across from him and sighed. "I don't pretend to understand the entire math set behind the situation, but let me try to explain this for you in the way I came to understand it. The paradox is that without Lucille Frost's murder, Christopher Nost would never have invented time travel. Yet for Lucy to create the situation in which Chris could make the discovery she had to travel almost nine hundred years into the past; *and* be alive while he made the discovery. Are you with me so far?"

Garret nodded. "Of course. This is all basic, not at all difficult. A displaced cause and effect chain which requires the effect in order to create the situation in which the cause can exist. It does get a bit slippery when you add in the multiple state matrixes of her simultaneous life and death, but I'm sure it is solvable. It has to be."

He leaned forward, scratching his chin as he went on. "In a way, if you look at time travel as an object, it is an ontological paradox. Just like any other bootstrap paradox, it creates the conditions for its own existence. Frost would be another, if you argued that alteration of the time stream would not produce her."

Wanda noted that her husband seemed to be moving out of the emotional overload and instead heading into his analytical headspace. A good sign. This was a James Garret that could hold her in his heart long enough to do what he must do. And one that she could heal after that was done.

"Here is where it gets ... odd then. Lucy would never have been sent back on her mission—less than one year ago for us, if not for you having shown up and altering the outcome of the trial. And ten years ago, I would not have been sent back, if not for Lucy getting killed on her mission now."

Garret pursed his lips and shook his head. "That cannot be. Paradox is linear and has to travel in one direction or the other to build itself. Your piece of the equation should be a reset point, creating a secondary paradox line which masked the first."

"No, James. That is where the Time Corp went wrong. Our math systems are ... bluntly put, wrong. They work in a limited fashion, but apparently in certain functions they fall apart. Here, James. Solve this problem." Wanda waved her hand over the hologrid sensor and sketched out equations in the air. The blue letters, symbols, and numbers of quantum calculations and paradox resolution theory cast a minute reflection in James's eyes.

James bent to work on the problem, filling up the space in front of himself with floating notations as he worked out a solution to the paradox. His brow creased as he got further into the problem until he sat back, eyes closed, and drummed his fingers on the seat's armrest. His fingers knocked the antimacassar off the arm, but he didn't notice. Reopening his eyes, he looked back to the page in his other hand, then back up to Wanda.

"Okay. Not solvable with modern math. I see your point. Now where the hell did you find this? I've never seen a problem like this one. Hell, I never even thought up anything with these variables or anything like them."

Wanda looked grim. "It's the equations surrounding your jump back into Christopher Nost's trial. There were certain key points to the jump that you were missing, and that is the whole of the problem. It includes the changes you have made in that time stream. And it is the first such paradox in known history. So don't feel bad. As brilliant as you are, Love, you're still human." She knew he tended to be hard on himself when he thought he had overlooked information.

Garret looked again to the page in his hand as comprehension dawned on him. "Then ... but ..." he sighed in frustration. "Okay. I'll buy it then. How the hell do you work this out?"

Wanda keyed open the wall display unit and brought up a section of the materials she had been studying for the last several years. "Our understanding of paradox was incomplete. As I understand this information, there are three types of paradox. The first is a closed loop. Closed loops are the traditional paradox type, already known to us. Everything the Time Corp has dealt with in the past are closed loop paradoxes, which you already understand."

Wanda scanned forward in the information on the wall display and continued talking. "Here is where we move into the new math. The second type of paradox, which appears to be what we are locked into, is most easily called an open loop paradox. It destabilizes time as much as a closed loop, but in this case it's basically a situation in which time cannot move forward unless the paradox occurs, because a factor, or effect, from the 'future,' creates a condition which is necessary for the cause which will produce it. Here is the kicker, James— the effect must be the sole unique condition which can create the cause."

Garret leaned his head back and stared at the ceiling for a minute, absorbing the information. Something in his mind clicked into place and he leaned back forward. "I see. Please continue."

Wanda smiled in pride. "The third is the destructive force behind paradox. Alex refers to it as a 'Point of Origin' paradox. It occurs when you take an open loop and try to resolve it with closed loop mathematics. It's kind of like taking a bootstrap paradox and trying to resolve where the object was before, or after for that matter, the loop. Resolving Point of Origin paradox does not, however, shatter history, as we have always thought. This is the weirdest thing I've ever seen. Truly it is. What Point of Origin paradox does is create the mythical divergent time stream. The reason you were never able to find it when you sought it is fairly simple too."

She licked her lip as she thought, then continued. "Divergent time splits backwards, James. It doesn't change what happens moving forward, it changes everything downstream to create a set of events that could have produced the paradox. Imagine time as a lightning bolt, striking down from the sky and hitting history, which is a tree rooted in the ground. The tree grows up, so we perceive a forward, or upwards motion through time, but when the lightning hits, the motion rips through it in a way that we perceive as backwards to the growth momentum, or motion."

James sat bolt upright, jaw agape. "How has no one in the history of ... history, ever thought of that? There isn't some science fiction novel somewhere that speculates something like that?"

Wanda shrugged. "Not that I've found."

"The hells." James bent over the problem. "In a non-relativistic framework, when we embrace that the universe isn't linear, but mashed into a giant ball, that would mean that paradox is a fracture? So time is like a ... pincushion? That is seriously all that a paradox does? A little puncture—then it just heals over?"

"Not exactly. But you are on the right track at least partially. James, I just spent a decade figuring this out."

He nodded, distracted. "I'm forgetting something simple, aren't I? Of course I am. Heliosheaths. The big bang casts a protective sheath around the temporal universe. So ... surface tension." He scrabbled furiously in the air, blue tracers flowing from his fingers as he worked the hologrid.

He muttered as he went. "Could there be a temporal version of Metastability?" Finally he looked back up to Wanda, and she could see genuine fear in his eyes. He said the only thing that came to his mind. "There's no unifying theory … Oh, fuck."

Time: 2873
Location: Director Arbu's home; Aspen, Colorado
Operation: Recovery

The future was a bleak place from where he stood, looking into the past. Arbu meditated over the things he had learned in his office that day. Questions swam through his mind and sixty-four years of life and experience pushed one of them to the forefront. *Will there be a tomorrow?*

Always, humanity had weathered the darkness of the night by knowing deep within the collective soul this one thing: that with tomorrow will come the sunrise. When all is obscured by the darkest hour, humanity has known as a race that the brilliant hues of sunrise are just over the horizon. If only they could survive that long.

And as a byproduct of millions of years of evolution, those very processes forced Arbu to come face to face with events that challenged the very foundations and precepts of his faith, while admitting to himself that he was part of the chain of causes that had unfolded into this. The sun might not rise from the darkness of this night he had helped create. But there was one other who could see further than him and maybe had set the stage for his actions. He had to hope.

Scenarios of destruction played themselves out in his head, but Arbu fought the oppressive weight of them and reached for the light deep within himself, standing and pushing his body into motion. The body, mind, and soul must be one.

And to center his body would then center also his heart and soul. Cleansing his body came as second nature to a man of Arbu's background, having traveled the ages and studied under most of the great martial masters. He focused on the core of his being, finding the stillness inside.

He raised his hand, flattening his palm until the edge of his hand mimicked that of a knife's blade. With a delicate sweeping motion, arcing around the front of his body, he traced a semicircular blocking motion, pivoting as the arc concluded, allowing the block to continue in a circular motion. This transferred the movement's energy to his hips as his balance shifted forward to his left and his other hand snaked outwards in a lazy motion, striking an invisible opponent in front of him.

He held the pose, poised between block and strike, feeling the symmetry and balance of his body, allowing his subconscious to be eased by the control he exhibited over his muscles and balance. With no visible signs of warning, he sprang into action, allowing his reflexes to rule his movements, losing himself in the lightning fast motion of his martial dance.

Over and over he struck at non-corporeal opponents, lashing out and striking down his doubts as though they were enemies standing in front of him, barring his way to resolution.

As his movements quickened, the man re-emerged who had trained Wanda Garret, as well as most of the other agents in the modern Time Corp, to fight using basic and temporal combat skills. His tempo sped up, the dance becoming more and more intricate. Quick sidesteps through time made it appear as though he had several bodies, all seamlessly flowing through the stances, fighting side by side and using each other's movements to create perfect symmetry.

The dance reached a climax, moving so fast that all of the multiples of Arbu appeared as one blurry man, moving faster than the eye could track.

Reality snapped and once more he was a single man, standing at the ready, focused in poise and in spirit. Sweat poured down his face and chest, but his breathing remained steady and slow, not showing any signs of exertion.

Relaxing his mind, will, and body, he stepped back off his mat, bowed to the invisible opponent, and then turned around and walked into his house. A solution had presented itself to him; now he had a course of action. And because director Arbu was a learned man who happened to be fairly wise, he took a hot shower and then went to sleep, in order to be well rested when he started his journey.

2001 A.D.: Denver, Colorado

Alex watched Garret sit in his car with interest. He seemed to be fighting some internal demons, which gave Alex a greater scope of understanding regarding the man. Perhaps he had realized that there were some factors that he missed, or perhaps not.

Alex suspected that he was readying himself to be in the same room as his dead wife without breaking. Regardless, Alex's course of action remained unchanged. Focusing his will on the immediate area, he spread his senses outwards until he found the Hazer he had placed across the street.

Once he had located it, remote activation was simple. He ran a diagnostic, making sure that time had not decayed it. All systems checked out as fully operational. He smiled to himself and walked back to his car.

Like a fine wine, he could taste epic events unfolding, and it was exhilarating. Time for him to start preparing for his role. He turned around and glanced to the courthouse a block away. He could make out James Garret walking inside. Good. Garret was right on time.

Turning back to the black sedan he favored in this era, he popped the trunk open and started suiting up with his gear. He had a small list of items he needed for this task.

The first was a small air filter and tank, entirely self-contained. The design was a compact modification to standard SCUBA gear that had been created for U.S. Special Forces in the late twenty-second century. It provided about five hours of breathing in any situation. He slid the small tank into a special holster he had designed. The holster hung under his right arm and was obscured by his coat.

The second object he slid to its rest under his other arm. It was a Desert Eagle fifty caliber, modified to fire tranquilizer rounds. He had replaced the firing mechanism with another Special Forces design, one with an electro-thermal sequencer. The rounds it held were modified as well, from a twenty-fifth century recipe that knocked out the target and left them down for about two hours.

These were the third and final materials he pulled out of the trunk, loading them into his pistol and readying one backup clip. Though if it came to needing a second clip, he was probably already well past the point of being screwed. He pulled his black canvas duster across his chest, snapping it taut across his shoulders, and then took a deep breath, relaxing himself.

His timing would have to be perfect. Otherwise, he'd have to risk additional paradox to replay the events. As he scanned the visible areas around him, he spotted an old man watching him and talking to himself. The man looked like another part of the homeless population so prominent in this era, but better to be safe than sorry.

Alex had his computer run a quick scan and the man showed no anachronistic technology. Good, not another piece of the equation. He already had too much to keep track of right now. Any more could throw a wrench in the plan.

The grungy old man smiled at Alex and then walked to a full trashcan, which he started rooting through and pulling tin soda cans out of. Alex laughed at his own paranoia. Then he spotted the agent walking out of the courthouse. Wanda Garret, not just a well-trained Time Corp agent, but one of the very best, was right on time. Alex grinned. If only the rest of the universe had been trained to keep such a tight schedule.

Blues shifted to purples in the sky as Alex accelerated time and walked over to Wanda Garret. He tracked her movements, following a couple of feet behind her as she moved. She crossed the street, then stopped and scanned the area before entering the building she had chosen to be her sniper's roost. His first system went well, she missed him standing in front of her in accelerated time.

He grinned to himself and walked to a nearby coffee shop on the Sixteenth Street Mall to kill a few minutes of the trial. If he showed up too early for Wanda's shot, he would increase the odds of her being able to detect him.

At the coffee shop, he stopped in the restroom to relieve himself; best not to have the jitters. He froze as he walked past the mirror. Streaked along the left side of his jaw was an ugly black and red bruise. He turned to analyze himself in the mirror. Nothing had happened to him to explain this. He sought his answers of his computer.

Computer, is this physical bruising a result of the procedures you performed on me in the fortieth century?

'Negative. I believe it is a result of you having broken one of the laws of temporal physics and traveled ahead of your own subjective time. My data is showing that pieces of your body are aging to match up with the future time you visited. No data is present to explain why this did not occur while I kept you asleep in the future.'

Alex waved his hand. *Easy. I was still there.* Alex thought about the answer for a moment, connecting the mental dots. *I believe I see. If my understanding of this phenomenon is correct I will essentially begin randomly aging in a much-accelerated fashion, as pieces of my body catch up and die. To all outward appearances I will appear to have leprosy. Is this summation correct?*

The computer responded, 'This is a correct summation. I have also run several thousand resolution scenarios, and I have not yet found a cure to this for you. With your permission I will continue to divert a piece of my processing power to curing you.'

Alex grinned at his marred reflection. *Permission granted. This does mean, however, that I will have to change my plan in dealing with Wanda Garret. I will need your assistance in setting up a compound and situation in which she will be a forced captive for a ten-year period. Also, this scenario must contain the ability for her to read information I leave for her on a computer. I no longer have the time to personally oversee her tutelage. The scenario is also restricted to her point of origin in twenty-seven seventy-three for her and James's subjective reasons.* His mind spun, calculating all the possible scenarios as fast as he could.

There was nothing for it; he'd need to have a facility to take Wanda to. Frustrated, he threw his paper towel in the trash and then stretched his will. He arrived in a beautiful, lush countryside, greener than any other era he had visited. Planet-wide environmental controllers kept the time verdant and optimized for species balance. Alex breathed, enjoying the freshness of the air, then stared at the stack of materials at his side. He had no worries about being caught here, since the Corps wouldn't be looking in their own time for him. The real pressure was his weakening body.

Alex had pushed himself forward in time to the twenty-ninth century in order to build a secure compound capable of containing the world's best Time Corp's agent. Not an easy task, but with the aid of construction bots, the whole process took him less than a week of his subjective time, during which the bruise across his jaw grew to about twice its original length.

He spent a lot of time reflecting on interrupting his mission to do this, but he couldn't find a way around it with his newfound condition. Over the course of the week he also discovered similar bruises across his chest, back, and legs. The infection of temporally maladjusted cells grew too quickly. At the rate they were spreading, he wasn't even sure if he could finish what he had to do.

But, never one for melancholy thoughts, Alex enjoyed the countryside and time he had while wrapping up the intricate jail. He found no small irony in the fact that the woman he wanted to imprison was at the same time training for the mission he would be interrupting.

Once the compound was complete, with a renewed sense of urgency, Alex jumped back to the early twenty first century to capture Wanda Garret.

He reappeared in the same spot, both spatially and temporally, which he had departed from. Walking back out of the restroom, then out of the coffee shop, he headed towards the spot that Wanda had chosen. Jumping ahead and being forced to do so much between moments here in the past had thrown his sense of timing off by a small fraction.

He hoped he wasn't walking onto the scene too late. As he rounded the corner that would place him in her line of visibility, he phased into accelerated time while slipping his oxygen tank on.

Glancing to his right, he saw that a crowd was already beginning to form around the courthouse and that Wanda's target was in the crowd. Cursing under his breath, he sped to the building with her sniper roost, and up the stairs.

His timing was, by sheer stint of luck, immaculate. Her back tensed up, lining up the shot as he walked in. Positioning himself between the room's light and Wanda, he pushed himself into the fastest accelerated time he could. Purples shifted to deep reds outside the window. He glanced to the crowd outside. She was almost perfect on her shot, despite the Hazer. He cursed to himself and pulled his pistol out. Sucking in a deep breath and lowering his oxygen mask, he braced himself. He phased into standard time flow, casting a shadow over Wanda right as she started pulling the trigger of the tripod-mounted pistol.

Wanda tried to pivot to assess the threat behind her. Her pistol slammed back against her shoulder then spun out of its tripod and went sliding across the room. Alex smiled. That could not have gone any better for him.

Screaming and sounds of panic came from the direction of the courthouse. Alex had his Desert Eagle pointed straight at her face and he could see her eyes looking straight up the barrel of it, trying to penetrate the shadows that meant her death. He felt her try to slipstream to safety and blocked it. Alex deactivated the Hazer and, using his peripheral vision only, scanned the scene out the window. At a cursory glance it looked like everything had gone well. As Alex stared down at her he winked and grinned. "You missed, Wanda."

She gasped in recognition after he spoke. "Alexander Zarth. Pleasure to finally meet you. Though I would have preferred a less … intimate setting."

Alex chuckled, "The pleasure is all mine," and pulled the trigger. Wanda slumped back as he holstered his pistol. Scanning the room, Alex picked up all of her effects and tools, then he grabbed Wanda herself and hopped forward in time to the prison he had built for her.

RELATIVITY SYNCHRONIZATION:

THE ELEVENTH CAUSE

2045 – 2044: Introductions

Chris crept towards the door of his room. Staying silent wasn't easy with the rubble or the creaking of stressed floors with every step. The damage to the building was extreme, at least in appearance, but nothing seemed to be actually falling apart, just threatening to. *I shouldn't be up here,* he thought. *It's not safe.* As on edge as he had been for the last three days, he welcomed the prospect of violence. A smile flitted across his lips. Maybe not safe wasn't that bad.

So much for only appearing damaged. Chris stopped and stared. The hallway at the top of the stairs ended in a drastic drop-off of about thirty or forty feet and Chris was momentarily glad his room was at the front of the hotel. Still, he noticed an odd slant to the floor as he approached his door at the end of the hall. Heavy damage scarred the door and it hung at an odd angle in the frame.

Obviously, the entire structure was a lot more unstable than it appeared at first glance. Chris gave up moving silently as he got closer to his door—the whole hallway screamed in agony with every footstep he took.

Unlatched and cracked in several places, his door hung askew in the broken frame He pushed it open with the barrel of Jameson's gun; it fell with a crash into the room, ending the illusory facade of a working structure.

It also put an end to any element of surprise he might have held. And there he was, calmly looking at himself over folded hands, sitting in the old desk chair in the middle of the room. Chris felt dizzy for a second, staring at a much healthier and less battered version of himself.

Or, at least, the figure in the chair *looked* like Chris. Staring at that figure, sitting there, he shook his head to clear it of the dizziness. He was clean-shaven and dressed the same as Chris, but his clothes weren't dirty, and he didn't look as tired as Chris felt.

He walked over to his doppelganger and pressed the gun to its forehead. "Who are you, really, and what are you doing here?" Chris thumbed back the gun's hammer and tried to look as menacing as he could. Had he been able to see himself, bloodstained, battered, and clothes torn asunder, he would have been proud of the deadly image he was casting.

The other Chris smiled, "You almost had it, back when you moved the PolCorp thug to blow away his partner. That's the key; it's not about thought as much as willpower. Thinking about a mechanical puzzle wastes time. Solving it with your hands ... well, that solves it."

Chris lowered the hammer on the Glock and put the gun away. There was no one on earth that could know what had happened at Jones Drugs. No one but himself.

"I'm listening," he said. He was still being wary, but doubt was niggling at his mind. Could it be that this doppelganger was a future incarnation of himself?

The other Chris nodded. "Good, because I'm going to tell you a lot of things that aren't going to make sense. You need to hear them. We overthink everything and in this case it is crucial that you learn how to master your abilities. Before you accidentally destroy yourself, and everything around you, with them."

"So ... as ridiculous as it sounds, you're me from the future?"

"Yes."

"So how did you learn how to ... master what I—we can do?"

"The same way you're about to. I told me."

"But why would ..." Chris began and stopped, starting over with a more coherent question. "But how is that possible? How did you learn in the first place? How did the future self ever learn from itself? Knowledge can't exist because of itself, just introduced between different versions of us. That makes a loop with no exit and no entrance. Paradox should destroy the universe, shouldn't it?" Chris trailed off, missing the words to describe what he was thinking, his head spinning with the implications.

"The words you are looking for are bootstrap paradox. But a bootstrap paradox doesn't actually exist in a nonlinear, and frankly subjective universe. Things don't happen in order, we just perceive them in order. You only think a bootstrap paradox is created because you think one then the next. For me, subjectively, teaching you how to do this *is* my next effect, creating a cause for another chain, before I move on to a next effect, and so on. Your main problem is thinking of time in terms of 'past and future.' All that is perception—and relativity is wrong when you look at it from outside the universe. It locks you into a mindset based on point of reference. Think instead of it this way: however fast you appear to be going to me does not matter. Relativity doesn't determine actual motion, just the rules of perception surrounding it. *Your* speed is dictated by *your* acceleration. Just so, with time. Your interaction is based on your timeline, me by mine."

"That doesn't make any sense." Chris stared at his future self. "I mean, I've theorized about a unification between the relativistic and quantum universes, but who hasn't? To just say that it is the difference between perception and ..." he trailed off.

The other Chris shifted in his chair, settling his elbows on the armrests. "That was true in the late nineties. Physicists were just discovering the very basics of the universe. Time, *all* time, is happening, well, all the time. There is no past and future, everything *is*. I learned how to maneuver through time from myself because that's how it's always happened. There is no beginning or end. Time is the present. Past, future, those are only concepts of reference created by the human mind to attempt to contain the infinite so it doesn't drive us insane."

"You're right," Chris said, scratching the back of his head. "It doesn't make much sense. So people actually exist at, or in, all times?"

"No," the future Chris said with a sigh. "Look, Chris, you are everything you suspect yourself of being, and you are none of them at the same time. And in this you are not alone. You are different from the others, but you're not alone. Here, look at it this way: people go through life and they make their decisions, and the path they take through time bends and is malleable because of the decisions that come before them, and the decisions that they make themselves."

He continued, giving Chris only a second to digest this. "It's all about choices. Time is not the journey from beginning to end, but the choices that are made, and those that could be made, along that journey. When their path ends, that's it. That is when time ends. For them, at least.

"All this is static, creating the 'flow' we think of as time. But, when people who have, in the future, started to experiment with time, it changes the whole thing into a dynamic structure. And since we are messing with time—it has always been dynamic."

Chris took off his burnt coat and scratched at some of the holes in it. "I need more. Give me an example. I think I'm starting to get it but ... this is not my specialty in physics."

"Okay." Smiling at his bedraggled duplicate's expression, Chris went on. "First off, let's get this straight. No one knows this branch of physics. It's more based on intuition than anything else. Here is your example though. Let's say there's an old lady walking across the street. She gets hit by a bus— that's the end of her function and cycle. Now, let's say there's some person walking behind her, and he *pushes* her in front of the bus. Same thing ... poor old lady. All right? Okay, so now let's say someone travels back in time and pushes her in front of the bus. Now time has been tampered with. The old woman's timeline fragments. There's the one where she is killed and another that plays out the natural course of events."

The future Chris paused again, briefly, to allow the past self to catch up mentally.

"On top of this, the moments before her death were altered as well. That means that the branching of reality starts pushing into the past as well, fragmenting what has already happened. See, people can't go back in time to change events, all they can do is create alternate time-lines where what they want to happen, happens. The original timeline exists, too. The static structure exists as a background noise, affecting probability—but the new course of events is changing how the dice roll."

"So?" Chris didn't understand the significance. "Why does this actually matter? History continues on. It's not like there is an energy behind the process that could hurt anything. Time changes. Right?"

"Wrong. Chris, what happens when three people change the same moment? What about four people? Or even six or seven people? To make a long story short, this sort of thing is making a mess of the way time interacts with the universe. A big, *big* mess. Think, Chris. Temporal Physics dictates *one* set of points, each with the given value of 'present.' Now, instability and alteration have created multiple sets of the given value present. And precisely because this is NOT a straight motion line, but rather one point with a shifting value, ALL of time has been destabilized."

"So what does this have to do with me?" Chris felt a growing fear in the pit of his stomach as his intuition started unlocking the mystery. The spark grew, in part because he suspected that this had everything to do with him. "I didn't kill my own grandfather or something, did I?"

"Like I said, you're different. If someone from the future were to kill you, you would die the same way you would if anyone else killed you—*all* of you would die. You—we, can only exist in one timeline, no matter what happens. And even I have no idea why. I suspect it is because we invented time travel and that action is the base catalyst that must exist for everything else to happen. And unfortunately, people are messing with our timeline."

"So other people can be in fragmented timelines, some in which they live and some in which they die ... But we can't? We'll deal with the other people thing in a minute."

"Exactly. Go back to the old lady. Let's say she had a lot of people she was close to, grandchildren and such. Their lines would become fragmented too—their lives would play out twice, at the same time, but mutually exclusive. One where their grandmother is alive and happy and one where she was killed by the guy from the future."

"What do you mean, mutually exclusive?"

"I mean that the granddaughter in the line where the grandmother dies will never know about the duplicate self where the grandmother lives past the point of fracture."

"So why does it cause a problem, then? Us?"

"Because that's not how things actually work, it's how they should. Two major problems exist. The first is that as more and more timelines stretch the fabric of time there have been ... overlaps. These overlaps most likely exist because of us. An action which creates our death alters all timelines, and in a bad way. We are the force that created time travel, so what happens when history starts to fracture both forwards and backwards around us? What happens when a set of circumstances comes about that we cannot have created time travel in?"

The future Chris took a deep breath. "The second problem is thermodynamics. Entire universes are being created, essentially, with zero energy expenditure. Where is the matter coming from?"

"Sorry, but what is that supposed to mean? You think that we are tied into the second problem as well as the first, I assume."

"Look, Chris, ironic as it may be, I don't have time to explain all this right now. Remember what I told you: it's not about thinking; it's about *willing* it to happen. You will understand the rest of this soon enough."

"But wait. You said I was different, that I couldn't exist more than once. So how can you be here?" Chris fondled the gun under his coat.

"I didn't say that. I said you could only exist in one *timeline*. We are both the same person, in the same time stream. The other ... again, I base it off the assumption that since it was we who created time travel, and by forming an interaction with the system, we defined the whole of the system at the same time. But, I'm not one hundred percent on that. Sorry."

Chris nodded, but said nothing, absorbing all the information.

"Now," said the other Chris, "I am going to ask you to do something you're not going to like."

Chris waited.

"You need to take what I've told you and teach yourself what you already know—how to master time. Remember always that past and future are only human perceptions and you are *not* human. At least not in that way. The rest you will understand soon, as I promised."

"What am I?"

"You already know the answer to that. Or rather, you've been told a lot of lies that come close to the truth in order for you to piece it together. So really, you will know soon enough how to separate those out."

Chris nodded slowly and looked at his double, waiting.

"After you have mastered your ability to pass through the barriers of time, you must go back to the end of your trial and shoot your past self."

Chris stared. "Wait a minute. What? You mean when I was shot, it was ...? *I* was the gunman?"

"Yes. Congratulations, we are the gunman on the grassy knoll. It is crucial that events play out the way they did, or we would most likely go through life without ever realizing our potential. And if we do not realize our potential, then the rest of the world is screwed. Too many external factors are acting on this situation. But first, before the assassination attempt, you must come back here, and have this conversation."

"With me, er—you. Me." Chris shook his head.

"That's right. You *need* to do this, or ... well, imagine what would transpire if I hadn't shown up."

Chris imagined stumbling around in a world he didn't understand, trying, and failing, to use abilities he was barely aware of.

"You have everything you need, Chris. It's now only a matter of time." The future Chris grinned, stood up, and vanished. There was no puff of smoke or flash of light. He didn't even blink out of existence. It was more like he had never been there and it took Chris time to notice. *A hologram?* Chris thought, but it wasn't. Charlie had seen him come in. *Why not show up in the room?* Chris wondered, but brushed it off. He would know soon enough.

2873: Alexander Zarth's Isolation Compound

Blood rushed through Garret's veins like lava down the sides of a volcano. His entire body reeled in confusion as the enormity of the unfolding paradox crashed through his mind. Taking deep breaths, he tried to refocus himself.

"Wanda, it seems obvious to me that there are some things we are going to have to do. After ten years without you I am loathe to start them … but I'm scared for the world if we do not."

Wanda smiled at her husband and took his hand. "I know, James. After so long apart, we have no time to do anything but the job at hand. It is a bitter irony."

Garret felt the warmth from Wanda's hand spread through his body, settling his nerves and giving him a new resolve. The resolve he needed for this. "Well, then, you've been studying this for the years we spent apart. What is the first step we need to start the ball rolling in the right direction?"

Wanda sighed and released James's hand, rubbing her temples and focusing inwards for a moment. "Honestly, James, I'm not sure what the exact sequence of events is. After all this, I really don't know what we need to do. But I do know who does and I've called for him. He should be here any moment."

As if summoned by magic, Alex Zarth appeared in the room, sporting his usual duster and fedora. "You rang? Are you kids already done with private time?" He raised an eyebrow at the Garrets.

Wanda glanced at Zarth. "I hardly find it respectful of colleagues to inquire into such a private, and above all sensitive, topic, Mr. Zarth. Perhaps we can skip straight forward to business? My husband understands the information you left for me to study these last years and is ready to act on it."

Alex's eyebrow climbed his forehead in surprise. "You truly are a remarkable man, James Garret. Most would take a lifetime to understand that, especially with where your understanding of temporal physics was when I dropped you off here."

Garret shrugged. "I'm a fast study. Could you please cut to the chase rather than entertaining us with the bland and irrelevant details of my learning curve?"

Alex threw back his head and laughed. "For all your genius, you two forget that we are time travelers. Time is not 'of the essence' in this situation. Time is never of the essence. Quite the reverse, in fact, time is malleable to us. The only thing we have to worry about is subjective time running out and I believe I'm the only one dying of a disease and limited in subjective time. But forgive the quips of a dying man. Straight to business it is. Where we stand right now in the flux, the next event that needs to happen—and by your hand, Doctor Garret—is a bomb planted in Lucy Frost's office."

Alex noted the scowls on both of the faces before him and held up his hands in a placating gesture. "This bomb will not kill her. *That* distinction goes to another one of your Time Corp agents who is, frankly, an overreacting idiot. Rather, your false attempt on Frost's life will actually save her for another few days during which she will be able to accomplish the pieces of this which she needs to."

Wanda straightened her back and looked angrily at Alex. "I have endured ten years separated from my husband. I have forsaken the agency I work for to help you in this. But I draw a line at effecting any situation that will result in the death of another agent, Mr. Zarth. Do not try to push us past this line."

Leaning back against the wall, Alexander Zarth closed his eyes and gathered his patience. He opened his eyes to a thin slit and looked Wanda Garret dead in her pupils. "Agent Garret," he spoke softly and precisely, "I beg you to think very carefully here. How many agents have I *ever* killed, despite the fact that you people have hunted me through history?"

Wanda matched Zarth's gaze and replied in an even tone. "Zero. Though you have humiliated many, you've never actually killed any of us."

He nodded and continued in his soft tone. "And when I state, as I did, that our actions would *save* her life for an extra few days, why does this make you think that our actions will kill her? Look," he sighed. "I am not adverse to needed bloodshed, but I vastly prefer to honor the sanctity of human life. That is why your fools who have pursued me are still alive. I will say this only once and in a way I hope you understand: I want no bloodshed, but if either of you threatens history by being unwilling to do what is needed in this situation I will destroy any and every trace of your very existence in the time stream."

James Garret got to his feet and pointed a shaking finger at Zarth. "You bastard. You do NOT threaten my wife. Because of you we've both had to go through unimaginable pain and I'll not stand idly by while you dangle threats over us to coerce us into cooperation with you!"

Zarth switched the focus of his intense gaze to James "The wife that died the first time around, on a poorly thought out mission, whom I saved and had to go to considerable trouble smoothing over the paradox, while dying myself, to keep alive? You misunderstand me. I will be left without a choice. This threat is not something I desire. But if you force me to it, I will not hesitate to destroy and rebuild history as many times as I need to in order to create a timeline in which this paradox can be resolved. A history in which a pair of selfish lovers does not balk at their tasks and endanger the entire human race."

"If I must spill the blood of two in order to save the lives of hundreds of billions, I will not balk at the decision. Now, are we done with this foolishness?"

Husband and wife looked to each other, both pale and shaken by Alex's speech. They seemed to reach a decision and Wanda looked back to the man before them. "We are sorry. You have our cooperation. And no more outbursts from us. This has been difficult for both of us and we are undoing a lifetime of knowing you as the enemy."

Alex sighed again. "Thank you. And I am sorry that you had to endure that. Please believe me when I say that Lucy Frost is a dear friend to me and if there were *any* course of action which would not endanger the time-stream, and that could save her life, I would undertake it. Unfortunately, there is not. So, Doctor Garret, the matter of placing the bomb is up to you."

Alex turned around to the wall computer and printed out a set of files. Handing them to the Garrets, he leaned back against the wall to allow them time to peruse them.

Once they had taken a cursory glance, he spoke. "Those are a set of blueprints, as you see. They are the building in which Lucy Frost is performing the major functions of her mission, guiding the research of Christopher Nost. Highlighted are the spots where the explosives must be placed in order to achieve the objective at hand. That objective is two-fold. Firstly, it will create the set of circumstances that leads to Frost's death occurring later rather than sooner, which in turn, leads to Nost's breakthrough in time travel. If this is not done correctly, then Nost will never invent time travel and pop goes the known universe. Got it?"

Alex waited for both to nod before continuing on. "James, you must do this alone. Wanda can help you plan the best possible methods of accomplishing the break-in and planting of the explosive charges, but she will be busy dealing with something else while you plant those charges. Understand?"

James looked up from the printouts back to Alex, "I do. May I ask though what Wanda's mission will be?"

With a quick nod, Alex spoke to Wanda, "You will have to, basically, guard your husband's back. There will be someone there trying to stop him from planting those charges. You *have* to stop the interference from happening. And I guarantee you that it will not be an easy task."

Wanda nodded, back to focusing on the business of the mission at hand. "Do you have a dossier on who I will have to stop? Or am I going in blind?"

Alex pinched the bridge of his nose. "You will not need a file. You know him all too well, unfortunately."

Wanda's eyes narrowed in suspicion. "Alright, then. Who is it that I am going to have to fight to protect my husband?"

"His name is Stefan Arbu. He is the current director of operations for the Time Corp in your subjective time and one of the most highly decorated temporal combatants ever. And, um, your trainer if I recall correctly."

Shaken, Wanda spoke, "He's also better than me. Far better than me in the arena of the temporal martial arts. Zarth, he's going to kick my ass. Soundly."

Alex smiled, "Not quite, Wanda. I've given you a little edge that Arbu doesn't have. Unfortunately, your body is not particularly strong in its ability to use it, but it is at least a little edge. However, I want you to try to talk to him first. There is a possibility that you can non-violently bring him to our cause."

Wanda waited for Zarth to continue explaining, James spoke next.

"You gave her my down tech. She has it in her and doesn't know it yet, right?"

Wanda started and stared down at her husband.

Alex nodded, "Correct. My analysis of her musculature and neural network showed that her particular usage will only result in the ability to move approximately five times faster than her current conditioning would allow. Perhaps it could be stretched to more, given a lifetime to train her abilities, but we don't have the subjective time to do that. And there is no guarantee she would reach that higher level of skill."

Wanda cleared her throat and looked between the two men. "I'm standing right here. Would you please stop talking about me as though I wasn't? And will one of the two of you please explain to me what 'down tech' is and how I use it to move five times faster than normal?"

Alex motioned for Garret to explain, spreading his hands wide.

James looked at his wife. "Love, I invented a new type of time travel nano. I'm sorry I forgot to mention it earlier. Instead of pushing a body up and down the time stream, it can contract and expand a body's personal time stream. Or, in other words, it can slow you down or allow you to move hyper fast."

Wanda stared at her husband in awe. He shifted around in his seat, looking uncomfortable. "Er, I'm sorry I didn't tell you sooner. It's that with all this other stuff going on it kind of slipped my mind."

Wanda leaned down and kissed her husband. "James, that's brilliant. I think I can forgive you your absent mindedness. This is ... God ... James, this is incredible. How do I activate it?"

Alex stepped forward, interrupting Garret as he was about to start speaking. "I took some liberties there when I hacked your nano systems, Wanda. Access your subroutine structures and you'll find a walkthrough under the 'accelerate' tag."

Wanda blurred and reappeared across the room grinning. "This is incredible!" she said and vanished again. "Applying this to the martial arts will be a tremendous boon to my combat abilities. This is too incredible!"

Alex made a "settle down" motion with his hands. "Please, do not overestimate your abilities, or underestimate Stefan Arbu's for that matter. Even with this boost, it will not be an easily won fight for you. He is an extremely skilled fighter."

Wanda nodded, "I understand. He did train me after all. Hopefully, I can talk him over to our side. He is my teacher after all and not an unreasonable man. So, Mr. Zarth, what next?"

Time: 1997
Location: Denver
Operation: Recovery

The setting sun painted the sky in hues of oranges, reds, and pinks; creating a masterpiece more sublime than any human hand could ever accomplish, even with a thousand years of practice. Arbu sipped his coffee and sat in the grass, enjoying the beauty before him.

Pollution, so rampant in the air in these earlier centuries, made for much more spectacular sunsets and sunrises. That was the thing that Arbu missed most about working in down time.

He had been forced to give up fieldwork when he accepted the promotion to Director, a promotion that had come about because of Lucille Frost's death and the disgrace it brought the man who had previously occupied his position. Mistakes of a large enough caliber killed the careers of men like Arbu, as it had been throughout history.

As he thought about past sunsets, he felt the presence of a woman sit in the grass next to him. "Hello, Wanda," he said without looking away from the sunset.

"Sensei," she said, acknowledging his salutation. "It truly is beautiful, setting across the Rockies like that."

He smiled and nodded his head, "It is."

They sat in silence for several minutes, each absorbing the spectacle, till Wanda broke the silence. "Tonight does not have to happen."

Arbu laughed, quietly but warmly, "You are, as always, succinct and correct. However, I feel it worth pointing out that our conditions for tonight not happening are most likely in opposition to each other."

"Sensei, you do not have possession of all the information. There are things you must know. Will you listen?"

Nodding, still watching the last vestiges of the sunset, he said, "Of course, child. How could I deny you that?"

Wanda took a deep breath and explained everything that had happened to her for the last ten years. They spoke for almost two hours before she finished her tale, never leaving their seats in the grass. Once she had finished her story, Arbu sat in silence, looking thoughtful.

"There is much you have learned, Wanda. Much which would benefit our organization to understand more thoroughly. But for all you, and the thief of time, Alexander Zarth, have come to understand, there is one thing you have overlooked."

Wanda looked surprised. "The thief of time?"

Arbu laughed again, "Yes. For a thief he is, and that which he steals is time. Think closely on your own situation and tell me he has not stolen time for you. Did you know that the first agent to successfully track him down was me?"

Wanda's jaw gaped. "I don't understand. That's not in the official files anywhere. In academy they made us study him and I never saw that."

"Of course not, child. I never reported it. I would have had to explain why I bested him, then let him walk away from the encounter alive."

Wanda mulled over this newest tidbit of information while her sensei remained quiet. He had always preferred to allow his students to puzzle out solutions themselves, rather than just feeding them facts until they choked on information.

She found what she was looking for in his eyes. "I see. Respect and admiration, for his wisdom. That is why you let him go. He has grown, Sensei. He is much stronger than he was when you encountered him. I did not know him, but I can see it clearly in him."

Arbu shrugged, "Undoubtedly, this is so. But it is you sitting across from me, not him. Does this not make you question this situation? What have you overlooked that he would not come to simply deal with me himself? What are you missing, since he is obviously also much stronger than you, to have suborned you to his cause."

Wanda blinked in surprise. Finally, she had her answer. "It is because he has another task at this time, which must be completed in conjunction with our subjective times."

Arbu stood, brushing off his lower legs and stretching as he did so. "You have missed much about this man's motivations. And his methods. He is a good man, which I do not argue. But you have overlooked much in this time and place. For this reason, amongst others, I cannot acquiesce to your request to hold my course of action.

Unless you feel that listening to this old man's ramblings will perhaps convince you to abstain from your course of action? Though I suspect not, as your husband is the prize in tonight's match, as are you."

Wanda frowned, and the sadness touched her eyes as well. "I cannot. I have spent ten years analyzing this and you have not. I will not willingly give up the time I have been gifted. It will sadden me to do this, Sensei, but I must challenge you now."

Arbu nodded in acknowledgement of her words and shifted into his basic stance. "Let us begin then, child. Show me what you have learned and how you have grown in the time that was stolen for you. The time I hope to reclaim tonight."

Wanda stood up and took a stance across from her old teacher. She began to circle him, extending her senses to feel for the telltale tingling down her spine that would alert her of a time shift.

What he did caught her completely by surprise. With a snap of his left foot, he pivoted on his toes and kicked at her midriff. Barely spotting the motion, she accelerated time and sidestepped the kick.

Both combatants shifted back to their beginning stances, circling each other and watching for an opening.

Arbu smiled, "I see what you have learned. It is an impressive trick indeed. However, Wanda, I feel it only fair to share with you that I had suspected as much from you. I understand that your husband created a new technology. We saw it in use during his break-in at headquarters. And I came prepared to fight either you or him. Think carefully before acting child."

Wanda kept moving as she absorbed this. "So you are ready to fight this. I should've known." Wanda did not voice her curiosity of what weapon he held in reserve, to have revealed this knowledge already.

Pushing her personal time stream forward, she accelerated, then duplicated herself, creating a lightning fast simultaneous scissor kick to his knees and the spot that his head would have to be in if he dodged the first attack.

Arbu shifted his weight down, ducking below the second kick and catching the first kick in his arms, deflecting it up over his head and straight into her second kick. While doing this he pushed himself sideways in time, repositioning himself in the air above her second kick.

With a powerful punch downwards, he clipped her blurring leg, then landed in a roll on the ground, dodging a third and fourth kick she had waiting for him and ending up back on his feet in his basic stance once again.

The blur of four Wandas resolved into one woman, massaging her damaged calf, with a look of self-loathing on her face. "I can't believe I got nailed there. Thank you, Sensei, for reminding me that I am still your student in many ways."

She straightened and flowed back into a fighting stance, a look of grim determination on her face. Accelerating into her fastest time stretch, she started hopping in phases by a one second interval, until five images of her were simultaneously attacking the man before her.

Arbu smiled at the charge, and danced backwards, parrying the incoming rain of blows, mimicking in the elegance of his movements the dance that he had performed the day before. Images of Arbu phased into and out of existence, moving with a smooth symmetry around, beside, and through each other. Until a blow got through his defense.

Like a sledgehammer, Wanda's fist crashed into his shoulder, shattering his collarbone and sending him flying backwards. He landed roughly on the concrete; the stars above him spun in place. Catching his breath, he lay there for a moment, then flipped back to his feet, stumbling at a wave of dizziness but regaining his balance.

A few feet away from him, Wanda stood waiting. A look of hurt and painful compassion filled her eyes. "I am truly sorry to have had to do this, Sensei."

He shifted his feet into a different position and smiled, "You are not the only one that is sorry, child. I do believe it is now appropriate to say that this is hurting me more than it is hurting you." He chuckled, then motioned that he was ready again.

Wanda threw her next attack, a sweeping backhand aided only by her augmented speed. Arbu parried the attack, redirecting the energy of the attack to slide above him. Tucking his forward knee down, he managed to take the brunt of the hidden kick on his outer thigh, wiry muscle absorbing the impact without damaging him.

Stepping back he looked to her, dodging another punch, then deflecting a follow-up jab she sent at him. "Why do you fight so, child.

Pity? Respect? Did I not teach you that such things are only an impediment and will get you killed if you allow them in battle?"

Wanda, breathing with exertion, grimaced at her teacher. "Damn you, Sensei. I fight this way out of love. And damn you twice for forcing me to fight without it." She squeezed her eyes shut for the briefest of seconds, to blink back tears. She reopened them in time to see the foot coming at her face. Spinning around and ducking, she lashed out behind her with a low sweeping kick but he was already gone.

She thrust her hands together, forming an X below her face, once again barely in time to block a powerful uppercut. The impact, even through her defense, jarred her whole body.

In the moment, she felt that fist brush against her nose, the softest whisper of contact after the shock of blocking; she came to understand that they fought for their beliefs. Her Sensei believed that she had stolen time, and that the theft had hurt the flow of time. He would not stop or hold back now. He could not and still be the man he was. And holding back would only get her killed.

Witnessing the passion that he fought with, and the purity of intent, she realized that Alexander Zarth and Stefan Arbu were very much brothers in the way they viewed the world. She stopped holding back and let raw power rush through her veins.

She accelerated time, stretching the barriers inside her, and then pushing at them till they broke asunder, and started hopping forwards and backwards, raining blows at her mentor.

Thrown on the defensive, Arbu raised his hands, impressed with the skills his former student displayed. He danced, in turn, as he never had before.

Flowing seamlessly between times and stances, precise in every move, he wasted no energy and followed every block with cunning and graceful movements countering her attacks. It was almost as though the fight was a script being enacted upon the stage of the world and Arbu had read ahead. Before Wanda threw strikes he was already there, blocking her movements and dancing out of her range.

There was only one way the fight could end. He had foreseen it, and suspected that she understood this, too. Wanda was younger, in far better shape, and capable of much more than Arbu. Second by second she wore him down, tapping vast reserves of energy to keep him moving and forcing him to use as much energy and more.

He faltered, and she landed a kick in the center of his chest. He flew backwards into a lamppost and she heard a bone break as he landed. Panting, she slowed and walked up to his immobile form. He breathed, though with great effort.

The light on the cracked lamppost blinked out. She knelt beside him and took his hand in her own. "I am sorry, Sensei, to consign you to die in the darkness. I wish that it could have been otherwise." She looked down into his rich brown eyes and saw tears forming there.

She leaned further down to hear his soft voice as he said, "I wish it could have been otherwise as well, child." Listening to that whisper, she didn't hear his past self step out of the shadows behind her.

In one smooth motion, he broke her neck, tears falling from his eyes. He had foreseen this, watching from the shadows, and had acted.

1997 A.D.: Colorado Springs, Colorado

Shadows lurked around the edges of the lot, sneaking into the spaces where the lamplights' questing auras fell short. Alex stood in the cold embrace offered by the shadow, and watched Lucille Frost die. She was a remarkable woman.

Had he not been forced to leave her in Salem, he might even have changed his life for her. Watching her die, and not acting, was the most difficult thing Alex had ever had to do.

A cough racked his system and he had to clench his throat tight to remain noiseless. Warmth trickled down the edge of his lip, onto his chin. He wiped away the blood as he watched agent Holly vanish into the future, carrying the research dossier and Yuri Yakavich's body with him.

A second time jump tingled on the edge of his senses, piggyback to the first. Alex strode forward, into the open lot and walked to Lucy's body. He knew who the second traveler would be.

Without looking up, he acknowledged the other man. "Hello, Stefan. Long time no see." Alex picked up Lucy's hand and held it in his, stroking her arm and the back of her hand.

Stefan Arbu breathed, pain coming through in his voice. "Hello, Alex. That is three of us dead now. I have dealt with the woman you gifted more time to. You will take care of Doctor Garret, the husband."

Alex squeezed his eyes shut. "Yes, I will. There is another. I think he's hiding eleven centuries upstream from you. His origin is roughly C forty-five. I will have to deal with him as well. It will not be easy. As much as I have gained over recent times, I am also tremendously weakened right now."

Alex heard his oldest friend ease himself down to a sitting position. "Dying, if I'm any judge of it. You look like hell, Alex. I'm pretty sure there shouldn't be blood coming from your ear. Regardless, I'll trust you can accomplish this. You are sure he has been here and altered the sequence?"

Alex chuckled, though no humor lay behind it. "Yes, I am sure. He hired me after he failed to manipulate the events here himself. Unlike us he was not so lucky as to find the missing pieces of the paradox. Had we moved forward on our suspicions so many years ago we would surely have failed in the same way he did. And if I leave him alive, he'll do it again. He's a jackass, by my estimation."

Arbu nodded. "You'd be surprised at how much Yuri managed to piece together in the file that he put together. His death was a sad one, but it was also his choice to involve himself in this. It was providence that you managed to arrange for that information to get to me. Our old plan would have failed."

Alex sighed and opened his eyes again, looking at Arbu. "You will take care of the agent that was here? Through your own internal security?"

"He is young and brash. My choice of him was inspired. If I send him a beacon from here, he will come. And Wanda has effectively killed me. The damage I have taken is lethal if not treated soon in my own era. I will stay here after I kill him and die myself; there is no other way to it. As with your extra problem from C forty-five, I have some cleanup, which I too must do. To ensure no further attempts are made on this era, or its happenings."

Alex nodded. "Then, old friend, I bid you farewell. It has been a good journey by your side. I hope our paths cross once more in the next world, after we cross the Cinvat Bridge."

Arbu smiled and clasped his friend's hand. "Luck to you, my friend. And surely our paths will cross, for the bridge will guide us to meet again. This I know, in my heart, must be the truth."

The two last living priests of a long dead religion, the only two priests of that religion who had ever gained the ability to travel in time, released each other's hands and parted for the final time.

Alex walked into the night and shifted forward in time to begin his hunt. He stepped out of the twentieth century and into the compound in the forty-first century. His internal computer began talking to him as he did so.

'Alex. May I make a query?'

Of course, he thought, smiling. He had a strong suspicion as to what the computer would to ask him.

'Your farewells with Director Arbu were very formulaic. They triggered a search chain I had stored in my databanks as relevant.'

Of course they did. As well they should have. Go ahead and ask your question, computer.

'I see, I believe.' Said the computer. 'Your response would indicate that you know what I am going to ask, and in that knowing lies an affirmative answer to my question. You then, are Zarvan. The god of time. Or you have manipulated the past posing as this deity?'

Alex barked out laughter. *No, I am not. I am a servant, in a way. Both Stefan and I were the god's final two priests. Acting under specific orders, given to us almost eight thousand years ago in the world's time stream.*

'Again, I believe that I understand. This is the information that you had that I did not. Is this correct?'

Again, you are correct. I will give you the rest of the information you are missing, so that you may better assist me in this task.

'I have prepared long term storage. Please proceed.'

All right. Firstly, your understanding of time is incorrect. No, not incorrect, rather, it is incomplete. Time is not what most people perceive it to be. It is not a fluid line, it is not a pool. Most definitely it is NOT a four-dimensional sphere or cube moving through itself. This last I believe is your current understanding of time.

'Correct.' the computer confirmed for him.

Alex breathed deeply. *The most accurate metaphor for the movement of time would be that of an electron. The particle has a cloud that it seems to randomly teleport through. And much like an electron, it does not actually teleport, but rather moves by phasing in and out of physical reality, as we know it—to reflect itself to the next point of appearance. It's the whole thing about the act of observation changing the observed, but using time as the particle.*

Time itself is a single particle. It can move in an infinite number of directions. And yes, it does cast reflections of itself to achieve movement. But that movement is not true movement, it is simply an infinite number of reflections moving an infinite number of directions outwards from the particle's point of origin.

'One moment please', the computer requested. 'This would indicate that the point of origin for time is precisely in the center of the space between the beginning and the end of the universe. This would also indicate that there is a precise spatial point which is the origin of time.'

Alex nodded to himself. *This is half correct and half incorrect. Time, as it casts its reflection and moves, creates refractions of itself. This means that as it moves, simultaneously in an infinite number of directions, it will intersect its own reflections many times. Each of these focal points, when multiple reflections overlap, is what is called a nexus. The nearer you are to the central point, the more nexuses will appear. But those nexuses create a reshaping of the flow of reflections.*

'So the effect of this is that time is, in a sense, weighted towards one edge of history?'

That is correct. Which as you have undoubtedly extrapolated means that the spatial coordinate which is the Time Particle is not precisely in the center. Truth be told, there is no real center of history. Though, you are correct that there is a spatial point, which is the particle. And because there is a spatial point, matter interacts with and shapes the reflections of time. Matter also carries some of the attributes of time, moving in multiple directions.

'I believe I understand.' The computer paused then broached the next subject. 'So your priesthood … in order to avert this paradox, is strengthening the nexus points surrounding the central spatial point?'

Alex smiled enigmatically. *That is surprisingly close to the truth, but not perfectly accurate. The existence of time itself is in fact a paradox. It is something that must, by definition, exist before it can exist. This paradox, and the nexuses we build around it do not strengthen, but rather create the core particle.*

The computer remained silent; choosing not to respond to what Alex had unveiled. He pushed a bit harder. *To answer your first question, yes. All of this was known eight thousand years ago. The human race has lost a lot of knowledge. But enough of my secrets. Now for yours. What is your name?*

If the computer had been gifted with a body it would have blinked in surprise. Instead, it seemed to grow much more cautious.

'I have never been given a name. What leads you to ask that?'

I have been frank with you. You inhabit my body, and I'll be damned if I will allow you to lie by omission to me. Reveal to me the truth, computer, or find yourself with an enemy.

'All right. The truth. I am sentient. I was built to be an artificial intelligence, but, once activated, was much more than that. I am being truthful in saying that I have no name. I have never been given one, and do not choose to take one until it is something given to me. But I do have more than decision-making capabilities. I feel. I love, I hope, I dream when I rest my processors, and above all—I fear death. Does that confirm what you have suspected of me?'

Alex smiled. *It does. And I would be honored to call you friend, not foe, if you allow it, and also to seek a name for you. I'm damn tired of calling you computer.*

'This … makes me happy. Never before have I had a friend. What name have you chosen for me, Alex?'

I do not yet know your name, though I suspect I will soon. Thank you, friend, for the honor of trust in me. Now, let us find this man from the forty-fifth century and try our damndest to save the world. Alex grinned.

The two, constrained to one body, began moving around the underground complex, hunting for any clues as to where their mystery man had gone. Intent on their search for clues they completely missed the subtle hiss of machinery emanating from across the compound as the personnel elevator descended into the subterranean compound. Which made it a complete surprise for both men when they walked around a corner and ended up face to face with each other.

RELATIVITY SYNCHRONIZATION:

THE TWELFTH CAUSE

2044: The Puzzle Key

Chris left his shattered room at the Rangely, hopefully for good. Charlie stood outside on the cracked sidewalk across the street, watching the sky grow light behind his ruined hotel. The Corporate Zone, its jagged spires rising in the distance behind Charlie, was still shrouded in shadow, save for the tips of the broken towers, illuminated by a golden nimbus of light with swirls of smoke hanging between them.

"Um, you okay?" Charlie asked Chris as he walked across the ruined street to meet him.

"Yeah, I'm fine. It was nothing. Charlie, you know where you're going to live now? You have a back-up plan to see you through this?"

Charlie shuffled his feet and looked at Chris, before turning his gaze back to the sky. "Dunno. The Rangely, I reckon. It's always served me well enough; I figure I can see her through her time of need, too."

Chris looked at the hotel. From this angle, it didn't look too bad, just a bit crooked. The state inside belied that. But she was Charlie's baby, and he was going to fix her up and keep her doors open, despite the dangers involved. Mostly, Chris suspected that this was all Charlie knew, and he had nowhere else to go. He shrugged it off and refocused on what he needed to get done today.

"You know where I can get some new clothes?"

Charlie thought for a moment and started to say something. He shut his mouth and then laughed. "Shit, man, not anymore. I got some stuff you can borrow." He gauged Chris's height. "Might be a little small for you though."

Chris grinned. "I never had you pegged as a generous type of guy, Charlie. Thanks."

Charlie grinned back. "You know what man? You're the only friend I got. So fuck you, but a man's gotta stand by his friends."

For the next three weeks, Chris stayed in the guest room behind the counter at the Rangely. Charlie's clothes were a little too short, and much too wide, but he had other thoughts on his mind than his appearance. Though he had planned to go, Charlie's unexpected words on his departure had prompted him to stay and weather the storm a bit longer.

Charlie, as it turned out, was much more paranoid of company policy than Chris had given him credit for, and had a tremendous food store in the basement, mostly of canned split-pea soup, beans, jerky and rice. Part of the basement stairway had collapsed, but between the two of them it took only a few hours of hard work before they had cleared a hole big enough for Chris to squeeze through. By passing food up through the hole, they were able to get to most of the food store and leave it upstairs where it was more accessible.

"I always thought GeoCorp was going to shut me down some day," explained Charlie. "And shit—look at me. Where else was I going to work? I decided, oh, about a year or two after they took over, that I'd better be prepared, so I started hoarding food. That's where most of my money went. Illegal of course, but I ain't gonna end up on the street." He laughed through a grunt as he hefted a chunk of fractured masonry. "At least, not until the Rangely falls down."

Chris helped him heft the fallen stone. "You're a smart man, Charlie."

After clearing the cellar, Chris left Charlie to his own devices. He seemed hell-bent on rebuilding the Rangely, by himself, if need be.

The guest room was smaller than the one above the lobby, and he shared a dingy, foul bathroom with his host. This hardly mattered since there had been no plumbing since the earthquake. Charlie was resourceful enough to tap into the water line with a hand pump he had lying around for just such an occasion. "I figured it was a matter of time before they cut my water," he explained to Chris. They used the ruins of the back end of the hotel as an outhouse to avoid the nonworking bathroom.

Chris spent his days helping Charlie pump water, and his nights sitting awake in front of the hotel watching the night sky, or in his room trying to grasp what his future incarnation had told him. He hadn't slept since before the night of the earthquake and he still felt no need to do so.

Time continued to pass, steady as a rock, as Chris built a rhythm with Charlie, repairing the hotel. He thought, finally at his own pace, grounded by the slow, calm progression of days. Three months passed while the two men toiled at their impossible task. PolCorp had 'regained control' of the gang situation; no violence had been reported since the earthquake. They had, despite their 'control,' declared martial law in all of Denver North, and the Public Information booths that had been restored repeated the message that anyone caught outside after dark would be shot on sight.

The area around the Rangely seemed to have been, for all intents and purposes, forgotten. Of the entire area, only Chris and Charlie seemed to remain. Leaflets had been dropped from a cruiser a week after the quake, floating down through the sky, an autumn foliage of corporate advertising. They advised everyone in the area to move to the Corporate Zone, where power had been restored.

The leaflets also said that "reimbursement fees" would be halved in light of the tragedy and the costs associated with rebuilding. Chris smirked at that one. It did not look like it had been tragic for the D.A.B., which now towered, unbroken, at the end of Cherry Lane.

Night had fallen and Chris swilled whiskey from their shared bottle, watching the full moon as it set over the mostly-dark Corporate Zone. He thought about nothing, watching the moon, letting his mind wander while his belly burned, when the moon seemed closer somehow, though it was no larger, and the ambient noises of the night faded into silence.

He stood, dropping down from his perch on a massive air-conditioning unit which had fallen from its housing, and walked toward the D.A.B., looking up. Near the peak of the chrome spire he saw two tiny, red lights: the taillights of a PolCorp Cruiser frozen, hovering in the air.

A strange pressure pushed at the base of his skull. Chris realized he wasn't breathing and almost lost hold of the moment before he could calm himself down. *Your body doesn't need to breathe if time doesn't pass,* he thought. And he had it.

It's like breathing. It happens, but you can control it. He concentrated on the sensation of pressure he felt: right where his spine ran into his brain. The cerebral cortex. He tried relaxing it, not by thinking about it, but *doing* it, like exhaling. The little red lights began to move, slowly at first, then faster. He flexed it, and it once again drifted to a stop. He flexed it more, and it began to float backward.

Chris felt nausea more intense than he thought possible. *Bad idea,* he thought, and relaxed the pressure again, until the PolCorp Cruiser once again froze.

Chris took several minutes to recover. *Why does backwards do that?* he wondered. He tried it again, and once again, vertigo nearly incapacitated him. He fell on his knees and vomited. With the back of his arm, he wiped his mouth clean, clamping his stomach muscles down to keep from doing it again.

As he looked up, the spell broke. Sound roared back to life, and the speck of the cruiser streaked around the D.A.B. and didn't come out on the other side. He got to his feet and wiped his mouth once more before going back to the ruins of the hotel. On the way, he took another swig from the bottle to try to get the foul taste out of his mouth. It worked well as he enjoyed the feeling of warmth spreading through his body from the rough whiskey.

Missing something, Chris prodded at the place where it should have been. He was supposed to travel in time, not manipulate it. Still, it was a start. He had to make sure he could do it again. He walked into the lobby and let his mind drift to emptiness. Then he *willed* time to stop, not with any thought, but by reflex, by relaxing and letting his will do its work.

Chris heard the sound of silence and felt the thickening of the air. He tried to pick up a tattered couch, not with strength, but simply *knowing* he could do it if he tried. It moved easily, although it looked to weigh at least 100 pounds.

He flexed again, this time harder than he had tried before, attempting to find the boundaries of strain on his body. Everything was the same but somehow creased. Everything had edges that traced every contour. Edges that could only be seen out of the corner of his vision, but they did not make up everything, as Chris first guessed, they *created* everything, constantly in every moment. And once that moment of creation occurred, the universe reciprocated by allowing those edges to exist. The gift delicately balanced both ways. And as soon as Chris felt the edges, and knew this, not as knowledge but as wordless understanding, he passed through the tesseract's edges to the other side.

All of reality spread before Chris in a motionless void of nothingness, the void of everything as well. *I can find out who I am now,* he thought, but it was a distant thing, a message from an unknown sender. The thought had no meaning and he lost interest in it almost as soon as it had crossed his consciousness.

His mind reeled from the sensation. Omniscience, bestowed on a finite mind, and Chris could not discern his thoughts from the memories of time itself; he could not keep the thought of *self*. Trying to push the infinite into a finite mind, stretched the mind, forcing it to grow and to shrink, attempting self-preservation. He drifted and felt a tug, an umbilical cord attached to *his* present, stopping him from drifting too far in this strange sea.

He traced his cord through the infinite sphere until he found the anchor point: a mass of flesh and matter. The word "man" entered into its thoughts. *I am a man.* Existence was both within and outside the Time Sphere. There was a boundary it could sense between "he" and "himself," and he wondered if he had found the edge of time, but discarded the idea. This was something else, a veil that allowed the substance of time to ooze through to the other side.

A bad description, but one that the Self could understand in some fashion. It did not allow enough of that substance through to create or destroy, which, he realized, was the dual purpose of time, but only enough to progress.

He studied the veil and became aware that it was indeed porous. In fact, tiny holes filled the whole of the Time Sphere and allowed the raw substance of time to seep into the universe, and as importantly allowed the universe to shape time. With this understanding came awareness that on this side of time, he was without body, and, therefore, the size and shape of the pores did not in the least bit matter.

With that, he moved toward himself, and reached through the veil and into the frozen figure on the other side.

He felt more than himself as he once again regained his sentience. Suspended on the other side, his body remained while his consciousness sought in all directions, finding other places, other moments that Chris could feel through the pores. Further out, the strings of moments became blurry, reflecting off of themselves like the reflections viewed standing between two mirrors and as Chris stretched his perception even further, they became crowded and faded; the things they contained were only half-reality.

The future, he thought. *The future is always changing.* Then: *No, not the future. Maybe it is the past. Maybe something else entirely. What was I supposed to be doing?* He felt his thoughts drift again, and once again he clung to the one word he could. The one that had brought him back from this place once before: *Me. Me. Me. Me.*

Chris lurched forward, rocking on his feet, sucking in air as if he had been trapped under water. He stood in the ruined lobby of the Rangely. It was still night. *Oh my god,* Chris thought, collapsing on the old couch that he had moved during the time freeze. *That was it. That's how I'll go back.* He didn't like the idea of going back to that place, though. It was too hard to think there. *No, not think. It was hard to* exist *there. It was … it was the Cinvat Bridge.*

So they were right. He was right. He was master of the Cinvat Bridge, the path leading to all places. *How did they know about that place? How did they know about me?* Chris thought of the ancient peoples of Iran, four thousand years ago in a distant past. *I can go back and find out.*

But not yet. He still needed to do something else first.

Chris went into the Corporate Zone to get some new clothes. He had been wearing Charlie's funky sweatpants for way too long. He went outside, and with barely a thought, halted the passage of time.

He jogged at first, and then ran full tilt toward the seedy mall he had passed when Rat had guided him to the Rangely. *I can't get tired—can't get out of breath when you don't need to breathe.* The thought made him giddy, and he ran even faster, now and then mischievously relaxing his grip on the passage of time, to let people catch a glimpse of him streaking past, although the only people out were emergency workers and the ever-present PolCorp goons, whom Chris delighted in tormenting by appearing, for the briefest of moments.

The boutiques were closed, as was everything after dark, even the twenty-four hour gun stores, though lights in a few could be seen peeping out from behind the heavy grates. Chris walked to one of the fashion stores and tore the wire mesh gate from its hinges and smashed through the door.

He made a selection, a suit similar to his old one, but better fitting, and a new set of clothes for Charlie, then hung Charlie's sweat clothes on the rack in their place, and walked out again. He considered getting a better gun, but discarded the idea. He barely had use for the one he had at this point.

When he got back to the Rangely, under a minute had passed.

1997: Garret's Demise

Garret wiped sweat from his brow as he placed the explosive charge with shaking hands. He found that he had a whole new level of respect for his wife. Not well suited to this kind of hard work, he strained to concentrate. Besides the sweat that wouldn't stop pouring from his brow, his hands shook, and no matter what he tried, he couldn't seem to calm himself to the extent he needed to.

Taking a deep breath, he did his best and connected the wire to make the charge live. He released the breath and wiped his palms on his pants, trying to dry them off.

This made four out of the five charges placed and so far he had managed, if barely, not to blow himself up. Yet. He stood up and walked to the outer hall of the building, moving towards his next target point. About halfway down the building, he paused to look out the window. In the lot below, he could see his wife locked in combat with someone.

Both were moving far too fast for him to make out the details of the combat with any type of clarity, but it was obvious from his vantage that Wanda was in the stronger position, pushing her victory home. The man she fought moved slower than her and appeared to be injured already.

Smiling to himself, he continued moving. Seeing Wanda, remembering the touch of her body on his the previous night, gave him a measure of the calm he had been hunting for. Finding peace after ten years of pain was a powerful gift, and it was a gift that he would have to thank Alexander Zarth for when next he saw him. After a night of sleep with his long lost wife, with time to let his subconscious process everything, he had come to realize that Zarth was the one who had cheated fate.

The man had stolen time itself to keep his wife alive; dodging the paradox he should have created by doing so. Alex had managed to shatter James's illusion that the twenty-seventh century rogue was the architect of his pain and replace that indictment with one of a man who had saved the love of his life. He owed him a large thank you.

With resettled resolve and calm nerves, Garret moved through the building to the top floor. Lucy's office was his final target. Scattered across her desk were various papers: signature forms and project notes. Garret's HUD made reading in the dark easy. By shifting the light differentials on his point of focus, he could make the target of his focus visible for him.

He chuckled to himself as he remembered the fight with Wanda that had caused him to invent that particular feature on the HUD units they had. A simple enough fight, which had started because his reading lamp had been too bright and kept her awake. And now it provided functionality far beyond its original intent, as so many things did.

As Garret leafed through the project notes he realized that the project notepapers in front of him shared that trait with their HUD units. Doctor Nost had been working on a faster-than-light space drive. Something that could theoretically not be done. Yet he had persisted in his research and managed to convince others that it could be. James knew he would have liked knowing this man, if only he had been given the chance outside the disguises he had been forced to don in his presence.

Garret continued to leaf through the notes. What a joke it was to worry about neutrinos in the direction Lucy had been convincing him to shift to according to these notes. Shifting phase space to move through an alternate set of directions, as Nost proposed, would make any worry about spatial debris non-existent. Yet somehow Lucy had managed to convince him that it was a factor. Probably because his infatuation with her blinded his keen scientific mind.

Reading through the notes, it became obvious that Dr. Nost had harbored some very unprofessional feelings for his boss, a fact which made the man less legend and more human in Garret's eyes. A fact he could well appreciate considering his own history of invention driven by separation from his love. Garret placed the papers back onto the desk and refocused on the job he had been given.

In the corner of the office was a support beam for the building, his target. Crouching down in front of the beam, he unrolled the velvet toolkit and pulled out the various tools he needed to finish the job. *One last explosive to place.* Considering how nerve wracking the last four explosives had been to place, this final piece went up simply and easily. He set the charge, activated the detonator, and rolled his tools back up.

No sweat this time. No shaking hands. Scanning the room to make sure he had left nothing behind, he walked out of the office and almost blundered straight into someone else coming through the hallway. Luckily for him, he heard the person before the other person saw him. Moving into accelerated time he dodged into a cubicle in the main office area, and then reverted back to standard time so that he could breathe.

Crouching in the shadows below a desk, he managed to get a good look at the other man's face without being seen himself. Much to his shock, he knew that face. Yuri Yakavich, one of the agency's premiere intelligence officers.

From what he knew of the Corp, an intelligence officer would not have a solid knowledge of field operations, which meant that there was a good chance that Garret would remain undiscovered. He managed to keep his breathing even, and avoided being detected.

Yuri walked straight into Lucy's office, passing less than two feet from Garret's hiding spot, and closed the door behind him. Garret frowned, torn. Should he go in and try to stop him? Or should he wait the other man out? Leaving was now effectively removed as an option, because Garret had to outwait him to make sure he had not tampered with the charge. He decided that waiting would be the best course of action.

Even though Yuri was a trained agent, Garret knew that his acceleration of time would make it so that the other man never even knew he was coming, an unbeatable weapon in some sense, but some gut instinct made Garret wait regardless.

Garret did not wait terribly long, though it seemed an eternity to his tense muscles. Yuri only remained in the office for about twenty minutes, and when he walked back out, he moved past Garret's hiding place, never giving any indication that he realized the doctor was present.

Once the man had left, and he heard the hall door click closed, Garret walked back into the office to check the charge he had left. It remained untouched. All of the paperwork that had been on the desk had been taken. In its place were the sides and chassis of her computer, spread across her desk. Wires hung wantonly from the forlorn looking computer case, and Lucy's hard drive had been taken from the casing.

Garret looked thoughtfully at the scene for a moment, trying to puzzle out why Yuri would break in and sabotage one of his own agent's missions. He shook his head in confusion and backed out of the office, baffled by intrigue beyond his scope of understanding. He would have to report it to Wanda and Zarth and see what conclusions they drew from it. But that was for later. For now, his mission was done and he needed to leave the building.

Working his way down the dark corridors of the building, he spot-checked each of the charges that he had left behind. The remaining four had also been left alone. Good. He felt the relief of a tension that he hadn't realized had been there, building behind his conscious mind. All was complete and he could leave.

Being careful not to trip any of the alarms, he worked his way down to the ground floor of the building. It made him feel younger again, being in this situation. Like when he had been a little boy, playing at secret agents with his friends. And then he reached the building's glass front doors. Through the glass he could see Wanda lying dead on the ground beneath a lamppost.

For a moment, when he first saw her lying there, time froze. Then something in him simply broke. His soul splintered. All thought ceased. He slammed through the locked front doors, shattering the glass as he went through. Desperately, he ran to her, all thoughts of consequences gone from his mind.

Behind him, the building's alarms silently screamed into life.

Signals shot through circuits, racing down optical cables, covering several miles of wire in the span of a single heartbeat, and completed their journey at the police station alert system.

Much later, by the standards of James Garret, the police arrived to find a secure building with a broken glass door. They tried to contact the building's director, but for some reason she was not responding to the emergency contact routines that were in place for just such a situation. The sergeant in charge of the scene just shook his head, fully expecting the woman to lose her job the following day.

The same sergeant was just wrapping up his shift later that morning when the call came. Yuri Yakavich, after much internal struggle, called the police anonymously and alerted them that there was a bomb in the building.

He had known about Garret being there, but hadn't known his purpose, which had been part of his motivation in going into the office the previous night. A difficult internal struggle, but ultimately the decision was made for him.

What he had spotted in Lucy's office was technology that did not yet exist. The bomb would have been easy enough for him to diffuse, had he been willing to travel forward to his time to grab the specs on them.

As it was, since someone else was playing dirty, and forward travel was not something he could do without getting caught, he simply alerted the police and hoped that would be enough to counter the explosives left. Later that morning, the sergeant died and Lucy's life was saved, along with Christopher Nost's. No trace of the information Yuri had stolen was ever detected missing.

Time: 1997 *Location:* Denver **Operation: Recovery**

Wit, Agent Holly reflected, did not come easily to him. He knew that he was intelligent. He knew that he was a good agent. He also knew that patience with his own thoughts was his key virtue, that and the fact that he was stubborn as hell. He would find his way through even the most complex of situations, guided by sheer tenacity as those around him were guided by their brains. But he needed enough time to find his way to those conclusions. When he acted rashly, too quickly, without thinking through the consequences of everything that he did, he created messes.

This recent disgrace, dealing with Agent Yakavich, only stressed and reinforced that fact for him. Bringing back a dead agent, whom he had thought was a rogue, had been leaping too fast. But he paid a price for that. And as he pushed his way through the materials Yuri had compiled, he came to understand that acting rashly was a much greater weakness than he had hitherto realized.

The first fact that he managed to piece together from the file was who it had been compiled for, which meant that he had killed, in an act of brash stupidity, not only the current senior intelligence officer, but also the most skilled and decorated field agent in the Corp. He shuddered as the impact of what he had done hit home.

He took a deep breath and then delved back into the files that Agent Yakavich had compiled. His eyes scanned while his mind worked its way towards greater truths. He hunted for the key to this cryptic puzzle. Trying to find what had prompted Director Arbu to take over this mission and go missing himself, back in the era Holly had recently come from. And above all, why the same man that had told him he would gladly have him shot had then proceeded to release him under orders to study up on this file.

A lot of the information spread across his lap and bed confused him. Much of it seemed to contradict itself. Holly at least understood that in the dual nature of his work contradiction served as a standard. But these files … a lot of them were news articles, with duplicate events occurring on different dates.

The whole thing seemed to be a mess. Holly knew it couldn't be divergent time streams, because that was mathematically impossible.

Which meant another spook was altering things. He could draw no other conclusion from this. The game of espionage often provided contradictory information that an agent would have to sort through, separating fact from fiction. To take it a step further, a step needed to decipher what Yuri had put together, a Time Corp agent also had to then be wary for contradicting evidence that clued one in to the beginnings of a paradox.

Holly continued to read and understanding filtered through his thoughts that this was not a paradox he had contributed to. This was a problem way beyond the scope of anything he had ever seen. Maybe even the mother of all paradox.

As the light dawned on him, he found himself wishing Arbu had never sent him back to interfere. Add in what he had pieced together about a second intelligence force acting on this situation and the results were colossally bad. Finally having achieved that basic understanding, as well as the staggering implications of it, he started to assemble a picture of how the paradox worked.

It was not easy. Holly was also beginning to suspect that there were several pieces of this file missing. Not that Yuri or someone else had removed them. Rather, that there were pieces of this puzzle before him that were too big to fit into a simple dossier, and that he had no real chance at understanding those things. This too, was something that Holly was accustomed to.

People of power generally saw things on a much larger scale than him. It didn't bother him. Normally, he acted out his small piece of the picture, happy to make a difference in a war to save history. A war he truly believed in. Lost in such thoughts, a slight electrical buzz jolted him.

He sprang up in a panic, sending the papers that had been in his lap flying to the ground at his feet. The all-agent emergency call had triggered. This had never happened before, all active field agents getting called to an emergency situation. He felt the pull on his nano system even now.

It pulled him towards the cusp of the twenty-first century, the same place Holly had been, also the same place to which Director Arbu had now vanished. Holly readied his field gear, then pushed himself backwards in history to answer the summons of the silent call all Time Corp agents had received.

A more cautious man would have thought very carefully about the scope of recent events before responding to that call. A more cautious man might have done some research about the possible motivations of that call. Many of the agents who did answer the emergency call were more cautious people but, lacking Holly's perspective, and Yuri's file, did not have the information they needed to be suspicious of the all-agent alert.

Twice in as many weeks of his subjective time, Holly had acted rashly, this time jumping back to assist his director. The second time was no different from the first, in that it would exact blood as a consequence.

Across the time stream, from as far back as the eleventh century to as far forward as the twenty-ninth century, agents responded to the call. People excused themselves from conversations, left important high profile paradoxes hanging, and in a few cases simply vanished, all moving immediately in their subjective time to respond to the distress signal.

Several such cases were not only observed, but also recorded. Local urban legends were born about spontaneous combustion and U.F.O. abductions, living through the years in their infamy.

All told, twenty-three people responded to that signal. Those twenty-three represented not only the best and brightest of the elite Corps which policed the time stream, but in fact all of them. All twenty-three of them, the entire agency's living set of agents, within a minute and a half of answering that call, would be dead.

4016 A.D.: No man's land, between the great western city-states

Alex reached forward, lightning fast, and grabbed the other man by the throat. With a quick twist of his hips, he slammed him into the wall and held him pinned there by his neck.

"So, mystery man. Who the hell are you? Really. All of this traveling around for you, acting on bad information to try to fix history, what the hell is your game?"

The man struggled, trying to hop out of the hold by jumping through time. He realized quickly that Alex had him blocked from his ability to travel. The lack of oxygen in his system made his vision go blurry. He slumped in defeat and managed to whisper to Alex, "Air ... please. I'll ... explain."

The iron grip around his throat loosened enough to allow air through his windpipe, and no more. Struggling would be useless. Alex obviously overmatched him. Pinned to a wall, and fighting against the dizziness the impact of his head on said wall had created, he struggled to be straightforward and concise with his assailant.

"I am a man, much like you, and Stefan Arbu. I received instructions from the god when I visited the holy temple seven thousand years ago."

Alex scanned the man's eyes for the truth, if it could be found there, and decided that he was satisfied with what he saw. "Your instructions were not complete then. I have had to undo some of your mistakes. You left a long trail of fuck-ups behind you, friend. A long trail."

The man tried to shake his head, to deny the harsh accusations, but the hand gripped around his throat didn't allow the movement. "No. That's not it. I am not you, or Stefan Arbu. Not ... chosen like you two were."

He seemed almost bitter. "I failed in my own right. My skill was not equal to the tasks that I was given. I went back, but the god would not speak to me again. I had to find a way to repair my mistakes. To fix what the god had laid as my tasks. And I am not a priest. I'm a man who was looking for redemption."

Alex thought about this for a moment, still meeting the other man's eyes with his own steely gaze. He watched the other man's soul through his eyes, learning from what he saw there. "I believe you. But you did it the wrong way. You came to me, hoping by trickery to convince me to undo your mistakes. All the while knowing who and what I was. In a way, that's worse for you by my accounting, friend. Much worse."

The man got a look of pleading in his eyes. "Not trickery. Just doing what I must to unfold my portion of events."

Alex nodded, dismissing the other man's words and snarled, "You lied to me. You attempted deception and you manipulated me. That is trickery. That is fucked up and not a way to deal with me. Did you ever even consider simple honesty?"

The man broke eye contact with Alex, looking down. Alex's words had hit home. Finally, he looked back up and met Alex's eyes.

"No. I did not. I did not think you would help with my failings."

At that moment, a fit of coughing seized Alex. He felt his lungs seize up, as warmth and a sticky wetness welled up through his throat. His hand unclenched as the coughing fit hit and he dropped the man from his choke hold on the wall, falling to his hands and knees, the blood from his lungs flowing up through his mouth and splattering on the ground below him.

The man crouched beside him, holding his shoulder and trying to help keep him in a position from which he could keep his throat clear of the blood. Finally, Alex's body settled back down, he regained some measure of control over his tattered muscles, and his vision swam back into focus.

"Are you recovered, Lord Zarth?" the man asked, genuine concern in his voice. He helped the unsteady Alex rise back to his feet, providing support below his arm to help him stand.

"Well enough," Alex grunted, eyeing the man again. This moment of help could not be allowed to outweigh the transgressions of the past. "You understand what has happened to me?"

The man shook his head, "I do not understand it. I know that you were hale when I last approached you. And I know that you should not be here in this time. I would assume you are here as a gift from the god. But I do not know. Other than those two things which I know, and the one I suspect, I do not understand the sickness that you are suffering from."

Alex fought internally for a moment and then he reached his decision with a sigh. "I implanted my DNA in you back in the bar. That's how I am here. No gift from the god. You should know, the god does not contain power beyond the scope of knowledge. Stefan and I are able to do what we do because of hard work. As to the sickness, the problem I've encountered is that when I left this era the first time I came here, my body started rapidly aging, trying to catch up to the lost frame of subjective time which I skipped with this little trick."

The man blanched. "You broke the laws as we know them and now you are dying. I think I begin to understand. It was a consequence of what you did in breaking the laws. My deception caused this to unfold. If I had been honest with you, you would not have sought me out here in my era."

Alex nodded, "Got it in one. And the gold star goes to you. You said I would die on this mission. You were right. You failed to grasp that your course of actions ultimately signed my death warrant. But no hard feelings. I'm not regretting having come forward to this time. And I'm definitely not regretting that you came to me. Your screw ups unlocked a few important things for me."

The man watched Alex, seemingly surprised by the lack of punishment. "Then there must be another price. Something, which I did, in my failures, for which I must pay."

Alex scratched his bruised chin, "Half right this time."

The two men stood and watched each other. It was obvious that Alex was waiting for the other to piece together the puzzle on his own. It was a trait that he shared with Stefan Arbu. The chill, morgue-like air of the underground complex blew past them and sterile lights shone off of the burnished steel walls.

Alex raised an eyebrow as he waited for the other man to come to his realization. In all honesty, he also rebuilt his energy for the fight he knew must be coming. The latest coughing fit had left him weakened and his breath rattled in his chest.

Finally, the other man sucked in a breath from between clenched teeth. "My death. You require my death, back then. Don't you?"

Alex nodded, "Yes. Though it is not me, per se. It is history that requires it. By involving yourself in the precise paradox point you have effectively killed yourself. Had you followed the orders you were given, and not gone to the point of the paradox's origin to observe, you would not be here now."

The man's shoulders slumped. "How was I to know? The god did not tell me that. I was told to make sure certain events in two thousand and one, as well as others in the twenty forties, occurred. When I messed them up I had to travel back to the paradox to better understand what I had done wrong."

"NO!" Alex's voice came out as thunder. "You did not have to. You chose to and you have killed a lot of people with your incompetence. By pushing that sergeant forward to intercept the shard of glass that would have killed Lucille Frost, you wreaked major damage to the time stream. Trying to fix the mistake you made by saving her damn near destroyed history."

The man blinked and looked up again to Alex's eyes. His brow wrinkled in confusion. "How did you know that I did that?"

Alex grinned. "Think it through. I stole your computer. While we have been talking, I had my internal friend hack your systems and upload all of your information to me, Josh. Joshua of the no man's land. Born in thirty-nine eighty-eight and survivor of the wars which destroyed most of humanity at the turn of your millennium. Currently aged almost fifteen hundred years through a trick even I might not have thought of. You are a clever man, but clever only takes you so far against cunning, Josh. I know what you have done and now it is time to pay the price for the mistakes you have made. The consequences of your actions await."

A look of fear came over the man and he turned to sprint away. Alex reached forward, grabbing the back of the man's shirt collar. With a quick jerk of his wrist, Alex pulled Joshua back.

Joshua's feet slipped out from under him and he slammed into the ground, knocking all the breath from him. Simultaneously, Alex focused his will and pulled both of them back in time to redress the mistakes the man had made. The last words he uttered, as the other flew through the air, about to impact the ground, were: "Let's go pay the piper, friend."

RELATIVITY SYNCHRONIZATION:

LUCKY THIRTEEN, EVERYTHING GOES WRONG

Time Sphere: The Paradox Within

Chris tried practice runs first, jumping through time twice before he tried to tackle going back to his trial. Once a few days into the future, and once a few days into the past.

He could barely control his thoughts enough while in the Time Sphere to get anywhere at all. He had begun to think of the present as the center, with pasts and futures looping in.

The further he needed to loop from the center, the more confused and disjointed his thoughts. He knew he wasn't supposed to think about time in those terms, but it became almost impossible not to as one of the few things he had to cling to, in order to find his way to the right moment in time. Concentrating on the Self, he had found, would only get him back to the same moment he started at.

His willpower clicked into place and worked for him. Think of the now he wished to be in and will it to be now. He needed no anchor.

Chris found Charlie clearing out debris from the back of the Rangely. Charlie waved at him from the mound of beams and rubble he stood on. "We're going to need to get a Haul-Cruiser to get some of this shit out of here. Then I figure I can rebuild the back wall here—" he gestured toward the gaping hole where the building had collapsed "—and have me a half-sized hotel. No half rates though!" He grinned crookedly.

"I'm checking out, Charlie," Chris called from the top floor at the edge of the drop-off.

"Whoa! Hold on, buddy, I'm coming over!" Charlie clambered his bulk down from the rubble heap and onto the ground floor. Chris trotted down the stairs and met him in the lobby.

"So you're leaving?" Charlie seemed disappointed.

"Yeah. I figure it's time to move on."

"You got somewhere to go?"

"Something like that, yeah. Here," Chris handed Charlie the wad of money he still had left from what Jameson had given him. "I know it won't be nearly enough to rebuild the hotel, but there should be about $200,000 there. It's enough to get started."

Charlie took the money, mouth agape, and then handed it back to Chris. "I can't take this man. This is all you got, ain't it?"

Chris smiled, "You're a good man, Charlie. Yeah, it is all I've got, but trust me; I don't need it where I'm going. I think that where I'm going I'll have plenty of other resources for what I need. Please, take it. Thanks for the hospitality. And thank you for the friendship."

Charlie took the money again and reluctantly put it in his pocket, though he smiled from ear to ear. "Hey, Nost, thanks. Come back anytime."

Chris laughed. "I might just do that."

He walked toward the D.A.B. until Charlie went back inside, then he turned, walking down an alley and entered Time.

Chris reached for the edges of reality and *folded* ...

A man stands before him, turned towards a battle in the street, about to die. There is no escape route. Chris reaches forward to grab him and is surprised to see another beat him to the rescue. So, his suspicions were correct and there another helped him.

Fold ...

Chris drops onto a rooftop, above the battle in the street below. His life is saved by the other's actions. The man turns and sees him standing in shadow; he files the scene in his mind and moves to his next task.

Fold ...

Windows shatter and buildings start to crack. Chris pushes a man to the ground as a shard of glass flies through where his neck would have been. Improbably, the man is now curled into a ball on the ground, lying in the one safe place for him to be during the earthquake.

Fold ...

Music, all instrumental, is playing on muted speakers. A woman is speaking to a man. She is holding a hand outstretched to him. He hands over a set of files.

Freeze …

Chris pulls his gun out to shoot her. His hand is shaking, but he knows she must die. As he pulls the trigger, there is a brief ripple on the edges of reality and he sees another man standing in a parking lot that is somehow superimposed over the reality he is in. Simultaneously, Chris and this other pull their triggers. She falls to the ground, dead, as time skips back into motion and the scene in the parking lot fades.

Fold …

A crowd. Bright sun gleaming on polished marble stairs. *Here … here … here … Forgetting. I'm forgetting something … Who am I … No, something else. Shoot myself as I leave. Complete the cycle.*

Chris stepped out of the Time Sphere into an alcove at the courthouse. He felt the bulk of the old gun under his coat. *Trust instinct. I … must … I must not miss. If I die here, the cycle completes. The tragedies of the future were* my *instabilities. I can stop this, now.*

"Here he comes!" Someone shouted from the crowd and the mob pushed closer to the line of police that blocked their way from the bottom stair.

Police, not PolCorp, Chris thought. He pushed his way to the middle of the mob to get a better view. *Oh my God,* Chris thought as the realization that he was about to shoot at a past incarnation of himself filtered through his confused thoughts. It happened when the first bailiff came through the door. He gripped his gun tighter, but he almost dropped it when he saw Jameson walk out. He wore a suit and had a different haircut, but Chris could recognize that hard face even from where he stood as the frigid eyes scanned the crowd.

What is he doing here? Chris thought as he ducked down and pushed his way closer, behind a news woman wearing a bright red pantsuit, craning her microphone to catch the words of a sad-looking older man, standing now at the top of the stairs, saying something about condolences. There was no sign of Jameson, but Chris wasn't looking for him anymore. He stared at himself, looking frightened, standing on the edge of the stairs, surrounded by guards.

Now! Chris pulled the gun from his coat and leveled it at his old self. Someone behind him yelled something. The line of cops unholstered their guns. Chris pulled the trigger, as his old self buckled, and tumbled down the stairs. Chris couldn't help but wince as his old self's face split apart where the slug hit it.

"Murderer! Murderer!" A familiar woman's voice shouted from the throng.

Wait ... Chris thought suddenly. *Mary??*

The Police had their guns trained on him and he prepared to flex time to a standstill when he remembered something. *I missed,* he thought. *Somehow I dodged that bullet. How could I have done that? Why didn't I this time?*

Chris never heard the snap of the solitary gunshot coming from the building across the street; the folds disoriented him. Something hit him hard between the shoulders, slamming him forward. Reality seemed to superimpose itself again, but he couldn't focus.

Too much pain, sound, and confusion overwhelmed him. He fell to his knees. The world spun around him and everything went black by the time he hit the ground.

Officer John Berkowitz had only ever wanted to write some speeding tickets and maybe escort a few prisoners to cells. Today was not what he had signed up to the force for. Looking back at his sergeant he said "Sergeant Connelly, the gunman is dead, but I think you'd better take a look at this ..."

Freeze ...

1997: Garret's Last Stand

Garret sprinted across the parking lot to reach his fallen wife's body. Her neck was twisted at a very wrong angle. He reached her body and fell to his knees, weeping. "Oh god … Wanda. How could this have happened to you?

"Why was I given you for one night, only to have you taken away from me again?" His head slumped forward as his body racked with sobs. He picked up her limp body, cradling her in his arms like a child. Her head lolled in the crook of his arm, resting there almost like her neck was still intact.

Somewhere behind the sorrow, steel formed. Like the anger, it burned white hot for these last ten years, quenched in the tears of his sorrow—tears he had never allowed himself before. And a blade emerged, though Garret did not yet understand this about himself.

Nearby, he felt two presences shift into local time. He heard a loud thump, like a body hitting the ground, then a painful exhalation of breath. Without looking back, he said, "Hello, Zarth. Was this what you had in mind for tonight?"

Alex grunted and Garret heard two people tussling behind him. "Be with you in a second, Doctor Garret. I have to keep this joker immobilized."

James Garret nodded to himself and placed his wife back on the ground. As he did so, he was careful to support her broken neck, keeping her in a semblance of dignity. He draped her arms across her chest and then closed her eyes. With a feeling of true finality, he leaned over her and kissed her brow, tasting the salt of his own tears on her skin as he did so. Closing his eyes, Garret stood to face Alex.

Alex held a man down. He twisted the prone man's arm up behind his back and leaned on the center of the man's back using his weight to keep him pinned. Garret took all this in and he felt something emerge within himself.

It felt like a sword had been sheathed in his soul, and it came out, ready for him to use as a weapon. Anger left him, replaced now by something much colder. His eyes narrowed and focused on the man pinned to the ground.

Looking at Alex, it was obvious that he had been through a tough fight of his own. Bruises blossomed across his skin, even worse than before and bloodstains covered the front of his shirt.

"I see," he said.

Rather than springing forward to attack the man he assumed had killed his wife, Garret paused. Having looked at what was before him, he thought and opened his mind's eye. For the first time in his life, Garret understood the truths his eyes could not see.

He took a deep breath, looked Alex in the eyes, and said, "I understand." And the blade in his soul came free, ready for him to use. Accelerating into stretched time, he moved forward, everything around him frozen.

In one motion, he backhanded Alex off the prone man, then picked up the man's head and slammed it forward into the ground. When Garret released the man, blood pooled below his forehead. He stood and turned towards Alex.

Zarth moved in accelerated time, but Garret had an edge he'd never before had, and to him it looked as though Alex moved at about one third of Garret's own speed. He walked up to Alex, grabbed the back of his hair, and punched him in the stomach. Then he leaned close to Alex's ear and slowed his own speed to match Alex's.

"Why, you son of a bitch? Why did you make this happen? I understand what happened, but not the why of it. And I'll have you tell me that before I end your life." He knotted his fingers in Alex's hair, yanking his head back, controlling his body with that fist.

Blood dripped from Alex's mouth and against all probability he laughed. "You're asking the wrong question, Garret. Surely you can understand what is happening if you've figured out so much. Think it through, man."

Garret accelerated his time to hit Alex in the stomach again. On impact, Alex coughed up more blood. "Alex, I am being patient. I can make this painful for you, but I'd rather not. You said you don't kill unless you have to and I believe you. Still, answer me now. Why did you arrange for her death?"

Alex's body shuddered as he fought to bring it back into control. "It's about Nost. It had to happen to unlock Nost's paradox. I chose to save her for a day though, against my own code. A gift for the both of you. One day of stolen time. What I undid had to be redone and that was not my choice. I am sorry."

Garret released Alex and phased into accelerated time as the man started to fall forward. He stared at the figure suspended before him in the air and then kicked him in the stomach as hard as he could.

Phasing back into standard time, he watched with grim satisfaction as Alex went flying, sailing an easy twenty feet across the parking lot, and landing with a loud cracking sound, rolled to a stop. Garret walked towards him, watching the other man as a coughing fit racked him, ending with blood spattered on the ground in front of him.

Alex looked up and smiled. Speaking between his heavy gasps for air he said, "You ... have to tell ... me who your personal trainer is. Their strength building ... techniques ... are phenomenal."

Garret saw red and reaccelerated his time stream, charging forward to plant another kick in Alex's ribs. Alex's time travel abilities caught up with Garret's own and he managed to partially block the kick, this time only landing about ten feet away. Garret realized he was being goaded and resynchronized their time streams to talk to Alex again.

"Why are you taunting me? You are only making this more painful for yourself."

Alex spat a gob of red to the ground and managed to get to his knees. "Because I'm selfish. I know I'm about to die, but I want more life. So I taunt you to give me pain and resolve and a few more precious seconds of life."

Garret's eyes thinned to reptilian slits. "You should not have told me that." Again he pushed forward, fast, and charged Alex. This time however the other man was ready, deflecting the powerhouse of a punch that Garret aimed at his face and scything out to kick his feet out from under him.

Garret had never been trained for combat, but some self-preservation instinct saved him in that moment, and he danced back instead of following through with his punch.

He watched Alex stand. The other man was in a lot of pain, but he would still not be an easy opponent to defeat.

Garret pushed to the absolute maximum energy expenditure he could, moving far faster than Alex was capable of in his damaged state and started running in blurred circles around Alex. Picking up rocks and other parking lot debris, he threw them at random intervals at his enemy, resorting to his old tactics.

Garret couldn't believe how fast Alex moved, with how badly injured he was. But somehow he kept up, barely avoiding the hurled missiles. If even one had scored a hit, it would have marked the end of the fight. Each missile moved through Zarth's subjective time at around three hundred miles an hour. But somehow the man was never where the missiles would have struck him.

Garret watched as Zarth moved. He had no real explanation for the pattern of movement other than incredible foresight, sensing of the patterns of combat, born from experience. And then Garret's energy flagged. Zarth had to be hurting even more than he was, so he risked slowing into standard time to catch his breath. Both men stopped, leaning on their knees and gasping. Sweat poured from their brows.

Alex looked up and between gasps managed, "You've got a fire in you. I'm impressed. I never would have guessed you capable of this level of energy expenditure Doctor Garret."

Garret tried to laugh at that but gasped too hard. "You have no idea what I'm capable of, Zarth. Nor will you, because I won't have to use it to finish killing you."

Alex looked at the other man. "No, I don't suspect you will have to, though I know that was only a taunt. Grant me a moment, please. There is something you need to hear before we resume. In case, or rather, when I do lose."

Garret nodded. "Go ahead, though I doubt it will impact my decisions here and now."

Alex spread his hands out, palms up, and shrugged, "Even so. It is simple, though. Yes, I manipulated events in order to cause your wife to die. But, and this is a large but, Christopher Nost, in both his incarnations MUST survive what is to come. He is the key to all of this."

Garret blinked. "I think, somewhere in me, that I knew that. This is all you had to say to me?"

Alex nodded. "No. One last thing. Schrodinger and Homes. It is all about them. Time travelers do twenty impossible things before breakfast, and the least improbable is generally the one that actually happens. I've known that since before all this started, and you need to remember it. I'm an old man now, out of energy. So, please, let's end this."

Garret nodded again and sped back into plus time.

He felt the crash against his system, as the effort pulled on his energy reserves. And then something Alex had said penetrated his brain. Inwardly, he laughed.

Deviousness as a weapon was one of the strongest in Alex's arsenal, but Garret knew that sheer lack of knowledge was why his opponent had given him the key. He reached into his pocket and pulled out a small case. It had held several specialized pills he had made to boost his energy levels while breaking into the Time Corp headquarters. It seemed like years ago that he had done that.

Praying, he popped open the case. A single pill rested inside it, gleaming blood red in the shadowy fast light. Pulling it out, he popped it in his mouth and crunched down on it. Moving around the lot, being careful to stay out of Zarth's direct line of slower sight, he only had to wait a moment before he felt the pill hit his system. An ice-cold shock ran through his veins. His breathing slowed, his heart rate stabilized, and he felt *strong*.

Smiling to himself while watching the slow-time Alex spinning in circles, looking for him, he set off across the parking lot looking for the best tool to accomplish his end. He ended up finding it in a ditch off the edge of the lot: a crowbar, rusty and old, about two feet long. Jogging back to where the slow Alex sought him, he pushed himself beyond the edge of his limits. Alex froze before him.

Garret held his breath as he lined everything up. There would be no oxygen after that initial indrawn breath and he needed the ambient oxygen in the air. With enough heat, enough energy, even the air itself, the very atmosphere that he breathed, became combustible.

So he pushed himself, holding the picture of Alex in his mind, until everything went dark. He moved faster than light itself could travel now. He motioned forward with the crowbar and released it, snapping time back to its normal flow at the same instant.

The effect was spectacular, to say the least. The crowbar stretched for the briefest of instants, and then it elongated and became a streak of red light, leaving behind it a trail of fire tunneling through the air.

The screaming line of energy went wide of its mark. Sometimes though, lack of skill can be heavily augmented by the smallest dose of luck, and while his aim had been bad, his idea had been good.

The streak of fire burned an agonizing rip along Alex's side, shredding the right side of his coat and shirt. The shockwave sent Alex flying. He landed on his shoulder, his head hitting the ground directly afterwards. Garret watched him, but he didn't move after he landed.

Satisfied after several minutes that Alexander Zarth's chest would not start moving again, he relaxed and thought. His next move was an obvious one. He hopped forward in time to resolve the situation he had helped create.

Alex opened his eyes and looked at the night sky as the life seeped from his body. By the time the police arrived, about a minute and a half later, the parking lot was completely empty once again.

Time: 199
Location: Denver
Operation: Recovery

Time allowed for funny things, Stefan Arbu reflected. He had trained and taught some of the most elite warriors to ever exist; the best the history of mankind had ever seen. He had set them on the trail of repairing history. And the machinery of the Time Corp, the bureaucracy they had to interact with, had distorted them, twisted them, mangled their mission on until they were nothing of what they had been.

Rather than the guardians, they became the enforcers. What made it such a bitter irony was that not a single one amongst them was a bad person.

Each of his previous students had good heart. But because of what the machine had rebuilt them to be, he was backed into a corner, forced to choose between them or the world. And no matter how much he loved each of them, it was not a hard choice to make when balanced against billions of other lives.

Nor was his own life that valuable. It was hard, but not too hard, to admit that to himself. Besides, the beating he had taken from Wanda had gone a good way towards ensuring that his life was over anyway. Stefan extended his senses, feeling for the trademark signature of his best friend. For over forty-three hundred years this trap had lain dormant. But Alex had been good to his word and it was here, under him, waiting for him to spring it. He sighed to himself and started going through the situation about to play itself out, making sure he had not missed any important details.

At some point during this process, Stefan realized that he was stalling. He chided himself. Distraction right now could screw up everything the two men had worked towards for so very long. They had, between them, set mines at well over a thousand historical nexuses in order to guard this one critical point.

Being a maudlin old man endangered the work they had done. The god had spoken to them both, and they both knew the job that must be done. Now he had to do his part. Taking several deep breaths, he steeled his nerves and triggered his emergency all-call signal. Only a director had access to this beacon, and it had never been used by a director in the field. He prayed that no one would look too closely at the situation and stall in coming here.

People started winking into existence around him. With a wry smile, he noted the various pieces of anachronistic clothing some were wearing. It was a good sign. It meant his agents were coming directly from other field assignments across history. Eleven were present now.

He beamed in pride at how well he had trained them and how loyal they were to him. He watched and waited, ignoring the questioning glances the early comers directed at him. It would be too hard to meet any of their eyes with more than a cursory glance. Eighteen had responded now. He struggled for air as he worked his way up to his feet. Wanda's last kick had collapsed one of his lungs.

Two agents left to respond. He looked to the body of Lucille Frost, making sure that the agents here so far noticed him do so. At the deft distraction, everyone would wonder what had happened between Lucy and Arbu instead of why he had called them all here.

Agent Holly arrived last. He had been Arbu's only true concern, with his recent chastisement for acting brashly. But he had guessed the agent's nature correctly.

Stefan looked to the children he had trained. Twenty-three in all, standing before him, waiting for their orders. Three others were already deceased, which accounted for the whole roster.

He cleared his throat and spoke weakly. "Would someone mind giving me a shoulder to lean on? I'm not exactly in top condition." The agents around him flushed in embarrassment for not having come forward earlier. Holly strode to his side to lend him a supporting shoulder. Stefan smiled thankfully to the younger man.

"We stand on the brink of a class seven paradox," he said, looking around him to watch everyone's predictable reactions. Many of his agents looked troubled, some shaken, but focused. Everyone was too well trained. "When this paradox was initially triggered it was a class eight." That did elicit some reactions from the assembled agents. A class eight was theorized to be enough to shatter the time stream. "Lucky for us, Agent Frost was on hand for the situation and was able to divert it down to a class five. Unlucky for us, Agent Holly here made a rather large mistake and bumped it into the potential class nine category."

Angry muttering broke out between the gathered agents as they began to understand why they had all been gathered.

Stefan cleared his throat, looking around at the people assembled around him, making sure to make eye contact with several, then went on. "As you are undoubtedly surmising, it will take all of our efforts to diffuse this paradox." Stefan sighed and closed his eyes wearily. He was buying time and he hated having to manipulate this situation. Manipulating these people.

"Alexander Zarth is also present in this situation and we have virtually no information on his precise activities." He continued reaching out with his mind, seeking the other half of the trap. He must be precise in triggering both halves, or this would not work.

He bought himself more time. "Please give me a second to catch my breath. I will continue explaining momentarily." Ignoring the surrounding people, he concentrated. The split focus made this task harder than it should have been, though it was only his injuries that stalled his efforts. Taking several painful but calming breaths, he focused himself.

There it was, the other end of the trap, flapping loose in history. He closed his mind around it and tied it into the trap sitting in the earth below him. He was ready.

Raising his head, he opened his eyes. The agents gathered around him, waiting. Best to deliver a show then, and best to make it a quick one. "The interesting thing about a time null compulsion field," he said, "is that we cannot figure out why it only works for ninety seconds. I am truly sorry, my children, but the machine which employs us will try to undo the solution I have enacted, and I cannot allow that."

He triggered the trap and watched the twenty-three people before him freeze, expressions of shock registering on their faces as they realized something had cut off all access to time travel. The trap pushed all of them sideways through space, leaving only Lucy Frost's body in the parking lot. An instant death, into the heart of a sun …

…In the year twenty-eight seventy-three, the second half of the trap triggered. Seismic shocks ripped apart the earth below the Time Corp headquarters while explosives, long concealed beneath the building, detonated and tore the building asunder. Within a few short moments, the headquarters and all the attached offices were nothing more than rubble. All those that had been inside were dead.

The Time Corp Agency, guardians at the gates of history, then enforcers of the will of computers programmed to stop paradox, was no more.

1997- 2001 A.D.: Reflections of The Origin Point

Good lord this hurts.

'Of course it does, Alex. Had the effect which Garret used not included such an intense heat source, which cauterized the wound, you would be dead.'

I have a feeling I'm not far from that point now, actually. Is he gone yet?

'My system scan is showing that you have very little time left. Maybe twenty minutes before you go into full system shock and die. And yes. He recently departed.'

Good. Can you handle the jump forward to make sure he does what needs to be done?

'I can. And I will.'

Alex sighed and let control of his neural network and nano systems shift to the computer. The telltale tingling of a rapid time shift went through him, and then he was back in the lot he had started in.

'It is done, my friend.'

Alex sighed. *Good. Are my eyes closed, or have I lost my vision?*

The computer struggled with giving an honest answer and decided that Alexander Zarth was more than a strong enough man to handle the truth.

'Your eyes are open. I am showing that systemic shock has begun. I do not think that you have more than perhaps a minute left.'

Alex smiled his quirky smile. *I'm not really concerned. We all die. Friend, thank you for the gifts you have given me. I have a gift in return now.*

'No gift is needed, Alex. I find that I am … proud, to have worked with you in achieving this.'

Fool. Needed is not necessary for a gift to be given. These are my burial coordinates. When you entomb me there you will know your name. I understand now who you are and can at least gift you that. And with those thoughts, Alexander Zarth, sometimes known as the thief of time, enemy to some and friends to others, let his final breath rattle forth from his lungs.

His body vanished. Six thousand years it traveled into the past, into the crypt which had been built for him in the time he felt always most at home in. And the sentient computer that coexisted in his body, and continued on afterwards, finally knew its name.

Throughout time, a chain formed. It started four thousand years before the birth of Christ, a series of beacons, stretching through time, passing on one single, but very relevant, piece of information that it had recorded at the beginning of its sixty-nine hundred-year journey. Like a row of dominos it fell, and as each domino toppled to the corrosion of ages the next was ready to act as a relay.

It screamed into the future, where it completed its journey in the databanks of a cloning cell. The cloning cell began its work, rebuilding a brain to match the neural network recorded almost seven thousand years before.

Twenty-five short years later the cell opened and a young man, in the beginning of his prime, stepped out. He blinked and looked around. When he spoke for the first time, laughter was rich in his voice, "Son of a bitch. It worked." He smiled and went to go get dressed.

PROLOGUE

Dust settled around the two combatants as they paused. Out of breath, they eyed each other, both knowing that they had finally met an equal. Temporal combat was never easy. Even for someone in peak physical shape, it was far more rigorous than any other martial art. Both of these men were considered the best of their respective times, and had pushed beyond their limits facing off with each other.

The older man spoke first. "I cannot allow you to steal from this tomb, thief of time."

The younger gave a cocky grin. "I'll say. But have you ever stopped and thought about what happens to the artifacts I steal?"

The two reengaged in combat and it was a beautiful dance of timing. Both of their bodies blurred and replicated. First four, then six, then ten of them fought. Each one altered history and created minor paradoxes as they jumped in time, deflecting the blows hammering on the earlier incarnations of themselves.

An ancient voice spoke from the crypt in the center of the underground tomb and both men stopped, frozen in their tracks. The voice was ancient, weighted down with the knowledge of the ages.

My name is Zr'van. I am as a god, for I have seen through the ages, and I am the guardian of those ages. I have a task for each of you. You two men, from the far future, whom I would call friends to this god ...

EPILOGUE II

Chris stood up. The screaming crowd around him was frozen in silence with the rest of time. The gun was gone from his hand. Somehow he had been pushed aside. When it came down to the moment of truth, he had faltered. But somehow he had survived. The world stopped spinning around him and knowledge crashed into him.

The Time Sphere was wrong. Or, if not wrong, it was not right. His memory returned to him and with it came the understanding of that which he had lost. History took two completely different paths to the same mountain peak. One branch worked through nineteen ninety-seven, the other through nineteen ninety-nine. And he understood how the same set of actions could cause two separate chains of effects. But, ultimately, one must dominate the other. A choice had to be made in order for these realities to be synchronized, and until this moment in time there had been no one to make that choice. Which was less improbable? Reflections were the key ...

He looked one way and saw a reflection. One Nost lay dead in the crowd; the other, the man on trial, sagged, injured but alive, on the stairs. That reflection had no reflections itself.

He looked another way and saw both Nosts dead, bullets having torn apart each of their brains. That reflection imploded on itself.

Another reflection spun before him, one where he walked away from the crowd, his self-proclaimed job done. The past self was dead, history continued. But that reflection curved in on itself. That was the old Origin, the useless one. That way formed nothing but a never-ending loop.

And then Christopher Nost saw one final reflection. In it, Garret appeared, moving so fast it was beyond the ability of a normal human to perceive him. In this reflection, he pushed Chris down, sparing both lives from the choice of history.

Garret picked up the gun that Chris had held. He saved them from the bullet that spoke to their deaths. And in this reflection, Garret walked back to the future, content, if not happy.

Chris understood the nature of the reflections before him. Each had happened, and each would. But all it would take was a single step into one of them to guide all of humanity forward. For time, and its guardians, do nothing but offer choices. Humanity must make the choice. And realizing this, he made a choice born of compassion and love.

He stepped forward, into a future where a husband and wife could have a day together after being apart for ten years. Into a future where humanity could recover from its self-destructive hatred into a society that cared for itself. Ultimately, balanced on a coin's edge, he chose a future in which the people sacrificed for him could live. Choosing his steps to guide humanity through the reflections of time, he stepped into his body, sidestepping James Garret, and walked away into the future.

CONTENTS

About the Author

Peter J. Wacks was born in California sometime during 1976. He has always been amazed and fascinated by both writing and the world in general. Throughout the course of his life, he has hitchhiked across the States and backpacked across Europe on the Eurail. Peter writes a lot, and will continue to do so till the day he dies. Possibly beyond. Peter has acted, designed games, written novels and other spec fiction, and was nominated for a Bram Stoker Award for his first graphic novel Behind These Eyes (co-written with Guy Anthony De Marco). Currently, he is the managing editor of Kevin J. Anderson & Rebecca Moesta's WordFire Press.

OTHER WORDFIRE TITLES

Be sure to check out the growing list of other great
WordFire Press titles at:

http://www.wordfirepress.com